# DIAMOND HUNTER

## MADELLE MORGAN

MCBRIDE PUBLISHING GROUP

**Diamond Hunter**

Library and Archives Canada
ISBN 978-0-9939881-2-7 Paperback

McBride Publishing Group
Electronic book publication January 2015
Paperback publication January 2015

First published as Diamond Lust by Ellora's Cave, 2010
ISBN 9781419923517 ePub edition
ISBN 9781419961663 Trade paperback

www.MadelleMorgan.com

Disclaimer

No real persons, incidents, or organizations are depicted in this work of fiction. Any character resemblance to persons, living or dead, is purely coincidental. The descriptions of diamond mining and processing and related security procedures are per publicly available information or the product of the author's imagination. Any mistakes are the author's.

# Acknowledgement

I'm grateful to several people who lived or are currently living in Yellowknife, Northwest Territories, Canada (the Diamond Capital of North America). My good friend Karen Taggart, Tourism & Parks, Government of the NWT, introduced me to Randy McBride, an RCMP officer and helicopter pilot who, together with Cliff Robertson and Michael Hohm, a former bush pilot, patiently answered questions. My thanks also go to Diavik Diamond Mines Inc. for the mother lode of information at their visitor centre and on their web site. Editors Tracy Peverett, Sue-Ellen Gower, and Marie Lilly helped whip the manuscript into shape.

# CHAPTER ONE

"We need you in the back." The burly aboriginal's thick thumb jerked toward the aircraft cabin behind him.

Seth removed his headset and, with a nod to the other pilot, unstrapped and bent to follow him down the aisle between men trying to make themselves heard above the battering thrum of two propellers slightly out of phase. The Twin Otter was older than its nineteen passengers. Hell, it was older than most of their fathers.

A small man lay curled across two seats, his thin face gray and beaded with sweat. No deep tan like the others, Seth noted. No calluses on his hands. Must be one of the processing plant operators.

"What's his problem?" Seth shouted over the din.

The aboriginal patted the gut that stretched his clean white T-shirt with the Ptarmigan Lake Mine company logo. "Started five minutes ago. Thought he was going to puke on me. He's not just airsick. This is worse."

Seth agreed. The flight was as smooth as they get. Too cool and overcast for thermals. Besides, these guys were used to turbulence. They'd been flying in and out of the remote northern diamond mine site on a two-week rotation for almost a year.

He moved closer to loosen the man's belt and unbutton his denim shirt. "What's your name?"

"I'm fine. Just gas," he managed before his eyes rolled back and his jaw sagged.

Gas, my ass. The man was in serious pain and going into shock. "Put a jacket over him and don't move him," Seth shouted over the engine roar at the aboriginal hunched awkwardly in the aisle. "And return to your seat."

As he hurried back to the copilot's seat he ignored the other passengers' questions. If his suspicions were correct, they didn't have much time to save the fool's life.

After slipping on his headset, he flipped the rocker switch on the control yoke to "intercom" and shouted into the boom microphone bobbing at lip level, "We've got a medical situation. I'm calling ATC to request Medevac Priority and an ambulance to stand by our arrival."

"What's his condition?" responded Jason White, unfazed. At thirty-five, he was Northern Lights Air's most senior pilot, and a veteran of countless emergencies arising from bad weather and mechanical failures.

"I'm no doctor, but I'd say the guy's in deep trouble." In more ways than one. After Seth radioed Yellowknife Air Traffic Control, he checked their position. The desolate treeless plain rolled out like a carpet beneath them as far as the eye could see, dotted with small blue lakes that all looked the same to him. Unlike Jason, who'd been flying this route into the Canadian subarctic for eight months, Seth relied on the plane's satellite navigation system to determine their location. At their current airspeed, they'd arrive at their destination, Yellowknife, with the only hospital in a thousand miles, in forty minutes.

"Let's see how fast this old bird can fly."

\* \* \* \* \*

Two hours later Seth paced the airport cargo area. The passengers had long since piled their duffel bags into pickups and headed into town to blow their paychecks in the northern capital's many bars. Not one had accompanied the unconscious man to the hospital. A bad sign. Seth speculated that the guy's workmates must know something about the cause of his condition and backed off so as not to be implicated. The cause would land the sick mine employee and his associates in jail for a very long time.

The cell phone at his waist vibrated. He quickly flipped it open.

The voice on the other end didn't bother with preliminaries. "He didn't survive the surgery. Perforated colon."

"You were there?"

"Yeah. Plink, plink, plink onto a tray. You were right."

Rough diamonds.

Seth's contact at the Royal Canadian Mounted Police headquarters wouldn't say more. Cell phone calls could be intercepted. By prior agreement he knew the RCMP detective would drop off the details, including the name of the unlucky diamond smuggler, in a keyed box at the Yellowknife post office.

He snapped the phone closed and resumed pacing. It helped him think. Finally, a break in the month-long undercover investigation. He didn't expect official interviews to pry any information out of the coworkers. He understood the mentality. When you're holed up in an isolated open-pit mine camp with no way out except by air, you don't want to piss off any of your four hundred roommates.

The background files on each of the employees indicated that new trade school graduates and their older male relatives from tiny northern communities made up the majority of the heavy equipment operators and mechanics. The drillers, blasters and process plant operators came from other mines in southern Canada. He'd taken a close look at those with gambling and alcohol addictions and support payment arrears, but nothing connected any of them to an international diamond smuggling operation.

He sensed the brains behind the operation were spooked and in a hurry to ferry out their stash. Otherwise they wouldn't have risked drawing more attention by recruiting a man to stuff himself with rock. The miners weren't talking to cops, so he had to get to them unofficially. Tonight he'd hit the bars. Early tomorrow he'd fly in the replacement crew for its two-week rotation.

Seth scanned the filmy clouds threaded across the sky. Ten o'clock on an early July evening and it was as bright as late afternoon in his hometown on the US-Canada border between Washington State and British Columbia. This time of year in the far north, the sun merely dipped to paint the horizon a glorious mess of reds and oranges for an hour or two before rising again. No darkness meant no excuse to overnight at the mine site.

He needed to find a way into the camp before another man lost his life.

\* \* \* \* \*

Petra scanned the cold drink menu on the dispensing unit. Yellowknife bottled the best water she'd ever tasted. Ah...there it was. She dug around for Canadian dollar coins and purchased two plastic bottles.

A speaker crackled with the announcement that the jet she'd arrived on minutes ago was accepting passengers for the return flight to Edmonton, where she'd spent the worst Wednesday night of her life. A DJ in the atrium adjacent to her hotel room had tortured her until 3 a.m. with the chicken dance, polkas and schmaltzy wedding reception standards. Unfortunately, changing her room hadn't been an option. Wedding guests had fully booked the no-star hotel. Who got married mid-week? Civilization had given her this headache. She'd take a tent pitched on Godforsaken tundra thick with black flies and hungry bears any day. For the few precious moments until luggage appeared on the conveyor belt, she slumped forward in the chair and rested her forehead on the frame of the big backpack propped between her legs.

"Petra Paris?"

Raising her thousand-pound head slowly, she tracked a male body that seemed to go on forever—beat-up safety boots, muscular tanned legs and scarred knees under baggy shorts, a worn black leather jacket hanging open to frame a flat stomach and solid chest, determined chin, even white teeth in a tanned clean-shaven face and eventually intelligent eyes fixed on her beneath a thick forelock of straight black hair. She blinked. Blinked again. Men in the boonies weren't allowed to be that handsome. She liked them smelly and grubby, with at least a week's facial growth. That way she could keep her mind on her work.

But then again, she wasn't working yet.

She pushed the backpack aside with one foot, stood, and extended her hand. "Call me Petra. And you are…"

His strong fingers gripped hers a fraction longer than necessary. "Seth Cooper, your pilot for the charter to Ptarmigan Lake Mine." His rumbling baritone sent a shiver down her spine.

Sexy voice. Fantastic body. Now this was a perk she hadn't expected. Fatigue shed like a second skin. "How'd you know who I am?"

"You're the only woman in the terminal with steel-toed boots and Excelsior Exploration & Mining Co. plastered across your back. You had to be the geologist."

"Oh yeah." His grin was doing bad things to her insides. Bad things.

He was no less attracted. She knew men. She recognized the sudden awareness, the instant animation of his even features that meant he'd been pleasantly surprised.

He didn't move for a long moment. Just stared, that cocky grin fixed. She had the impression of a whirring and clicking of circuits behind calculating smoky emerald eyes.

"Hello?" She waved a hand in front of his nose. "Anybody home?"

He returned from the ether and focused on her. "Right. Are you ready to go? Where's your baggage?"

She had lots of baggage, for sure, but he meant the physical kind. "Over there." She pointed to the two long aluminum cases rotating around the massive stuffed polar bear guarding the luggage carousel.

He maneuvered them off the belt. "They feel empty."

She nodded. For now they were. In three days she'd need assistance to lift them, despite muscles honed by weight training.

He strode toward her, each big hand gripping a case. "The plane's outside one of the hangers. Want to grab something to eat before we take off?"

She nodded again. Sitting across from a gorgeous pilot for a half hour sounded good. She liked looking at him. He was a welcome contrast to the geriatric seatmate on the flight from

Denver who'd hit on her, and the pimply teenager with the nose ring who sniffed beside her continuously for the hour and a half from Edmonton. Maybe her luck with the male half of the species was changing. She hoisted the backpack straps onto her shoulders hopefully.

When he led her to the food machines, disappointment pushed out her bottom lip.

"Salmon or tuna," he asked as they surveyed the meager selection of cellophane-wrapped sandwiches.

"Salmon, I guess."

At her tone, he chuckled. "Don't worry. I hear the camp food is terrific," he said, misinterpreting her disappointment. "We have to recalculate the passenger weight every time we bring a crew out at the end of their rotation."

"You fly the scheduled flights in to Ptarmigan Lake?" Her mood jacked up a notch. Maybe she'd see him again over the next few days. "You're new, aren't you?"

"Yes, I'm co-piloting the skeds, but I've only been flying for Northern Lights Air a month." He inserted coins and retrieved sandwiches and coffee. "Should I know you?"

She took a sip of bitter coffee and grimaced, wishing for more sugar. "I was on the drilling team three summers ago that did the bulk testing and delineation mapping of the Ptarmigan Lake kimberlite pipes."

"Kimberlite?"

"You really are new up here. Kimberlite is the type of rock that contains diamonds. A kimberlite pipe is a carrot-shaped funnel with the wide end at the surface. We found two at Ptarmigan Lake." Pride suffused the words.

"Maybe I should have let you buy." His green eyes crinkled at the corners, teasing.

She stiffened. "I'm an employee, not a major stockholder." A frosty echo hung in the air between them. She caught him searching her expression, and quickly suppressed unsettling thoughts about Excelsior's major stockholder that served no purpose at the moment. "Let's get a move on. I have work to do."

Seth Cooper led the way through the terminal, onto the tarmac and over to the Northern Lights Air private hanger. Instead of approaching the four-seater Cessna 185 waiting on the apron, he ducked under the wing and headed for another C-185 parked inside.

"Balloon tires?" Petra cocked an eyebrow at the thick oversized tires on the second tiny plane. "My last trip, the Ptarmigan Lake air strip was in good shape."

"This plane has been hauling fishermen and supplies into various lodges. We needed the tundra tires," he said as he relieved her of the backpack.

"Why not take the other plane? It's obviously prepped to go."

"You ask a lot of questions." His broad back to her, he arranged the pack beside the metal cases.

"Well, why not?"

Sighing, he turned. "We're running flat out this month. All our other planes are booked." He waved toward the back of the hanger. "I forgot to ask. Do you need to use the facilities?"

She flashed him a frown. "I've been flying up here five seasons. I certainly know what to expect."

"Got your pilot's license?" Consternation briefly ruffled his smooth expression.

"No. I meant I've been flown to various exploration camps in helicopters, single engine prop planes like this, you name it. Besides," she opened the door to the passenger side, "it's only two and a half hours to Ptarmigan Lake in this little baby."

"Whatever you say."

She knew the pre-flight drill. She waited patiently while Seth secured the cargo and walked around the plane for the visual check. After the requisite run-through of the fuel, fluid and equipment checks, he taxied out to the runway. In short order they soared into a powder blue sky.

"Should be a smooth trip."

Petra didn't bother to answer. As the plane climbed and banked sharply, she became absorbed in the view vertically under her window. The modern City of Yellowknife, with its multistory office buildings and housing for twenty thousand inhabitants, sprawled along the north shore of Great Slave Lake. Indigo water, stunted trees, scrub bush, and rocky outcrops splashed with muted silver-gray, gold and orange lichens framed the government hub and mining town.

A mile beneath the downtown core, worked out stopes criss-crossed gold-bearing Precambrian rock. They used to say the gold was paved with streets. In the new century, diamonds, not gold, drove the current economic boom. Her heart swelled. Though she loved the Colorado mountains, the deceptively monotonous terrain north of the sixtieth parallel was her spiritual home.

She'd once seen a painting in a local gallery that captured her love and respect for the north in a way she could not articulate. A Gulliver-sized naked woman reclined on pink and gray granite under a limitless sapphire sky. Miniature evergreens spiked into her underside. That was the subarctic—incomparably beautiful yet harsh without mercy underneath.

As they approached the tree line, low brush began to predominate. For a while she watched the pilot competently handle the controls. The engine drone, familiar and comforting, softened the edges of her thoughts until her head lolled and she slipped into a deep, dreamless sleep.

\* \* \* \* \*

The plane touched down with a tooth-loosening thunk. Petra bounced into lucid and cranky awareness.

"What the hell!" she shrieked as the plane imitated a kangaroo for several hundred feet.

"Sorry about this," the pilot shouted over the bellowing noise.

No stranger to rough landings, this one felt different. Panic thickened her throat as she braced herself and watched him fight to maintain control on the uneven ground. When the plane eventually joggled to a stop, she sucked in a deep breath and released the fear in a torrent of words.

"This is the absolute worst landing I've ever experienced. You missed the runway entirely. You're a menace to Canadian aviation! Who'd you bribe to get your pilot's license? Didn't NLA test your skills before hiring you on?"

Without waiting for answers, she unbuckled, pushed open the door and slid down onto not so firm ground. Her boots sank into spongy moss. Wobbling legs distracted her for a second while she found her balance. But only a second.

She peered left then right. Empty, undulating tundra extended to the horizon in every direction. This was no mine camp.

"Hey!" She fought down a bubble of hysteria. "Where are we? What happened?"

The pilot from hell came up beside her, slightly unsteady on his feet himself. "The ground looked relatively flat from the air."

He seemed surprised. Her temper spiked. "How many times have you landed on the tundra?"

"This is the second," he admitted.

She smacked her forehead. A green pilot. Her luck with men was holding big time. The next question had to be asked. "Is there a mechanical problem?"

"No."

Relief quieted her for a moment. They were safe. The plane was fine. Then fury that he'd risked their lives for nothing took over. "Are you insane?" she seethed between clenched teeth. "What are we doing here? Why did you land?"

He threw up his arms, palms facing her, in a placating gesture. "Relax. I'll explain everything."

She gasped. Was that a gun holster she spied under the flap of his open jacket? A sickening dread squeezed aside the anger. Adrenaline spurted. Her heart pistoned blood. Man oh man, how did she get herself into these situations?

She peered into the "too damn cute to be good news" face of Seth Cooper, if that was even his real name. Crazy, dangerous men often appeared normal, even exceptionally handsome men. Blast it all, she'd walked right into this abduction. Mustn't hyperventilate. She drew one deep breath and then another. If she lost control of her emotions, couldn't think, she was done for.

Breathe. Think. Her satellite phone was safely tucked in her pack. She took one step backward. Slowly. Then another. Two more steps and she'd reach the point where she could hitch herself up into the plane.

The pilot advanced step for step. "I'm not going to hurt you. Give me a minute."

She abandoned the stealthy retreat, scrambled up into the plane and slammed the copilot-side door closed. Before she could secure the other, he wrenched it wide.

"I-I don't have much money. A few credit cards and a return plane ticket. That's all."

"I don't want your money." He kept his distance.

"You want to have sex with me?"

"Jeez no! Listen—"

"You lie! You want my body."

He reddened. "Okay, maybe I do. But not here, not now, and for sure not against your will. I've never forced a woman in my life."

Petra's thoughts spun. "Who's paying you?"

"Northern Lights Air."

He was toying with her. She leaned over and slammed a fist into the pilot's seat. "Why in Heaven's name did you land this plane in the middle of Godforsaken nowhere?"

"I've been trying to tell you. Will you give me five minutes? Out here?" He indicated the rocky outcrop to the left of the plane.

She wasn't ready to put herself in a more vulnerable position. "I'm calling for help. I have a satellite phone."

"Not anymore." He pulled her phone out of his jacket pocket and waggled it.

Her stomach dropped to her knees. The creep. He'd been one step ahead of her the whole time. He'd even searched her pack. "I'll use the radio then," she muttered, scanning the controls and gauges on the console. She'd watched pilots tune in to air traffic control dozens of times from the adjacent seat. Or she'd take off out of here. Surely she'd manage. How hard could it be?

"Don't even think about it!" He growled, closer now. "You told me you don't have a license."

"Doesn't mean I can't fly." She clambered into the pilot's seat.

The man cursed. "Woman, you're testing my patience." He reached in, wrapped one long, muscled arm around her waist and hauled her down out of the plane.

"I'll get your license revoked for abducting me," she swore, legs kicking as he carted her toward the outcrop. She thumped her fists against his chest, then stilled when she hit the hard bulge near his armpit. "Kidnapping is a felony offense."

"This is Canada. The laws are different. Besides, I didn't kidnap you." He set her down fifty feet from the plane and swept one arm toward the horizon. "You're free to go."

A trek across the bleak, lonely tundra days from the nearest settlement with no phone, no food and only two bottles of water did not appeal to her.

"Or you can listen to what I have to say."

"Fine." She squatted on springy moss and bent her head. She didn't want to die. People were counting on her to come through for them. The company stockholders. Members of the board of directors. They trusted her to drill new kimberlite cores and carry them to Colorado to be analyzed before the stockholders' meeting in eight days. Her dad's reputation and millions in stockholder equity depended on her collecting diamond-studded core.

The pilot squatted opposite. "That's more like it. First, I want to apologize for scaring you."

She observed him through slitted eyelids. Sincerity dripped from him like slime. She remained unconvinced. Her breathing hitched, jerked. She was a sitting duck, ready to be plucked.

"An idea occurred to me, and landing here to discuss it seemed like another good idea."

"How so?"

He shifted to plant his boots more firmly in the soft ground. "Well, no one can overhear us."

"You got that right," she said dryly. "What's wrong with a nice chat during the flight?"

"I didn't want to discuss it via headset."

"Nor could you coerce me into doing whatever it is you want me to do. Instead you kidnapped me."

"I'm an RCMP undercover cop—" he began.

"Yeah, right." Just like the so-called cop who'd tried to detain her at the Denver airport. At the check-in counter, the uniform had demanded to see her ticket and passport. His scuffed shoes gave him away. Not standard issue. She'd threaded through the crowded departure level at a jog and made it to the customs area before he caught up. "Let's see your I.D."

He extracted his wallet from a back pocket. She scanned the Northern Lights Air photo card identifying him as Seth Cooper. "If what you say is true, that's your fake ID. What kinda proof of anything is that?"

"I'm an undercover investigator attached to the Diamond Protection Unit," he continued, ignoring her. "We ran a background on you. Twenty-nine, single, now living in Boulder, Colorado and employed by Excelsior since graduating with a geology degree from the University of Colorado. Your father is Edward Paris, the head of the Denver assay lab that confirmed the economic viability of the Ptarmigan Lake diamond mine. Excelsior's stock price sank like a stone a month ago when it became public that the diamond yield from the mine is well below forecasts. You flew up here to supervise the collection of new core samples. Shall I continue?"

"Do you know my landlady's name?"

"Jessica Harper. You live in an apartment at 14 Cougar Drive."

Dizziness hazed her vision. Either Excelsior's Chairman and CEO Tony Athlone had briefed his hit man exceptionally well, or Seth was telling the truth.

"I still only have your word as to who you are. Not good enough."

He reddened. With anger? She wasn't taking any chances. As she half-rose in an attempt to make a run for it, he grabbed her upper arm.

There was no better place than the subarctic tundra to dispose of a body. Only ravens could ever find it. She decided she'd rather know his intentions and get it over with. "Are you going to kill me?"

"Jeez." He dropped his arm and swatted at the low scrub between them. "No, I'm not going to kill you." He ground his teeth. "I want to be your boyfriend."

Petra scrabbled backward, crab-like. "You landed to have your way with me?" Better raped than dead, she supposed, but he wouldn't lay a hand on her without a fight. "Touch me and you'll regret it! I bite."

He stood, all six muscular feet of him looming over her, and she flattened against the rock outcrop. "You've got it all wrong. I want to pose as your boyfriend. You don't have to sleep with me." His lips quirked. "Unless you want to."

"I'm glad one of us thinks this is funny. In your dreams, Cooper. Or whoever you are." She levered herself upright and dusted off her jeans, not tearing her gaze for a second from the jacket concealing the gun.

"We have a mutual goal. The stock price is in the toilet and we both know why."

"We do?" Three directors on the Excelsior board suspected the company chairman of manipulating Excelsior's stock price.

They'd shared their suspicions with her at a secret dinner meeting prior to her trip, but to her knowledge no one else was in the loop. "Tell me."

Inner debate silenced him for several moments. "Smuggling," he blurted, watching for her reaction.

"Smuggling?" Surprise drew a hand almost to her mouth before she diverted it to tuck a curly strand of hair behind her ear. "You know about the…smuggling."

"Isn't that why you're here? To confirm the potential yield compared to the recent diamond production?" When she said nothing, he continued, "Half a dozen stolen rough diamonds were recovered a week and a half ago."

"They were?" She suspected Tony Athlone only of capitalizing on a poor production streak in order to artificially depress the stock price. The directors believed Athlone was attempting to secretly buy up thousands of bargain basement-priced Excelsior stocks through an agent. They trusted Edward Paris' assay results and expected that the stock price would recover when diamond production returned to projected levels. By then Athlone, unless stopped, would control the company. The possibility of theft had never shown up on the board's radar.

Detailed feasibility studies and preliminary drilling samples provided a pretty good estimate of the potential quantity and quality of diamonds in the ore body, but there were no guarantees. Edward Paris' assay reports showed the kimberlite pipes at Ptarmigan Lake potentially contained large, superior quality diamonds. The first six months of production had validated the estimates. Lately, however, the low-grade yield had stockholders in an uproar. Rumors leaked to the media accused Edward Paris of salting the preliminary drill core material with diamonds. Stock market analysts speculated the mine was a dud and the owners had perpetrated a fraud. Petra had her own reservations about her dad's honesty.

To prove the stockholders hadn't been bilked, the board had authorized an independent analysis of new cores. If indeed Tony Athlone aimed to seize control, he had a vested interest in delaying the results as long as possible. He meant to stop her, and he wasn't playing nice. Petra pressed a forefinger to her lips. Could Athlone be double-ending this? Manipulating the stock price as well as siphoning off the best diamonds? The greedy bastard.

Seth grew impatient at the lack of response. "Are you game?"

"For what," she said absently, still pondering the implications.

"I need access to the employees at Ptarmigan Lake."

"So? You fly in there every day."

He dragged in a heavy, chest-expanding breath. "By posing as your boyfriend, I have an excuse to sleep in the camp—"

"Over my dead body." Oops. That was probably not the most appropriate choice of words.

He took two steps, leaned forward, forced her to meet earnest eyes. "Listen. I won't disturb your beauty sleep. I plan to spend the evenings hanging with the boys, playing cards, shooting the breeze."

She bit back an involuntary grin. "Some boyfriend you are."

His brows lifted. "Does that mean you'll do it?"

"Get me proof you're really a cop. Then we'll talk." The smuggling presented a new, disturbing angle. If his story checked out, by keeping Seth nearby she'd have the opportunity to find out what he learned. Diamond lust twisted ordinary men, and Athlone was no ordinary man. She suspected he was prepared to stop her at any cost, and might have others in his pay on site. Even undercover, Seth unwittingly offered protection from her enemies.

Seth grabbed her cold, clammy hand and pumped it. "Deal." His sunny grin dazzled her, threw her off-kilter. "There's just one more thing."

"What's that?" She frowned. He had what he wanted.

"The men have to believe our relationship is real."

He hadn't released her hand. She tugged, but his grip merely tightened. "What do ya wanna do, hold hands around camp?"

"Practice."

His left arm snaked around her waist, pulling her close, tilting her into the crook of his shoulder. Firm lips swooped to cover hers, muffling her startled cry.

# CHAPTER TWO

Cool. Resolute. Experienced. The bold lips pressing hers revealed more than he could know. Petra froze, caught off-guard by a move she'd not anticipated.

He tugged her hard up against his broad chest and slid one hand around the back of her neck. Blood throbbed at the places their bodies intimately touched. Primal "you man, me woman" chemicals dissolved the self-preservation thoughts crowding her usually sharp mind. She was left with barely enough control to prevent her arms from crawling around his waist. She refused to give him the satisfaction.

She knew Seth's spur-of-the-moment abduction had him literally flying by the seat of his pants, and his "be my girlfriend" gambit was as much a surprise to him as it was to her. She couldn't decide whether to feel outrage at his audacity or to appreciate his resourcefulness. Or to simply enjoy the kiss. Without responding, of course.

But he was making that increasingly difficult. One big palm slid to the small of her back, pushed her hips against his. At the sizable evidence of his attraction, a lustful spiral of pleasure swirled through her nether regions.

Enough. She squirmed out of his arms. "You enjoyed that," she accused.

"Purely business. It has to look natural." The amused glint in his eyes belied his words.

"Yeah, right. I should slap you."

"Save it for an audience. A fight will make our relationship appear even more realistic."

"Excuse me?" was the best she could come up with.

"Speaking of realistic, that kiss wouldn't convince a ninety-year-old we're in love. You'll have to do better."

Anger roiled. "In your dreams, you—"

Before she could muster insults to hurl at him, he thrust one arm around her shoulders, the other around her waist, tilted her back, and planted his mouth on hers again.

Rendered immobile and off balance, she could only screech, "You a—" Big mistake. The muffled protest gave him access to her tongue and beyond. Swiftly he penetrated the breach and reconnoitered with the tongue desperate to curse him all the way to the North Pole.

Each plunge into the hot, wet depths of her mouth felt more wonderful than the last. She met the third. Tangled with the fourth. Sucked the fifth. Lost awareness of her limbs with the sixth. His inventive tongue curved into the deepest places, dipping, cajoling and tasting. He had a special gift, blast it all.

When he finally released her mouth, she slumped to the ground, her spine molten steel.

He grinned down at her, hands on hips. "That's better. Nothing like a little anger to heat the blood."

Fuming because she had no power over the glorious cocktail of adrenaline and hormones charging through her veins, she struggled to her feet, stomped off ten feet, and tucked the flannel shirt back into her jeans.

"Don't think you can get away with acting like a Neanderthal. I'm going to charge you with sexual harassment. If you're really a cop, you'll be drummed out of the force."

He laughed then, a deep rich roar that startled fluttering birds out of nearby bushes. "What's the point, when under oath you'd be forced to admit you kissed me back?"

She had to concede that point. Reluctantly. "Why should I help you?"

He sobered. "You'd be performing a civic service."

"I'm American."

He scratched his head. "Right."

"I want something in return."

He straightened, alert. "Depends. Name it."

"I'll pose as your girlfriend on three conditions." She raised her forefinger. "One, you provide proof you're with the RCMP."

"Agreed." He nodded.

"Two," she raised her middle finger, "you help me get my core samples onto a commercial flight out of Yellowknife by Sunday, whatever it takes."

He shrugged. "Sounds simple."

She shook her head. "I believe there are men at Ptarmigan Lake who will try to prevent that shipment. I don't know who they are, or how they will try to stop me." Her gut protested at revealing even that much to a man she didn't trust. A cop, and she was taking a calculated risk that he was indeed a cop, would do his duty to protect her.

"I'll need more details," he said quietly. "Why do you suspect someone may sabotage your work, for starters?"

"No." She shook her head more adamantly this time. "I've revealed enough. Prove to me you're who you say you are, and I'll decide what you need to know. Do we have a deal?"

He regarded her intently. "What's the third condition?"

She managed a weak grin. "Keep your hands to yourself in our bedroom. I've got a job to do, and I don't have time for any, uh, hanky panky."

Seth advanced several paces with his right hand extended. "Deal. But the third condition is void if you start something when we're alone." He waggled thick eyebrows suggestively.

She snorted. Her seduce him? Not going to happen. The mine operated twenty-four hours per day on two twelve-hour shifts. With round-the-clock drilling ahead, no dalliance with a handsome cop fit into the tight agenda. Every hour counted.

"In your dreams, buster." She snapped her hand into his and clamped down hard.

\* \* \* \* \*

After a featherlight landing on the asphalt runway, Petra's fake boyfriend maneuvered the plane adjacent to the Ptarmigan Lake aircraft refueling station, cut the engine, and reminded Petra to remain seated while the whirling propeller gradually whump, whumped to a stop.

A lean man in a blue coverall with a Ptarmigan Lake logo emerged from the prefab building provided for the private airstrip's operations staff and approached Seth as he swung out of the cockpit.

Petra memorized his features. Sparse mustache. Small, close-set eyes. Blond hair rimming the blue ball cap. Under the circumstances, every stranger on site posed a potential threat.

"You're overdue," the fuel technician said.

"We landed on the Barrens," Seth replied.

"A problem?" Petra overheard the tech ask as the men walked around the plane and stopped to pretend to inspect the prop. Seth murmured a few sentences she couldn't catch, even after she dropped to the tarmac.

She'd never encountered this particular tech on previous trips. Of course, turnover was to be expected. She assessed the men from her vantage point at the tip of the wing. They appeared too chatty to be casual acquaintances. Well, she wasn't going to find out more standing there.

When she moved toward the storage hatch, Seth quickstepped over to unload the baggage. Blue Coverall made himself busy hauling hose to refuel the plane.

"Who's he to you?" Petra asked Seth.

"That's Joe. He refuels planes." He handed over her backpack. "Your baggage has to be x-rayed by Security. You may be searched. Any drugs or alcohol in your possession will get you kicked off the premises."

"I know the drill." The lack of airstrip terminal meant security screening was carried out at the camp's administration and residential complex half a mile away. She refused to be diverted. "Is Joe his cover name?"

"What have I let myself in for?" Seth moaned as he carried her aluminum cases toward a vehicle parking area where a single pickup waited with its engine running. "You think this is TV where the cop discusses his case with—"

"With the woman posing as his girlfriend to help him solve the case?" Petra filled in.

Seth ignored her. A familiar figure stepped out of the passenger side of the pickup and lifted a suitcase from the truck bed. "The mine manager chartered my return trip. He's probably pissed."

Petra frowned. "Hank's leaving at a time like this?"

"At a time like what, exactly?" Seth's intelligent green eyes sharpened.

"Oh." She thought quickly. "What you said. The smuggling."

"Management's on a four-day-in, three-day-out rotation. I believe the boss is leaving early because he has a meeting in town this afternoon. Which he's likely to miss."

"Thanks to you. Maybe you'll be fired."

He guffawed. "Don't look so hopeful. Pilots are in short supply during the summer. You're stuck with me for the duration, babe."

Petra knew Hank Horvath well. An engineering geologist in his late fifties, he'd supervised three exploration teams, including hers, before accepting the mine manager job eight months ago. He'd lost at least twenty pounds since they'd last met, weight he couldn't afford to lose. His wiry frame radiated nervous tension. As she extended her hand, she met his gaze, noting the left eyelid now spasmed with a tic. "Hank, how are you?"

"Busy." He glanced at Seth, nodded a greeting.

"Do you have time for a coffee?" She'd expected Hank to give her the inside scoop on potential mine fields, so to speak.

"Sorry, kid. I'm late already. Your drilling crew is standing by. Carter's on duty and waiting for you." He remembered the stocky man with a thick mat of white hair behind the wheel. "This is Bob Scott, Chief, Security Services. He's Acting Mine Manager in my absence this rotation. Just ask him if you need anything Carter hasn't the authority to handle." He swung his attention to Seth. "Plane ready?"

"Ahem." Seth cleared his throat, threw an arm across Petra's shoulders, and peered down at her expectantly.

Hank's departure left her with only one other friendly contact, Carter Lee, the chief geologist. Bob Scott was an unknown quantity. She had no choice, really. "This is my…ah, boyfriend, Seth Cooper. He'll be staying with me while I'm here, so he'll need to be cleared through security later tonight."

"Boyfriend, eh?" Hank's brows lifted clear to what used to be his hairline. "Cooper has ferried me back and forth to Yellowknife a few times. I had no idea you two knew each other, let alone…" His voice trailed off. He shrugged narrow shoulders. "Will wonders never cease." A thin smile creased his long face. "Well, you're a rare man to pin this gal down long enough for a relationship, Cooper." Hank shook his hand and passed him the suitcase. "Scott will take care of the clearance."

"We'll have to check him out first," Bob Scott reminded his superior.

"Any friend of Petra's is good enough for me. Do what you have to do, but Cooper stays as long as she wants. Got that?"

"Yes, sir." Scott frowned, unconvinced.

To Seth, Hank asserted, "The faster you get me to Yellowknife, the sooner you can return to this lovely woman here. Let's get the show on the road."

The men tromped toward the plane, Hank's bony fists gripping briefcase and laptop case handles. Tears prickled behind Petra's eyes. Hank she knew. Hank she trusted. She'd never seen him so anxious to get the hell out of Dodge.

And, more worrisome, she didn't have a clue why.

\* \* \* \* \*

At the reception desk Petra phoned the Mine Planning and Geology Services office. Carter promised to send someone to collect the cleared aluminum cases while she checked into a guest room.

The four hundred-bed accommodation complex comprised a reception area, security facility, administration offices, the cafeteria, a fitness center, two lounges for watching satellite TV on big screens and a games room with pool tables and computers. Four dormitory wings extended like spokes off the hub of a wheel.

Modules for the mine's prefabricated buildings had been trucked over a winter road and assembled like a giant erector set. None of the structures were more than three stories high, and none had elevators. She puffed out a curse as she climbed to the third floor in the south wing laden with her heavy pack. More cardio training was definitely in her future.

They'd assigned her a deluxe room, a fancy word for slightly larger spartan quarters that boasted a double bed instead of a single. While she unpacked her toiletries, she evaluated the sleeping options. The bed posed a problem. A single-sized mattress pulled off a bed could have been squeezed into the space on the carpet between the bed frame and the easy chair, but not a double mattress.

In eight summers of field work during college and afterward, she'd often bunked in a multi-cot tent with male colleagues. Three men, totally bushed and driven to the brink of sanity by their craving for a female, had tried to kiss her. She tapped one finger against a tender bottom lip. Not once had she ever kissed back.

Heat seeped up her neck at the thought of sharing the double bed with Seth. He'd given his word he wouldn't touch her. She was less confident about her own resolve.

The other options were the floor or the armchair upholstered in a scratchy blue synthetic. Neither appealed. She decided they'd take turns on the floor, and phoned housekeeping to request extra blankets. That settled, she locked the room and went to find her old buddy Carter.

Petra paused at the reception counter to survey the site map. Colored spokes denoted enclosed heated "arctic" corridors which connected the hub with most of the other buildings. Many employees were able to walk to work in shirt sleeves. She didn't envy the blasting crews and heavy equipment operators responsible for extracting diamond-bearing rock at the open pit mine and hauling it to the processing plant. They needed to gear up to withstand frigid temperatures and gale-force winds during the long, dark winter months.

A whiteboard behind the counter proclaimed the record low temperature the previous winter to be -61 degrees F. Despite the generous salaries, turnover was a fact of life. Many abandoned their jobs after experiencing the desolate twenty-four-hour darkness and extreme cold firsthand.

The site map offered limited choices of destinations, really— the processing plant, where the ore was crushed and diamonds were separated out from the rubble; the sorting and valuation building, where diamonds were counted, graded, recorded and packaged for shipment; the heavy equipment depot; the power plant; the mine services wing where the heavy equipment operators, and drilling and blasting crews received training and daily assignments; and the water and waste treatment services in the Facility Maintenance complex. She traced the thin line that linked Mine Services to one of the main corridors.

Minutes later she pushed open the door of the cramped office Carter Lee shared with his alternate on a two-week rotation. He sat slouched over a drafting table, his shaggy head bent close to a spider web of lines demarking pit elevations on a topographic map.

"Still haven't given in and bought glasses, I see."

"Petra! About time. The crew has been on standby for an hour. Not that they're complaining, but," he checked his watch, "there are only four hours left in their shift."

"Nice to see you too, old friend." Carter's brilliance outshone his social skills by a factor of ten.

He swiveled on the stool to face her. "We'll catch up on the social chit-chat at dinner. Give me the sampling grid coordinates, angles of declination and depths you want for today's drill cores. I don't understand why you refused to e-mail them. We've lost hours."

Petra retrieved a USB flash drive with encrypted files from an inside pocket. "The locations of the cores are on a need-to-know basis. I told you that."

"But I'm Chief, Mine Planning & Geology Services."

Petra rolled her eyes. A stratospheric IQ had no correlation to people smarts. Shrewder managers at head office in Colorado had chewed Carter up and spit him out, and he'd washed up here in the middle of nowhere, highly paid but with his wings clipped.

"How's your wife?" she asked to divert him as she punched in the password and downloaded the information into his computer.

"Carol left me for the mailman."

"Seriously?"

"Yeah. Actually he's a counter agent at the Boulder post office. I wondered why I was getting so many parcels."

"I'm sorry."

"Don't be. I have a new girlfriend. I upgraded to a better model." He flashed her a pleased grin through his bushy beard.

"Yeah? What is she, a heavy equipment operator?"

He pursed his lips until the thick mustache brushed the tip of his broad nose. "You haven't changed. Just for that, I'm not going to offer you coffee."

"You never do anyway," she reminded him.

"Desirée's a cook. You'll meet her at dinner."

"Ooooh, Desirée. Sounds sexy," she teased.

"I sent Carol a picture of her. For closure."

"I'm seeing someone too," Petra threw in casually as the software churned out coordinates for the drill rig set-up.

"That's a crock. You haven't had a boyfriend in what…never?"

"I had boyfriends in college," she countered. "Well, one boyfriend. Besides, I do have a life before and after field work with reprobates like you. I've dated several men."

"I'll believe it when I see it," he muttered as he tapped the keyboard to scroll through the drill array coordinates. "The guys say you're gay."

She smiled, letting it ride. Truthfully, the rumor was convenient. "You'll meet Seth at dinner."

"What?" He punched the wrong key. "Damn, you made me erase the file." He entered commands to retrieve the data. "He's here? Who is the poor sap—I mean the lucky fellow?" he corrected when she swatted him with a rolled up map.

"Seth's a pilot. Are you done?" She stamped her steel-toed boots impatiently.

Carter slid off the stool and drew himself to his full five foot three inches. "Twenty feet of core would be over there," he pointed to a narrow steel-topped table dividing the room, "ready to log if you'd trusted me with the coordinates. What the hell is going on?"

Petra clapped him on the shoulder. "Office politics, my friend. You don't want to know the details." She sobered, aware of the risks if he pushed that big nose into places it didn't belong. The less he knew, the safer he'd be. "Keep what we're doing to yourself, okay? Refer any calls from Excelsior to me, at least until the cores are shipped out."

\* \* \* \* \*

Two hours later, Petra stood at the edge of the massive open pit watching the men operate the drill rig far below in a cordoned-off area. Grit blown on the breeze coated her hair and clothes. The ground shook under her feet every time one of the monster two hundred and forty-ton haul trucks with twelve foot-diameter tires rumbled by on the gravel road. She expected the next shift of drillers to reach the desired depth sometime about midnight. There was nothing to do but wait.

Her thoughts drifted unwillingly to Seth. She rehashed each of their conversations, searching for a weakness in his story. To trust or not to trust, that was the question. Had her judgment been affected by the bone-melting impact of his kisses? Smarter, tougher people than she had tossed aside common sense for the sake of physical gratification. Her own father, for instance.

But not her. A disciplined mind, not a craving for sex, controlled her body. Hard work filed the edge off stifled desire. The alternative was to expose herself to being manipulated. Or worse, not in control of the situation. Not an option.

One of the dusty, green, half-ton company pickups crunched to a stop beside her. Bob Scott extracted himself from behind the wheel and approached. He cultivated a well fed, jovial persona, complete with white hair and beard, but sharp gray eyes darted obsessively, cataloging every detail. He planted himself a shade too close. She stiffened.

"Quite a sight, eh?" he shouted over the din as the operator of a hydraulic excavator far down in the crater tipped a ten-ton bucket of ore into a waiting truck.

"Yeah." She dug her hands into her jeans pockets and silently cursed Hank for saddling her with an unknown quantity, namely this crafty old wolf inside a Santa Claus shell. How much did the chief of security know? Could she trust Hank's right hand man?

"The crew is drilling more core samples, I see. Funny you should fly in to supervise when we have a senior geologist right here at Ptarmigan Lake."

Carter outranked her both in experience and in the management hierarchy. They both knew it. She didn't bother to respond to the implication that head office didn't trust Carter. Hank had been advised of the purpose of her visit by the board of directors, but apparently had not briefed his head of security. She wondered why. "I'm simply doing what I'm told."

"Carter's a good guy. Does his job and stays out of trouble." He peered at her from under bushy white brows.

"I plan to do my job and stay out of trouble too." She smiled to soften him up a little. "I'll be out of your hair on Sunday. Sir," she added a fraction of a second later. They both had jobs to do. She definitely intended to stay out of his way. Get the cores and get out.

"I want an update on your progress every morning at 9:00."

Surprised, she met his eyes. "Of course, if that's what you want." When he lingered, she added, "Anything else?"

"I have a message for you," he admitted reluctantly. "Hank Horvath called me from Yellowknife." He paused for her reaction. When there was none, he continued, "He said to tell you these exact words—'in your dreams, buster'."

Petra laughed outright. Seth had found a creative way to confirm to her he was indeed a cop, and that Hank knew Seth's real identity, and approved. Best of all, they'd kept the security team in the dark.

"So you understand the code, or whatever it means?" His rounded cheeks flushed. "I don't like being left out of the loop, Miss Paris. Why are you really here?"

If what Seth said were true, Scott had to contend with smuggling on his turf. Or was potentially involved. She couldn't fault the chief of security for nosing into her business.

"Sorry, sir. What I can tell you is that I'm authorized by our employer to collect core samples and accompany them to Colorado. If you want more information, contact Hank or head office."

"I tried that." He glowered.

She shrugged her shoulders apologetically. "I'll report tomorrow morning in your office, as requested."

"You do that." Scott marched over the loose gravel to his vehicle, heaved his bulk inside and slammed the door.

As the pickup bobbed over rough ground toward the main building, she pinched her lower lip between two fingers. The RCMP appeared to be working undercover on the chief of security's turf without his knowledge. But Excelsior generally hired retired RCMP officers to run security. Ergo, Santa Scott couldn't be one of the RCMP's own.

Then who the heck was he and why didn't Hank trust him?

\* \* \* \* \*

Seth found Petra at 7:30 p.m. in the cafeteria. A bolt of pleasure shorted a heartbeat, still unused as he was to her exquisite coloring—natural deep, rich reds in her curly dark hair mirrored wine-tinted lips. Lips he'd tasted and fully intended to taste as often as possible while in Ptarmigan Lake. Opposite her sat a short furry man the spitting image of an Ewok in one of the Star Wars movies.

"Hi, babe." Seth set his food tray on the table beside Petra's and leaned over to bus her mouth. Her cheeks pinked and gold-specked brown eyes flashed in reproach. He grinned back, amused. If she expected him to feel ashamed for embarrassing her in front of her colleague, she was wasting her time. Petra had agreed to be affectionate in public for appearances, and damned if he didn't intend to take full advantage.

Carter stuck his hand out across his tray and said around a mouthful of lasagna, "You must be Seth."

"This is Carter Lee, the chief geologist," Petra said. "Are you in for the night?"

"Yes, ma'am, and looking forward to spending it with you." Seth tugged her thick, shoulder-length ponytail playfully.

Carter's cough sounded suspiciously like a chuckle. "You think this is funny, don't you," Petra glared. "I was simply wondering if Seth needed to make another trip after dinner."

"I didn't say a word," Carter complained, waving his fork for emphasis.

"You know each other well," Seth observed as he settled in to work his way through a small mountain of lasagna and Caesar salad.

"Carter and I spent a summer together on the tundra west of here three years ago. He's like a brother to me," she quickly clarified. "Nothing happened."

"Nothing happened," Carter said, "because all the guys including me thought Petra's g—" Her dinner roll unerringly bounced off his nose. "Hey! You made me spill food into my lap."

"Carter sometimes doesn't know when to keep his mouth shut," Petra said between clenched teeth. She spied a large coil-bound book Seth had placed in front of his tray. "What's that?"

"It's my sketch pad," Seth said between mouthfuls, well aware she'd changed the subject. She was feisty. Complicated. With secrets. And awfully attractive even with her curvy figure camouflaged in bush clothes. Man, he was beginning to enjoy this assignment. "I draw caricatures of people I meet. Helps break the ice. Make quite a few friends that way."

"Do you charge?" Carter asked.

"Of course not."

"Then will you draw my girlfriend after her shift?"

"Maybe Seth has better things to do," Petra intervened.

This time Carter waved his knife, and a dollop of butter landed in her drinking water. "You have all night for that," he said airily.

She scoured the vicinity for another roll, but came up empty. Instead, she leaned forward. "Don't forget I have work to do after midnight."

"We can log the cores in the morning. They aren't going anywhere."

First scanning the other tables to verify other diners were out of earshot, she said in a low voice. "The cores need to be guarded 24/7."

Seth straightened. Carter's features registered astonishment. Clearly the chief geologist had no idea why such a precaution was necessary. She hadn't confided in him, for some reason. Either she was paranoid, or there were other layers to the relationship he needed to probe.

Seth spoke first, directed to Carter. "Isn't your counterpart on duty from 7:00 p.m. to 7 a.m.?"

"I supervise two geotech engineering technologists, one of whom works the night shift. Unfortunately they've both been drafted by the supervisor of the Blasting Divison to replace guys who quit the explosives crew. I'm it this week." Carter crossed his arms, leaned back in the plastic chair, and swung his head from one to the other. "One of you better tell me what's going on here."

"I have no idea." Seth threw up his hands. He was keenly interested in the answer, himself. Hundreds of tons of rock had to be crushed and processed to fill a coffee can with diamonds, and most of those were industrial grade. The astronomical odds of finding even one high-grade diamond in a two-inch thick core sample left him perplexed. Why guard a dozen cylinders of almost worthless rock?

Both men stared at Petra expectantly. She relented. "Carter, I believe someone on site may try to prevent the cores from reaching the assay lab. We have to protect them from tampering or destruction from the instant they leave the ground to when they're stowed in the jet leaving Yellowknife in three days. That's all I'm willing to say."

Carter's bushy brows veed above confused eyes. "How are you involved?" he asked Seth.

"Seth's my bodyguard," Petra improvised before he could respond.

"Bodyguard? Hired by Excelsior? I knew it," Carter crowed. "Petra with a boyfriend was a real stretch even for me to believe."

Bodyguard. Good cover. While Seth appreciated her quick mind, he was sharply aware she lied with no hesitation to a superior she knew well but didn't trust. More troubling to his male ego, Carter implied she didn't get intimate with men. He rubbed his cheek. Yet their kiss on the tundra left her panting, her lush bosom trembling, if he did say so himself. Maybe she was manipulating them both. He made a quick decision.

"Keep all this to yourself, buddy," Seth warned. "Sabotage is serious business. Petra may be in danger, and by association, so might you. Watch your back."

Relief shone on Petra's well-scrubbed face. She pushed her chair away from the table. "Carter, please wait in the office for the cores." She glanced at Seth. "I'm going to sleep for a few hours. Alone."

"Of course, babe. I can see how tired you are." Besides, Seth had his own plans for the next couple of hours.

Petra sniffed suspiciously at his easy acquiescence. "Carter, I'll take over from you in the office at midnight. If the crew brings in the first set of cores before then, call me."

"Sure thing, boss."

She ignored the sarcasm. "I don't have the energy to play around, guys." She targeted both men with her words, hands on slim hips. "This really is serious business."

"Shit." Carter forked apple pie into his mouth after she walked away. "I don't know why the hell I don't just quit and leave her alone to collect the cores."

"The money?" Seth ventured.

"The money's good. Excelsior pays well." He slurped half a glass of water. "But there are other compensations. Hey, here she comes now. Desirée slips away for half an hour to have coffee with me after dinner."

A statuesque blonde woman in a white uniform approached them carrying three coffee cups on a tray. Long fingers tipped with scarlet unwrapped a cup in front of him. Seth hitched a breath and took inventory. The baggy white uniform didn't quite conceal curves in all the right places. Her back arched on purpose, pushing melon-shaped breasts against the permanent-press fabric as his eyes traveled slowly down from dyed, pale-blonde hair drawn back in a tight bun to a set of curious icy blue eyes and pale but exquisite facial features bare of cosmetics. Her figure, gussied up in better clothes, would stop traffic. He rationalized that a woman who lavished attention on polished nails but nothing else probably downplayed her femininity to defend herself against a camp full of sex-starved males.

Or found herself a protector. His eyes widened when Carter's hand grabbed her butt and she didn't slap his hand away.

"Have a seat, *poupée*," Carter invited. "That's French for 'doll'."

Seth rose to offer her his hand. "My name's Seth Cooper. And your name is…"

"Desirée. Desirée Dumont." She smiled, displaying perfect, capped, whitened teeth. Expensive set of choppers for kitchen staff. "I am so please to zee a new face around 'ere."

Sexy as hell French accent. Her mellow voice slithered down his spine like a cold ice cube on a hot night. "Are you from Quebec?" He named the Canadian province where most of the population spoke French.

"Nah. She's European, from Belgium." Carter lifted a muscular arm to drape it across her shoulders. "She works full time, because she's got nowhere else to go on her two weeks off."

Desirée's overgrown brows twitched with irritation. To Seth, she explained, "I love to cook. It is my life. And the money in ze north is, of course, wonderful."

"Sure," Seth agreed. Cooking four hundred meals at a time of plain, hearty food in an industrial kitchen was every cook's dream. So it had to be the money. Desirée Dumont intrigued him on many levels. "I've been telling Carter that I sketch people for my own amusement, and he suggested I draw you. What do you say?"

"Oh." Her eyes darkened and she snapped to Carter. "Why do you suggest such a thing?"

"You're so beautiful, *poupée*." Carter pulled her onto his lap, where she balanced precariously. Desirée had six inches in height on him, easy. "I want a picture for when I'm off-site to remind me of you."

"You took a photo already."

"Yeah, well, I lost it."

Seth opened his sketch book. "Have a look-see, Desirée." He flipped through the series of caricatures he'd drawn of some of the men he'd encountered on previous flights into Ptarmigan Lake. "These sketches aren't ever going to end up in the Louvre, but you might find them amusing. Recognize any of these fellows?"

Desirée pulled Carter's arms from around her waist and moved into the chair vacated by Petra. "They are what you call cartoons."

"Yes. I find a distinctive feature and exaggerate it."

"What would you exaggerate with me? I am so plain, so simple a woman."

A knowing glance passed between the men. Seth cleared his throat. "I believe Carter might prefer an emphasis on your figure." He extracted the charcoal pencil from inside the coil binding and commenced drawing a few curved lines on a fresh page. A voluptuous hourglass torso clad in a skintight mini-uniform emerged under the pencil tip.

A musical laugh escaped Desirée's lovely throat. "You are too kind."

"I need an actual sitting to finish the rest properly."

"You shall have it, but it must wait until my shift ends in an hour." She rearranged long legs ending in trendy thick-soled clunky shoes and rose to her feet. "I must return to help put away the leftover food."

"Tomorrow's lunch," Carter said in an aside.

"Oh you." She patted a furry cheek. "I will see you later too, *mon amour.*"

"Don't you have to return to your office?" Seth reminded him.

Carter's face fell. "Shoot. Sorry, *poupée*, I can't join you until after midnight. I have work to do."

"Then Seth will have me all to himself." She winked and waltzed down the aisle with a swing that captured the fevered attention of every man in the vicinity.

"Quite the woman."

"Yeah," Carter replied. "I still can't believe my luck." He smirked and leaned closer, confiding, "She can't keep her hands off me. So how are you going to kill the next hour?"

Seth stretched his fingers. "Oh, I may wander into the lounge and check out the Sports channel while I wait for Desirée."

\* \* \* \* \*

Shortly after eleven, Seth quietly let himself into Petra's room with his key card. Soft rhythmic breathing emanated from a mound under the bedding he could barely discern in the dimness. She'd closed the curtains to block the daylight. In mid-July this far north the sun barely kissed the horizon to mark the transition from one day to the next. He advanced in the gloom and cursed as he tripped over the duffel bag he'd left just inside the door.

The mound erupted. "Who's there?"

"Seth," he said in a normal tone, moving to part the curtains a crack. "Time to get up."

Petra levered herself into a sitting position and clutched the blanket to the neck of her white thermal underwear. "What are you doing here?" Sleepiness fuzzed the edge of her words.

A grin tipped the corners of his mouth. She apparently shopped for lingerie at Work Warehouse. "This is my room too, remember?" Seth dropped heavily onto the edge of the bed to remove his boots.

"What are you doing?"

He quirked a brow. "Isn't it obvious? I'm preparing for some shuteye."

"Oh no. Not yet! I mean, let me get dressed and out of here first."

"Don't panic." Seth patted the two lumps that were knees drawn up to her chest. "I'm so beat I can barely keep my eyes open. Besides, you're sporting long underwear like ever-lovin' armor. It's hardly a turn-on."

"These are my p.j.'s."

"Right. Well, I don't wear any." He shucked his T-shirt and tossed it on top of the leather jacket draped over the back of the chair.

"That's what I'm afraid of," came the mutter from the other end of the bed.

"Pardon me?"

"Nothing."

"Nobody's forcing you to watch." He unbuckled his leather belt and unzipped his fly to the accompaniment of a muffled moan.

"Where's your gun?"

"I'm undercover, remember? A gun sure woulda triggered the security alarms."

"Get undressed in the bathroom. Please," she pleaded, her voice pitched high.

"Too late." Seth, naked but for boxer briefs, yanked at the blanket she clutched in a death grip. "Move over, darlin'."

# CHAPTER THREE

Seth's muscled chest and shoulders were backlit by shards of light escaping the blackout curtains. The skin of the man's upper body flowed—a scenic landscape of smooth surfaces curving into sinewy mounds in all the right places. Petra dared drop a glance to white boxers swimming with rainbow trout before swiftly averting her eyes. Her independently minded stomach fluttered. She refused to be attracted. She refused.

"I have work to do," she said aloud as much for her benefit as his.

"Hop to it then," he said without a trace of sympathy. Or invitation to linger longer.

"Right." She pushed back the covers and swung her legs over the edge of the bed, perversely disappointed that he hadn't even attempted a peck on the cheek. The public affection was all for show. No nooky. That was the agreement. Then why was she feeling so peeved at his lack of interest? To answer that question required deep internal analysis, for which she had no time. Ever.

She gathered a fresh set of clothes and dashed to the bathroom before the desire to test his attitude elbowed aside common sense.

Hot water coursed down her limbs, beat back some of the energy-sapping fatigue. By late Monday morning, in just over

80 hours, she'd be on the scheduled flight from Edmonton to Denver, far, far from Seth and from the temptation to feel. As the hot water dissolved brain fog, rational thoughts slowly displaced the uncomfortable desire Seth stirred to the surface. Thoughts like what had he been doing for the last three hours. Who had he contacted? What had he learned? Blast it! She'd wasted a prime opportunity to grill him when exhaustion lowered his guard. But she could remedy that.

In four minutes she'd toweled off, dressed and scooted to the bedside.

Seth lay flat on his back, magnificent bare chest rising and falling rhythmically, blanket bunched at his waist.

She shook one muscled shoulder. "Seth. Don't fall asleep yet. I have questions."

He grunted and shifted onto his side, his back to her.

"Seth. It'll only take a moment," she insisted in the accessible ear.

His deep breathing didn't falter. He couldn't be in REM deep sleep already. Anyway, weren't cops supposed to be alert 24/7? So far he was giving a good impression of a hibernating bear, down for the season.

Petra bounced onto the bed and scrunched low to face him. "Seth. We need to talk."

"Kate." He flopped one arm across her waist. "Come to bed," he mumbled.

Kate. That stopped her. But only for a moment. Now she had one more question for the list. She gently removed his arm and placed it at his side. He immediately slid the hand under his cheek and breathed deeply. She rocked one relaxed shoulder. Nothing.

With a sigh she hitched to the end of the bed and stood. Her questions would have to wait.

A few minutes later she strode through the unlocked door to Carter's office in the Mine Services building. A rolling snore assaulted her ears. Figured. Carter slumped in one of the chairs, bearded chin on chest, comfortably fast asleep. A quick scan of the table top and rest of the cluttered room verified the first set of cores hadn't been delivered yet. It was going to be a long night.

She lifted the lid on the coffeepot and wrinkled her nose at the bitter aroma. Had to be six hours old, at least. She found a tin of coffee to one side and resolved to make a fresh pot. After dumping out the muddy liquid in a bathroom sink down the hall and filling the glass container with fresh water, she returned to find Carter still sawing logs. Some security guard. Looked like she'd be needing the coffee over the next couple of days. On full-time duty, sharing a room with Seth wouldn't be part of the picture, she thought with a disconcerting mixture of relief and regret.

She inserted a fresh filter and tipped a healthy scoop of coffee grounds into it. An eraser-tip-sized lump poked out of the grainy deposit. She fished the dull glass pebble out with a forefinger. Her breath caught. No way! Heart thumping, she blew to remove the grains of coffee and inserted the rough-surfaced stone under Carter's microscope. She adjusted the magnification, rotated the tiny pebble. Not quartz. An honest-to-God rough diamond. As her legs gave way, her rear automatically found a stool. The room whirled and then stabilized.

After rough diamonds were mechanically separated from worthless rock in the processing plant, employees transported them under heavy guard to the sorting and valuation facility. Only then, under the watchful eye of security cameras, did human hands touch the stones. This diamond, as manifest as the microscope holding it, did not belong anywhere on site but in a safe. She clapped her hand to her forehead. Unwillingly she sidled a step closer to believing Seth's story—smuggling dropped out of the hypothetical realm. A thin moan escaped her lips. This complication she didn't need right now.

For the second time that night she attempted to waken a man sunk deep into oblivion. "Carter, damn you! Wake up." She tapped palms against both fuzzy cheeks a mite more forcefully than warranted. "How did the ice get into your coffee tin?"

"Coffee tin?" He stirred, shook his head and pressed thick fingers to his brow. "My head is splitting. What did you say?"

"Get it together, man." She ran to close and lock the office door. "We've got a situation. I found a rough diamond in your coffee tin."

A horrid notion stole her breath. Maybe there were more. Swiftly she emptied the tin's contents onto the table. Two more stones clicked dully as they tumbled onto the metal surface. "Make that three rough diamonds."

Diamonds didn't appear out of thin air. The two of them were being set up. By framing her and Carter with possession of stolen diamonds, the smugglers would divert security's attention from themselves. She felt the truth of that crazy idea settle into her gut.

"Carter, we are so screwed if they find us with these," she squeaked, trying unsuccessfully to stifle the panic squeezing her vocal cords.

Carter swayed groggily to his feet. "Show me the ice. Where'd you find it?"

She lined up the three stones, at least a carat each in size, beside the spilled medium roast. "In the coffee tin."

He swung his head from side-to-side like a woolly musk ox to clear it. Bleary eyes focused on the unwelcome discovery. "They weren't there when I last made coffee."

"What, yesterday?"

"No." He shot her reproach for the insult. "Coffee lasts only a couple of hours in this joint. I made a fresh pot after dinner."

"Anyone drop in to visit?"

"Could be." When she glared at him, he shrugged. "How would I know? I fell asleep."

"Both doors were unlocked," she accused.

"Big deal. The cores haven't arrived yet." He peered left and right to make certain. "We're in deep doo-doo," he muttered as the implications sank in.

"You got that right." Petra tapped her fingers on the table hard enough to make the precious pebbles skip. "If we're caught with these, we'll never work in the industry again."

"More to the point, we'll be tossed into jail." Carter's eyes bulged, wide awake now.

Petra swung to inform him the RCMP was sniffing around for evidence such as this, and in fact one cop had already attached himself to her like Velcro, but thought better of it. Carter was a wild card in this game.

Whoever hid the diamonds in her temporary office wanted to remove her from the property permanently. Pointing the finger at her, she reasoned, solved two problems. First, the smugglers diverted the cops' attention to the geologists. Second, with her and possibly Carter in custody, the cores would never make it to Denver by the deadline. Her eyes narrowed. The chairman of the Excelsior board might be playing both angles. She wouldn't put it past Athlone to simultaneously rip off the diamonds and manipulate the stock price.

"What are we gonna do?" Carter whined.

"Get rid of the diamonds fast," Petra returned. "Take the stones and toss them on the ore stockpile outside the processing plant."

"Me? Why me? You should do it. It's your idea. You found 'em."

"They're watching me." As she said the words, she knew them to be true. They, whoever *they* were, monitored every move she made. With video surveillance equipment in all the corridors, that wasn't difficult. She debated calling Seth for advice, but demurred. Once Seth came running into camera range, he'd potentially be implicated along with her and Carter. If charged for possession of rough, she would need her only ally to be above suspicion.

Another painful idea occurred to her. "They may have hidden more ice in this room. We'll have to tear it apart."

"Okay. You win." Carter had meanwhile put that prodigious brain to work analyzing the situation. "There's a plot to cut you out of the picture, and no way I'm gonna be swept up in this mess. You search. I'm getting the diamonds the hell outta here in case security pops by on a tip." He swept the three pebbles into one fist and bolted for the exit to the outdoors.

"Act natural," she hissed. "Pretend you're going for a walk. Don't head directly for the stockpile, for goodness sake."

"Trust me," he flung over one shoulder.

She fervently wished she could.

With Carter absent, she paused to plan a systematic search of the cluttered office. If she were trying to frame someone, where would she hide incriminating evidence? Fortunately the wall and ceiling construction of this module, foam insulation sandwiched between metal skin like a freezer building, eliminated the possibility of hiding places in wall cavities and above a suspended ceiling. That left the tables, desk, and underside of chairs and stools. She dropped on hands and knees to crawl under the long central table.

Back-to-back shifts allowed the smugglers scant minutes to slip in and out of the room unobserved. Unless a member of Carter's team planted the diamonds. She rejected that as improbable. Why would a crook risk investigation because diamonds were discovered in his place of work?

Heavy boots clumped up to the exterior door, which swung open without the formality of knocking. "Put the cores on the table," a deep voice directed.

Petra scrambled from under the table to the astonishment of the middle-aged aboriginal drilling-crew boss, Charlie Wha ti, whom she'd met before, and his two helpers. "I dropped a pen," she improvised.

"Sure, Ms. Paris." Charlie had a more important concern at the moment. "Hey. What's our coffee doin' all over the table?"

"Oh, I had a small accident," she said as she swept the powder off the metal edge into the can.

"I ain't drinking that," a husky man in his early twenties complained. "You got dirt in it."

"We were anticipating a cup of hot coffee," Charlie admonished. "This is our break."

"Take your break in the cafeteria, guys." Petra's patience, stretched wire-thin, snapped. "Fifteen minutes then back to work. There's a deadline, remember."

"You got a new set of coordinates for me?" Charlie swung his gaze about the room, his ancestral sixth sense unsettled by the incongruities of walking in on a woman crouched under the table and coffee spilled far from the pot.

"Carter will be here when your break's over. Pick 'em up then."

"Fine." To her vast relief three sets of steel-toed boots clumped down the corridor.

Carter's head bobbed up to peer through the open window. "All clear?" He ambled through the exterior door as if he hadn't a care in the world, brushing the palms of his hands together.

"That was quick." Petra eyed him, concerned. "You couldn't have made it to the stockpile and back so fast."

"I got rid of the ice. What do you care?"

"What did you do with them?"

He smirked. "I walked over to the security office entrance and, well, dropped them."

She paled. "You pitched thousands of dollars worth of diamonds into the dirt?"

"It's the last place security will look for them." He snorted with laughter.

She didn't join in. "Carter," she began, then changed her mind. They had priorities—first to finish the search for cached diamonds, then to log the cores. And it was equally important to keep the cores rolling in. "Your drilling crew is waiting for the next set of coordinates. We'll start with those."

An hour later, deserted by Carter who insisted on some shuteye, in his bed this time, Petra slumped in Carter's chair nursing her second cup of extra-strong coffee from the cafeteria. A thorough search of the premises had been fruitless, to their mutual relief. Her next task lay neatly on the table. Five long cylinders of hard rock nested in wooden molds. She didn't intend to convey all the core back to Colorado, of course. It was her job to select a representative sample from each set of cores.

Yet fatigue cloaked her shoulders. Scratchy eyes burned. Speculation fractured her concentration. Who hid the diamonds? Which of the four hundred mine employees brazenly walked past a dozing Carter to salt the ground coffee? Someone with an excuse to be in the office, she reasoned. That narrowed it down to maybe, oh, one hundred staff.

If collecting cores for head office were merely about doing her job, she'd have chartered a plane homeward before breakfast. The smugglers were attempting to intimidate her, and they'd succeeded. But this job was personal. She needed to know if her father doctored the assay results. Only fresh analysis by an independent lab could confirm his credibility, not only to the industry at large, but also to a daughter who feared Edward Paris to be a cheat across the board. Once she knew the answer, she could get on with her life.

At 6:45 a.m., Carter cautiously pushed open the door. Relieved to find her upright and glowering fiercely at him, he stepped into the room. "Everything fine here?"

"No one's arrived to haul me off in handcuffs, if that's what you mean," she snapped.

"Not yet, maybe. Get ready, because two security guards are right behind me."

She started to her feet. "What—"

"Yup. An anonymous caller phoned in a tip fifteen minutes ago, just like I predicted. They woke me to get down here pronto. Some wake-up call. I haven't even had breakfast yet."

Two young men with "Security" embroidered on their white, knit shirt pockets and across their backs pushed past him. "Sorry to disturb you, ma'am, but we have to follow through on all reports of loose diamonds," said the taller of the two, with a bad case of acne and blond spiked hair.

"Do I have to stay for this?"

"If you wouldn't mind, ma'am."

His stony expression didn't give her an option.

While the two security officers methodically emptied every drawer and upturned the movable objects, Petra leaned against the interior doorjamb, arms crossed, vibrating with nerves and trying not to show it. Carter slouched at a computer monitor, pretending to prepare his weekly status briefing for the mine manager.

"Good morning, honey." Petra lurched as Seth's arm swung casually across her shoulders. She'd been too preoccupied with the search to hear his approach along the corridor. Defenses at low ebb, her eyes unaccountably welled with tears.

"You feeling okay?" He attempted to search the face she angled away from him.

"It's been a long night."

"What are these yahoos doing?" He frowned at the chaos generated over the previous twenty minutes.

"Searching for diamonds," she choked, wishing for once that their relationship was real and she had the right to turn into Seth's arms for a bolstering hug.

As if reading her mind, he pulled her to the other side of the corridor, still in plain sight of the guards, and drew her close to growl under his breath. "Tell me what's going on."

"Seth, I'm being set up." She unwrapped her arms, slid them around his waist and nestled her head into the curve of his shoulder, the better to whisper into his ear, she told herself. Part of the act. "I found three rough diamonds in the coffee tin last night."

"Where are they?" His arms tightened, pinning her close enough to feel the accelerated heartbeat beneath his navy blue T-shirt.

"Carter got rid of them." She winced, appalled a fellow geologist had been so cavalier about valuable stones belonging to his employer.

"Lucky break you discovered them before someone alerted security." His tone roughened. "Any unauthorized visitors yesterday?"

"Seth, this office is Grand Central Station. Anyone could walk in here."

"The video cameras in the corridor record everyone who entered from inside the complex, but the exterior of this end of the building isn't covered by cameras."

The shorter, swarthy guard approached. "What are you two doing out there?"

"Spending some time with my girl, sir," Seth replied. He cupped the back of her head and brushed his mouth over hers. She leaned into the kiss, starved for the comfort he offered unaware, glad down to her toes for the opportunity to experience one of Seth's marvelous kisses. But as his lips captured hers she remembered Kate and pulled away. Seth dragged his mouth across her cheek, rubbed one hand the length of her spine, tangled the other in her hair, caressing, keeping up the pretense.

The guard backed off. "Take five minutes, then I want you in this office."

"We're on camera," she breathed.

"Let's give them a show." He nibbled his way toward her earlobe.

As private time to talk, this would have to do. Under the circumstances, she shelved the possibility of a girlfriend named Kate and played along, tipping her head to give him better access to her neck. Exquisite tingles rippled down stress-taut nerves. She breathed deep, tried to focus. "As a suspect, Scott won't allow me to view yesterday's digital video recording. Can you get access to them?"

"Not without blowing my cover." Seth quickly sifted through his options. The last thing an undercover cop wanted was to attract attention to himself. By hooking onto Petra, he'd unwittingly stumbled into an entirely different drama. Or perhaps the smugglers had a reason to prevent her from completing her job. Either way, Petra's situation put him in the spotlight instead of in the background, and he didn't like it one bit.

Well, he amended, he enjoyed the interaction with this beautiful woman. She trembled in his arms, uncharacteristically compliant. He attuned his senses to her shallow breathing, the fingers digging into his waist, and tension radiating from neck muscles under the soft, soap-fragrant skin beneath his lips.

By staying on site as Petra's lover, watched, his movements restricted, he'd have limited ability to mingle casually with the employees and chat them up, thereby compromising the success of the undercover operation. In short hours word of the early morning search would have spread to the entire camp. He had no business staying on undercover. Procedures dictated he call in for a replacement.

Yet he couldn't bring himself to abandon Petra to these vultures. Experience taught him that as the perps became more desperate, the danger to those in their way escalated.

"You need to leave this place. Get out fast. Fly to Yellowknife with me this morning."

"No." She tilted her heart-shaped face up to him, a stubborn frown marring her clear brow. "I need the cores."

"Listen, woman." He wanted to shake sense into her. Instead he crooked his arm to swing her away and down such that his back blocked them from the camera's view. Mouth grazing her ear, he spoke quickly. "You're in danger. These guys won't stop at trying to frame you. They want you gone, one way or another."

She squirmed, supremely irritated at being rendered off balance. "I can take care of myself."

He ground his teeth and clutched her firmly against his chest. "I can't protect you," he explained with a patience he didn't feel. "My cover, as you know, is a pilot for Northern Lights Air—a real job. My boss has me booked on three flights today, bringing me back to camp by dinner, if I'm lucky. I have to leave."

"I never asked you to protect me. You're using me to get access to the employees here, remember?" she hissed.

"Are the cores worth your life?"

"You're overreacting. Let me go." She twisted forcefully from one side to the other until he relented and released her, cursing softly.

"Why are the cores so damn important?"

She cast him defiance spiced with determination. "That's my business. You attend to yours, and leave me to mine."

Before Seth could invent a suitable rejoinder to such a hell-bent-for-trouble attitude, more trouble erupted behind them. A cell phone warbled. One of the guards answered, gave half a dozen "yes" and "no" responses, and finally grunted assent.

"Sorry to interrupt," Spiked Hair said, approaching. Petra straightened at Seth's side. "Ma'am, Bob Scott wants to see you and Mr. Lee in his office."

"Tell him we'll drop in after breakfast," Carter ordered from his perch at the computer.

The guard swiveled. "I don't think so, sir. The chief of security wants to see you now."

"I'm coming along," Seth said.

"He didn't ask for you." The guard scratched his chin doubtfully. "But hey, you want to be questioned for an hour, that's your decision."

"Don't you have a charter to fly?" Petra interjected.

Seth read defiance in her eyes, yet her full lower lip trembled ever-so slightly. Scared, he intuited, though she'd never admit it, and with energy at a low ebb from hunger and fatigue. He checked his watch. "I've got twenty minutes. How 'bout I collect some breakfast for the three of us and join you in Scott's office?"

"What about the cores?"

An attempt to frame her for theft, security breathing down her neck, and she never forgot the effing cores. Seth dragged one hand down his cheek. "One of you guys is staying to secure this room until they return, of course."

The two guards consulted. "We have to stay until the new shift relieves us," Spiked Hair said. "In case there's evidence."

"Then it's settled." Seth ushered the geologists and shorter guard out the door before it occurred to the kid to call in to confirm their orders.

The security center in the main building consisted of four interconnected rooms. The largest, the access point to the mine facility for all employees and visitors, contained equipment to x-ray incoming and outgoing baggage. A pricey backscatter x-ray machine, which emitted less radiation and was thus safer for scanning humans, took up one corner. Seth had overheard one miner label the area "the SAC", for Search and Confiscate.

In the second room, monitors blinked with tiling pictures from digital video cameras mounted at various locations on-site. The third held lockers, desktop computers, and a table and chairs—a common room for the security staff. Finally, the Chief, Security Services' private office, with its one-way window wall onto the SAC, immaculate desk surface, and impressive communications center, doubled as an interview room.

"I'm carrying a hell of a load in Hank Horvath's absence," Bob Scott groused as Seth arrived with muffins, yogurt and fruit on a tray. "I don't need this aggravation."

"Believe me, neither do I," Petra shot back.

"So what's the story?" Scott fixed his small sharp eyes on Petra for the explanation, Seth noted, not the senior geologist, who helped himself to two bran muffins and eased into a chair out of Scott's direct line of sight.

"You tell me. Who phoned in the so-called tip this morning? Who's trying to set me up?" Petra vibrated with controlled rage.

Seth placed a warning hand on her shoulder while offering a plateful of food. She got the message. Shut up. Spooned yogurt between quivering lips. Waited for the questions.

Scott thrust his shoulders forward, took on an aggressive bearing. "We've established Carter occupied the office between 9 p.m. last night and 1 a.m. You arrived at what time, Miss Paris?"

"Doesn't the camera recording show that?" Petra poked her chin out, defiant.

"Answer the question." Irritation pinched Scott's fleshy features.

Not good. Seth willed Petra to cooperate. This wasn't the time to show her feisty side. Perps mouthing off tended to validate cops' suspicions. Scott had the upper hand, and he knew it. "Easy," he whispered from behind.

"Hey. No interference from you. What's your name again? Seth something? That charter pilot. What are you doing here anyway?" Scott lifted from his chair, voice rising. "Who let you through that door?" He pivoted to pin the swarthy guard at the entrance with an accusing scowl.

"My name's Seth Cooper. I'm Petra's boyfriend."

"Well, get the hell out of here, Cooper. This is a private interview. No wait." His brain clicked over a couple of scenarios, and a possibility slid into the wrong slot. "I want to talk to you after this interview."

Seth shook his head. "Sorry, I have a scheduled flight and two charters today. In fact, I'm late."

"You returning to Ptarmigan Lake tonight?"

He didn't hesitate. "Yeah." Petra's shoulder under his hand sagged with relief. Yet guilt gnawed. Only a complete heel abandoned a woman under fire. One crucial impact of staying—he'd risk blowing his cover, and when that happened his superiors would remove him from the field, leaving Petra on her own. Seth didn't bother to second-guess his gut's impulsive decision. In his daily report to his cover man back at the RCMP HQ, carefully omitting details of his and Petra's bogus relationship, of course, he'd request backup. This, he rationalized, compensated for his compromised position.

"Call me when you get in. I want to have a chat with you as well," Scott ordered.

Seth squeezed Petra's shoulder. "I should be in around seven p.m.," he said for her benefit.

"Search him before he takes off," Scott barked at the security guard. "Put him through the scanner."

"Yes, sir." The security guard tucked one hand into the belt where the holster would have been if he'd been allowed to carry a gun. In his visits to the mine site, Seth hadn't come across a security guard older than twenty-five, other than Scott. Wet-behind-the-ears kids, most of them, bulking up in the weight room in their off hours.

\* \* \* \* \*

Petra angled her head to watch Seth through the one-way window. Tall, nonchalant, he toed a yellow line within a cordoned off area and allowed himself to be zapped by the x-ray machine. He had no choice really. None of them did if they wished to remain on or return to the site. When the guard gave a thumbs-up signal, Scott, obviously disappointed, turned his attention to her.

"Tell me about Seth Cooper. Where did you meet him?"

"Yellowknife," she said truthfully.

"When?"

"Oh, on one of my trips up north."

He thumped the desk with one meaty fist, making her jump. "If you're not more forthcoming, this is going to be a long session."

She'd wondered how far she could push him. Apparently not that far. "We met when he piloted a plane I chartered."

"Not good enough, Miss Paris." He leaned back in his chair and folded meaty arms above a rounded belly. "We know who Seth Cooper is."

# CHAPTER FOUR

Seth waved thanks to the maintenance duo who'd given him a lift the quarter mile along a bumpy dirt track to Ptarmigan Lake. The unceasing clamor of monster truck engines and house-sized shovels scraping bedrock, interrupted at intervals by rock-blasting, was less intrusive here, muffled somewhat by the low hills separating the lake from the camp. There were few places at the mine site where two undercover cops could meet unobserved. This was one of them.

Once the pickup rattled out of sight around a bend, he sniffed the cool air and assessed the flying conditions. A stiff wind at twenty thousand feet thinned wispy cirrus clouds, but at ground level a western breeze merely ruffled the lake surface. Nothing stood in the way of a smooth takeoff. Except his own skills, of course. He'd only been checked out on floats a month prior. Most of his flying before this assignment had been recreational, out of a municipal airport in southern British Columbia. Fortunately he'd pursued a commercial pilot's license, or he'd still be home tracking growers attempting to sneak the infamous weed across the Canada-US border.

He strode briskly past a trailer-sized building, two sixteen-foot-high round fuel storage tanks, and a coiled fuel hose nestled inside an earthen berm. A separate pipeline suspended on pipe supports paralleled the gravel road down to the shore where it terminated at the water pumphouse, the source of the camp's water supply. The float plane he'd docked overnight after flying a foursome of orthodontists and their gear into a fishing lodge on Great Slave Lake bobbed at the end of a floating dock.

Joe, the only other cop on site, undercover as a fuel tech, flung open the Beaver's cargo door, swung out to balance on the float, and from there hopped onto the wood planks. "Was wondering when you'd show up. You're half an hour late," Joe complained, pushing back a dusty Ptarmigan Lake Mine ball cap to expose his artificially blond hair.

"Sorry to keep you waiting," Seth rejoined. "I crashed an interview with the chief of security in his office this morning."

Joe immediately sobered. "Trouble?"

"We need to talk. Things are heating up faster than we expected."

Joe extended a hand toward the Beaver. "A couple of off-shift guys showed up to take the rowboat out fishing so I already topped up your tanks. I'm officially outta reasons to be here. Let's be quick. I have info for you as well."

Seth satisfied himself the fishermen drifted well out of earshot beyond the island in the center of the two mile-long lake before automatically performing a visual inspection. The robust bush plane with a seventeen-hundred-pound payload capacity had been specifically designed for short takeoffs and landings on the rugged, inaccessible lakes and rivers of Canada's wilderness. This fifty-seven-year old float plane had thousands of hours on its original nine cylinder, radial, air-cooled engine, yet Seth trusted the de Havilland Beaver more than any other small plane in

Northern Air's fleet to get him home safe through any weather, no matter how brutal.

Joe passed under the high wing to press a folded piece of paper torn from a notepad into Seth's palm. In a voice lowered in case the sound traveled over water, Joe gave his report.

"Here's a list of the guys on rotation this week in the processing plant and sorting and valuation facility. Samson Smith, a plant mechanic who repairs the crushers and scrubbers, is twenty-five thousand dollars in arrears on his child-support payments. Aaron Wintergate controls the x-ray equipment that luminesces diamonds in the pulverized ore at the recovery end of the processing sequence. Heard a rumor he's racked up a substantial obligation from online gambling."

"I'll get headquarters to compare your list with the shift workers on duty when that unfortunate SOB with the diamonds in his gut bought it." Seth paused. "I have a bad feeling something's going down, and soon. Today's Friday. The rotation changes Sunday night. The mine manager is off, leaving Bob Scott in charge. But guess what?" Seth didn't waste time waiting for Joe's shrug. "The chief of security is suddenly distracted by an anonymous tip that diamonds are hidden in the geologists' office. He has the female rockhound in the SAC right now for interrogation. Coincidence?"

Under a frown, sharp blue eyes fixed on his. "Another rumor has it that the female geologist is sleeping with you."

Seth winced. "Keep it to yourself, will you? I had to get on site somehow. Petra happened to be "

"Petra, is it? You're a fool," Joe interjected. "Now you're tied to someone involved in this mess. She an official suspect?"

"Doubtful. She's too obsessed with drilling new core. She believes she's been set up, and it fits. She conveniently showed up at a time when I suspect the smugglers want to divert attention. They're spooked. Potentially they've gotten wind of the RCMP investigation. My hunch is that they plan to pull out with the shift rotation."

"Is our cover compromised?" Joe had good reason to be worried. Not only would the undercover operation be rendered ineffective, common knowledge of their true affiliation put both men in danger. When stakes were high, perps tended to take extreme measures to defend their interests.

Seth crouched to inspect the front end of the nearest twenty-foot-long float rocking gently a couple of feet below dock level, and Joe accordioned his lean length to suit. "I don't believe so."

"But you're not sure. I should report this."

"Give me another day."

"Give me a reason."

"The woman knows more about the situation than she's saying. The fresh cores are crucial, who knows why. If HQ pulls me out, I can't find out what she's hiding. I think it's important. It might even break the case for us."

The other man reluctantly nodded. Relieved, Seth added, "Watch your back today."

When Joe reached for the diagonal metal strut bracing the overhead wing to haul himself to his feet, Seth grabbed his arm. "Wait. There's something else. What have you heard about Desirée Dumont?"

"Not much. She's a cook hanging with that geologist Carter Lee."

"She's supposedly from Belgium," Seth relayed, deadpan.

"Antwerp!" Joe immediately picked up on the connection. Rough diamonds poured into Belgium's capital city from mines around the world to be cut and sorted into lots for sale to jewelers. "Could be a coincidence."

"If you believe that, I've got a nice oceanfront lot for sale north of here. Cheap." Seth playfully shoved Joe's shoulder hard enough to topple him onto his rear. "I tried to pump the woman for details while sketching her in the TV lounge last night, but she did that dumb-blonde, girly-girl act and giggled her way out of direct answers."

"So maybe she isn't who she says she is." Joe scrambled to his feet to swat at the grit coating his coveralls.

"I intend to find out. Or at least, to alert HQ to do the background check when I'm in town later this morning. We've been focusing our investigation on the processing plant and sorting facility workers." He pinched the bridge of his nose, cursing under his breath. "It's well past time to widen the net."

\* \* \* \* \*

"What do you mean, you know who Seth is?" Petra attempted nonchalance, but her heart pummeled her ribcage hard enough to be recorded by the seismic event station in Yellowknife. "He's a pilot. He's my boyfriend. What else is there?"

The security chief slapped a pudgy hand on his desk. "He's moonlighting, Ms. Paris. We know all about it. So if I were you, I'd explain exactly why you are here in Ptarmigan Lake, and why you need a bodyguard."

"A bodyguard?" Inside she seethed. Carter, the blabbermouth, had better get his affairs in order. "Why on earth do you imagine Seth is my bodyguard?" She leaned forward. "He's my lover." Her tongue tripped over the unfamiliar word. The only time she'd honestly been able to make that statement was back in college a lifetime ago. Come to think of it, his name had been Bob too. By-the-book Bob. Their relationship had collapsed when she realized he wanted two kids, a nine-to-five job, and a house in the 'burbs.

"Ms. Paris. You're wasting my time, and I—don't—like—it." Scott extended his short neck beyond hunched shoulders to squint directly into her eyes, the better to gauge her reaction. "You were overheard in the cafeteria."

"You bugged the cafeteria?"

He let that go. "I repeat, why are you here?"

"I'm not authorized by Excelsior to reveal that information. Neither is Carter." She aimed the last at her silent colleague doing his level best to avoid attention.

"Everyone in this room is employed by Excelsior, Ms. Paris. There need be no secrets."

Petra, fatigued and anxious to check on the cores, spoke before she thought. "If they wanted you to know, they would have told you." She stood. "Now if you will excuse us, Carter and I have work to do."

Scott's skin purpled above the open V of his white shirt. "I didn't give you permission to leave."

"Do you have any grounds to hold me here? No. Besides, where am I going to go? I'm here until the job gets done. You know where to find me. Come on, Carter."

Carter tentatively lifted his butt off the plastic chair, waiting for a barked order to stay seated. When it didn't happen, he scurried after Petra.

"You didn't make a friend back there," he stated matter-of-factly when they'd turned the corner and entered the corridor leading to the Mine Services building. "Are you sure you know what you're doing?"

Petra didn't break her stride, yet her bravado masked tension that cramped her stomach. With persons unknown intent on sidelining her, a hostile security team, and her so-called protector flying off when his own job took priority, she had only herself to rely on. And that's the way she preferred it. Men complicated life. Messed it up big-time. "I know what I have to do and that's enough. Are you going to help or not?"

"I have to work with these people after you're back in Colorado."

"But you want to be sure you're on the right side."

"Yeah, so to speak. I have a career to think of. After the fiasco with our senior manager two years ago—"

"When you suggested in a staff meeting that the VP had obtained his geology degree through an ad on a matchbook cover."

"Jeez. The guy has no sense of humor. I'm a little more careful now."

"No kidding." Affection softened the tightness in her jaw. For the first time that morning she smiled. "I noticed." Carter's eccentricities bugged her at times, but then most of the people employed in this challenging industry fell outside the definition of conventional. When you lived away from home for months at a time, your coworkers became family.

At Carter's office she was glad to see the guard had apparently received word to abandon his post. Assuming the office had been bugged in their absence, she pulled Carter through the disheveled room, out the exterior door, and far enough across the gravel yard for privacy.

"Listen," she said as Carter wheezed, barrel chest heaving from the swift pace. "The less I tell you, the safer you'll be. This is the story. I'm here to collect core and deliver it for assay in Denver Monday morning. Seth is a pilot I hired to get me out of here in time to catch the 2 p.m. scheduled flight to Edmonton on Sunday. That's why we have to work day and night." She grabbed his shoulders for emphasis. "Forty-eight hours on site, Carter. That's all I've got."

He checked his watch. "It's almost 9 a.m. Your charter will have to leave Ptarmigan Lake at noon Sunday at the latest, so you actually have fifty-one hours—"

"Carter!"

"I think it's time to get back to work."

"Good idea."

\* \* \* \* \*

Carbohydrate-heavy pasta leadened Petra's stomach early that afternoon. Lunch had been a mistake. Eyelids sank south with increasing frequency as she teetered over the closest set of cores stretched the length of the stainless steel-surfaced table and made notations in her notebook. Six other unlogged kimberlite cylinders lay in wooden molds beside the batch that had been delivered overnight. So far, the efficient drill rig crew had met every production target. She expected to have her samples with hours to spare.

With most of her blood diverted to processing lunch in her digestive system, her brain had downshifted into the slow lane. A ceramic mug at her elbow taunted her with its residual scent of dark Colombian. When her eyelids drooped, she became desperate and ready to beg.

"Carter, I can't survive another minute without a cup of coffee."

"You threw the coffee tin in the trash." Carter didn't bother to interrupt his computer game.

"I know that." She bit back an impolitic curse. "Can we obtain another tin, or do we have to keep running back and forth to the cafeteria for coffee?"

His back stiffened. "By we, I assume you mean me."

"Carter, please. You know where the supplies are stored. I don't."

He heaved a put-upon sigh. "I'm still on my lunch break. I'll go when I finish this game."

"You've been playing for twenty minutes! You haven't even eaten yet." Crazed by a ferocious coffee craving and his intransigence, Petra leaped off her stool, marched across to his keyboard, and pressed the escape key. "You're finished. Find something to eat and bring me back some coffee."

"There's a reason you don't have a boyfriend," Carter dared over his shoulder as he reached the door. "You're a control freak."

Ouch. Fuming, Petra attempted to resume labeling the cores, but Carter's observation rankled. Darn it all, the little twerp nailed a sore spot. Men did seem to be put off by her assertiveness. Then of course she regularly disappeared into the hinterlands for extended periods of time. That didn't help fan the flames of romance. Yet she'd rather live to a solitary old age than abandon adventure punctuated by dizzy exhilaration when hard work paid off in the discovery of a new mineral deposit.

"Assertive's a good thing," she grumbled under her breath. Look where it had gotten her—recognition as co-discoverer of the second richest diamond deposit in the north. The respect of senior management. A decent investment portfolio…and a sparsely-furnished apartment she shared with a solitary cactus that had miraculously survived two summer field seasons. Her bottom lip pushed out as a tiny twinge of regret wedged a crack in her self-confidence. Seth probably liked soft, pretty women in shirts that they had to iron, with lacy push-up bras underneath. And names like Kate.

No wonder he tore off in such a hurry.

Fortunately Carter's return a half hour later with a coffee can and a thick package of filters kicked her unpleasant ruminations into the basement where they belonged. To her amazement he was even so accommodating as to make the coffee himself. Her eyes narrowed. He seemed unusually quiet, sullen even. Never mind. She concentrated on the delectable aroma and drip, drip as the carafe filled with fresh hot coffee.

When Carter refilled their mugs and placed hers on the table beside her paperwork, she thanked him with a heartfelt smile. "I owe you for this."

Two tentative sips of the hot liquid later, the drowsiness hadn't dissipated. If anything, she felt sleepier and prayed he hadn't picked up a can of decaf by mistake. The uneven blip, beep, blip of Carter's computer game reverberated like a gong inside her skull. She blew on the surface to cool the hot liquid then swallowed a mouthful. Seconds later Petra's upper body silently slumped forward onto the table.

# CHAPTER FIVE

Seth taxied the Beaver onto the apron and one-eighty'd to park with the propeller facing the Ptarmigan Lake strip. He'd had some difficulty wheedling permission from Northern Lights Air's operations manager, Drew Hamilton, to keep the small plane out overnight. With almost twenty-four hours daylight in early July, downtime meant lost business. Lucky for him other pilots on the NLA roster had reached their maximum flying hours for that day.

Seth's reputation for methodical, detailed police work powered by astute observation had won him the assignment with the Diamond Protection Unit. His superiors recognized his secret weapon in the war against drug smugglers at the border—an intuitive understanding of the criminal mind. He anticipated a perp's next move even before he did.

Instinct told him now that he may have been too hasty in deciding Petra Paris' rock gathering assignment fell outside the scope of the case. He had not one fact to substantiate this feeling. Yet his gut insisted on a phone call to ensure all was well. She hadn't answered the office phone or her satellite phone, and he could not reach Carter Lee. Scott may have locked them up. If so, she'd be spitting mad. A grim smile twisted his mouth at the vision—a preferable scenario to the others his dark imagination created.

Security staff retrieved him at the parking lot and drove him to the reception area. In response to his inquiry, a guard confirmed Scott had turned Petra loose shortly after Seth's departure that morning. It wasn't the answer he wanted. His stomach muscles tensed.

Once cleared through security, Seth strode quickly down the corridor to the Mine Planning and Geology Services office and rattled the doorknob.

Locked. Dammit.

Swiftly he scanned the area. Once. Twice. On the third sweep, he detected the lack of reflection off the security camera lens at the end of the corridor. Closer inspection revealed glass coated with black tape.

Spurred by adrenaline, he shoved open the emergency exit door at the far end of the corridor with unnecessary force and charged around to the office's exterior door. Locked as well. And the window sill to the right hung above eye level. He spun through the options to gain entry and selected the quickest avenue—the security staff key cards.

En route to the SAC he poked his head into the cafeteria on the remote chance an auburn-haired firecracker and her sidekick were chowing down. As he scanned the packed tables of men for a rare feminine form, Seth retrieved his cell phone and attempted another call to her room. No answer.

Single-minded Petra would never stray far from her precious rock cores. Unease rattled the outer calm he projected. He'd discounted Petra's worry that her cores were vulnerable. Mere rock cylinders weren't significant in the larger picture, he'd concluded. Logic dictated that diamond smugglers had no use for practically worthless drill core, and they'd attempted to frame her as a diversion. Yet if they'd targeted her again, she had something they wanted. He forced aside dark possibilities crowding his brain to concentrate on locating her.

The red-headed young pup he'd encountered that morning held the fort in the security office. When Seth made his request, the thin, lanky guard blinked rapidly.

"The other security staff with access cards are either in the cafeteria or are on shift change rounds. I'm under orders not to leave the communications console unattended. Give me a minute and I'll radio for someone to help you when he's free."

"No time. Both Petra Paris and Carter Lee are missing. I need access to their office. Now."

"It's standard procedure." The guard remained adamant. Remained seated. Remained calm. Seth wanted to haul the matchstick out of his swivel chair, upend him, and shake the access cards out of his pockets.

"Wait at the Mine Planning and Geology Services office for a guard with the master access card and code," the guard continued as he adjusted his headset and flipped open a radio channel on the console.

Seth blew out his frustration. There was a time and place for procedure. He had one more arrow in his quiver. "The video camera covering that section of the corridor has been damaged."

His blue eyes widened. "I'll alert Mr. Scott."

"That's more like it. If someone's not there with a key card in two minutes, I'm going to break down the door."

Seth beat it back to Carter Lee's office and, with nothing better to do, inspected the rooms on either side. The door on the right swung open freely to a space of a similar size to the office. It appeared to be a locker room and storage area for picks, shovels, ear protection and other small pieces of equipment. An exterior door provided easy access to the outdoors. Left of the office, the corridor door to a communal unisex washroom hung ajar. Both rooms were unoccupied.

A person with an access card could enter the corridor via the emergency exit, disable the camera from behind, and proceed to attend to business. The first threads of fear wrapped his gut. Kate had suffered when he misjudged her degree of safety. It cost him his marriage. Now another woman might be paying the price for his miscalculation. He ground his teeth. This was taking too long.

The blunt end of a double-headed long-handled pick looked promising. He hefted the tool over one shoulder and reached the office door in four hasty strides. As he prepared to take his first swing, Bob Scott steamed down the corridor, two cohorts in his wake.

"What the hell's going on?" Scott huffed, his round face red above the white beard.

Seth dropped the pick and stepped aside. "Petra's out of contact. So's Carter. I need this door open."

"They're probably at dinner," Scott grumbled, but Seth's agitation proved infectious. He produced the key card and swiped it through the lock.

At the click of the tumblers, Seth wrenched the doorknob and threw the door wide. Shock immobilized the four men for several seconds. Crushed and broken debris littered every surface including the floor. Petra's upper body lay face down amid shattered rock core strewn the length of the table. At the foot of her stool, Carter stretched face-up, framed by more rubble, loose papers, and bits and pieces of his smashed computer monitor.

Seth reached Petra first. Dread dried his mouth as he lifted the silky swath of her ponytail from her neck. With two trembling fingers he felt for a pulse.

"Strong and steady," he announced. Mushrooming relief blanked his vision momentarily. She was alive. He sucked in a deep breath and the tension cramping his jaw eased slightly.

"Same here," Scott reported from a crouch beside Carter Lee. He pried open one eyelid. "He's breathing fine and there are no marks on him."

Seth quickly patted Petra's head and accessible body parts, equally relieved to find no bumps or broken bones. Her notebook's metal coil dug into the soft flesh of her cheek, and he gently raised her head to pull the coffee-stained book out from under. She'd dropped her coffee cup before she passed out. Unconsciousness apparently overcame her in seconds. "They've been drugged." He picked up Petra's overturned coffee cup and sniffed.

Scott didn't deny the claim. Instead, he instructed one of his men to call the nurse, and the other to request backup.

Neither casualty had revived minutes later when men arrived with two stretchers and crunched over the wreckage to the pair. Swiftly the men trained for emergency response loaded them onto aluminum-framed stretchers and evacuated them to the on-site medical facility.

"Where's the nursing station?" Seth demanded of the departing team of first aiders.

"Behind Reception," one answered.

Satisfied Petra would be close by to receive the medical help he wasn't qualified to provide, Seth stayed to glean as much information as possible before Scott ordered him from the scene. Fortunately his presence took a back seat to organizing an investi gation. Seth figured he had two, maybe three minutes tops before the distracted security chief noticed him.

What were the perpetrators of such malicious destruction after? While Scott briefed his staff in the corridor, Seth surveyed the room without moving, without drawing attention to himself. The computer hard drive poked out of the dented CPU casing under Carter's desk. Day-to-day operations were of no interest to the perps, he concluded, although the microscope had been deliberately whacked beyond repair and thrown to the floor. They'd scattered technical manuals, books and papers haphazardly. But under them, the bottom layer of debris on the floor comprised wooden molds. His eyes narrowed as he memorized the scene, reconstructed the sequence of destruction, and filed his observations for later analysis. They'd overturned the wooden molds and attacked the core first, fracturing the long cylinders with a sledge hammer as evidenced by the deep dents in the metal-skinned table, and then disassembling the chunks of rubble such that they'd be impossible to sort out.

His attention returned to the notebook. It had more to tell him. The dry coffee-stained pages indicated several hours had passed since the event. He flipped a few ruled pages. Neat columns of incomprehensible numbers and letters covered four right-hand pages. The perps had no need of the documentation. They were after the cores.

Petra had been right. He pinched the top of his nose between his eyes. This time a woman had specifically warned him of the danger, and still he hadn't listened. Guilt co-mingled uncomfortably with lingering horror at the discovery of her prone body. He'd feared the worst. He'd almost failed. Again.

"Cooper!"

Time's up. "I was just leaving," Seth maintained as he carefully avoided crushing the evidence on his way to the corridor. "Gotta check on my girl."

"You do that," Scott glowered from under thick white brows. "But don't even think of flying out of here with Ms. Paris. I have questions for her."

"If she requires care beyond what the nurse practitioner can provide, you're not going to stop me." Seth made his statement matter-of-fact.

A vein popped out on Scott's temple. "I'm not finished with you yet," he said as Seth began to walk away. "Where'd you find that pick ax?" He pointed to the double-headed geologists' pick Seth had discarded upon arrival of the troops. "It coulda created the havoc in there."

Seth tensed. Dammit. The old geezer might be retirement age, but he was sharp. "The locker room is filthy with tools. That's where I found it."

"Your prints are all over the handle, no doubt."

"No doubt," Seth agreed, not waiting to hear the rest.

"I'll need your prints so the RCMP can rule you out," Scott shouted after him. "Report to the SAC in an hour."

Hell's bells. "Not if I can help it," he muttered to no one in particular. HQ had scheduled to feed him results of background checks on Scott and several others on a protected satellite channel at 11 p.m. He'd report the on-site incident and discuss with his HQ cover team how to deal with Scott without blowing his cover.

* * * * *

The fluorescent light overhead shot burning bolts through Petra's eyeballs. The throbbing head she tried to lift wobbled on a too-weak neck. She gave up and relaxed into the pillow. A moan under her breath drew a stranger to her side. "Who are you? A doctor?"

"I'm the camp nurse," corrected an attractive dark man clad in a lab coat over jeans and a white T-shirt. "My name's Sam Erasmus. How do you feel?"

"I'd feel better if you switched off the light," she complained as she inventoried her body. Legs moved. Fingers twitched. Head pulsed with waves of shooting pain.

"But with the lights off how could I treat my patients?" the nurse responded cheerfully, fingers at her wrist to take her pulse. "Would you like something to drink?"

She eyed him then. The last thing she remembered was sipping hot coffee. "What happened to me?"

"We have no idea. We're hoping you can tell us." Stocky but solid, with pleasant, even features framed by brown hair escaping from a short ponytail, the aboriginal patted her hand with the intent to soften his next words. "We suspect you and Carter were drugged." At her startled attempt to rise, he gently pressed one shoulder into the thin mattress. "Carter is fine. I gave him a painkiller for his headache and he's sleeping off the drug's effects over there." He jerked his chin toward the opposite corner of the infirmary.

"Do they know who did this to us?" She squeezed her eyes shut to stem tears from the pain slicing her brain to ribbons.

"Sorry, I don't have any information. Your boyfriend asked to be notified the second you woke. Maybe he knows more by now."

"Boyfriend? I don't have a boy— Oh." Petra clapped a hand over her mouth. "Seth." Her heart thrummed a tattoo. "Where is he?"

"I'll call him," the nurse promised, and did so, returning a minute later with a glass of water and a bottle of a familiar brand of painkillers. "While we're waiting, I expect you'd like a tablet for your headache."

"How do you know I have a headache?" The man seemed harmless, but Petra's antenna were raised and acutely alert.

"Carter had one," he replied reasonably. "You have no contusions. My working hypothesis is that someone knocked you out with a powerful drug, not a blow." While she absorbed the implications of the alternative, he added, "Your pulse and respiration are in the normal range. There appear to be no long-term side effects. Without knowing exactly which drug was administered, I'm afraid I can't offer you any remedy other than painkillers and bed rest."

"I don't want any more drugs." Or water. Even to her own ears the quiet protest lacked her customary energy. For all she knew Sam Erasmus was in cahoots with whoever did this to her and Carter. The troubling thought subdued any strong reaction.

"Suit yourself."

A single tap on the door warned of a visitor. Seth angled his broad shoulders into the room through the partially opened door. Her pulse quickened. Stubbled chin, charcoal hair mussed, his handsome face pinched with stress, he still had the power to connect all her circuits. Relief chased a complex play of emotions around his eyes when his gaze landed on her.

"How are you?"

"Alive," she said. "My head is splitting like someone took an ax to it."

He winced and retreated a step, stricken. She observed guilt overtake the concern etched in his furrowed forehead, and wondered at the distance separating them. "Whatever I've got's not catching."

He edged closer. "I had to confirm for myself that you're okay. The chief of security wants you to spend the night in the infirmary, but I think you'll be safer in our room."

Heat swamped Petra's cheeks. With a meaningful glance she drew Seth's attention to the nurse busy at the sink. "Sam, would you mind giving us a few minutes of privacy?"

"Privacy. Right." Sam checked her vital signs, raising an eyebrow at her rapid pulse, then visually confirmed his other patient slumbered undisturbed. "No problem, but keep it down. If you need me, I'll be in my office." He collected two file folders and closed the connecting door behind him.

Stars danced as she elbowed her upper body to a sitting position. When the room stopped whirling, she opened her eyes to again detect the complicated expression crimping Seth's face muscles—a mixture of exasperation and guilt, she decided. Though what he had to feel guilty about, she couldn't fathom. He'd no doubt been sitting at five thousand feet when she'd sipped the tainted coffee. "Sam didn't tell me what happened. Care to fill me in?"

He ignored her request, his mouth set in a determined thin line. "You're not safe here at Ptarmigan Lake. I'm flying you to Yellowknife first thing in the morning. Then I'm putting you on a jet to Edmonton."

"No way." She wagged her head for emphasis. Big mistake. When the room settled, she continued, "I have a job to finish."

He shook his head.

"I don't have a job to finish?" A dreadful suspicion flared. "Tell me the cores are safe." Her breath hitched and held as she waited for his answer.

He advanced to sit at the foot of the cot, out of reach of her fists, she noted. When the bad news came, it was mercifully brief.

"Pulverized."

Lips pressed tightly to help fight the nausea, she nodded wordlessly. A tear triggered by the agony of unwittingly moving her head escaped and dripped off the tip of her ear. "A day's work gone," she stated when able to speak. "Tell me what happened."

"I wish I knew. I landed about 7:30—"

Petra lifted a wrist to peer at her watch. "It's 9:30. We've lost half a shift," she wailed, closer to full-blown tears than she'd been in years.

Seth rolled his eyes heavenward. "Good grief, woman." His tone spiked with reproach. "You're lucky to be alive, and all you can think about is your damn job."

She stilled. "How lucky?"

This time he didn't hold back. "Whoever drugged your coffee proceeded to total the office. He or they deliberately smashed every core and scattered the pieces before trashing the rest of the contents."

"I wonder if the drill crew safeguarded the afternoon's production." Hope neutralized the bile rising in her throat.

Seth jumped to his feet. "Don't you get it? Those responsible are ruthless. You could have been killed. Next time they may put you out of commission permanently. I won't allow it."

"Shhhh." Petra pointed a forefinger at the softly snoring figure on the cot a mere ten feet from hers. "Carter's asleep." Killed? Her own instincts maintained Seth overreacted about the incident. Athlone's men wanted to destroy the cores, not her. Otherwise they'd have physically damaged her and Carter, not merely drugged them unconscious to get at the cores. Another unwelcome idea poked through the fussiness clouding her thoughts. "Carter might be faking in order to eavesdrop."

"The guy's snoring, Petra. You may have a point, though, about the eavesdropping. We should defer the rest of this conversation until we're in our room."

Seth's proximity in the relatively public infirmary she could handle. Hours locked up in a small bedroom with him was an entirely different type of proximity. She lashed out to cover her discomfort—the other kind of discomfort. The kind that arose from stifled sexual longing. "Since when do you tell me what to do?"

At that impertinence, he leaned over to position an arm on either side of her body. Quietly, for no one's ears but hers, he said with an edge that bespoke a barely controlled temper, "You have a choice. Stay here to be questioned by Scott now that you're awake, or come with me to sleep in your own bed."

His hot breath fanned her cheek, stirring an impulse to curl up in his arms for as long as it took to rid her body of the drug and the lethargy it induced. The prospect of being waylaid by Scott should she attempt to return to the office held no appeal in her current condition. The attraction to Seth, she figured, was easier to handle.

"When you put it that way, I don't have a choice."

\* \* \* \* \*

Seth leaned against the bathroom doorjamb, arms crossed, while Petra rooted in her backpack for a bottle of water. "I sincerely doubt the perps contaminated the camp's potable water supply in order to poison you."

"I'm not taking any chances. I don't see you drinking the tap water either." Flushed with the minor exertion and his scrutiny, she continued to search the various pockets in her quest for a safe beverage.

"After this particular day, I'd prefer beer. Several, in fact."

She waggled a raised brow at him from her cross-legged perch on the bed. "Ah. You're a drinker."

"No, I don't have a drinking problem, if that's what you're implying."

Her attempted diversion didn't work. He noticed the tremor in her fingers as they fumbled with the buckles. She belonged in bed. He strode to the bureau, retrieved her white thermal long johns and matching long-sleeved top from the top drawer, and hustled her into the bathroom.

"Do what you need to do. I'll find the water."

With a sigh, she acquiesced, but lobbed a parting shot as she closed the door. "You won't find anything interesting by snooping through my backpack."

He rolled his eyes. So she considered him a snoop. What else did she expect from an investigator? At least she allowed him to stay in the room. That represented progress and a smidgen of trust.

Several minutes later she emerged smelling of scented soap and mint toothpaste. Brushing had liberated rich burgundy hair that curled around soft shoulders. Amber-streaked eyes burned golden with simple desire in a too-pale face. His gaze froze on the dark, dry lips she licked, thirsty. The deepest part of him responded to her unintentional sensuality, drove him a step forward to touch, connect, until, like a man emerging from a trance, he abruptly halted on the precipice of sealing his mouth to hers. Only a jerk contemplated a romp with a woman barely returned to consciousness.

Straightening, he shoved the bottled water into her hand and extended a palm bearing a bottle of extra-strength acetaminophen tablets. "The painkillers are mine, straight from the Yellowknife Drugstore to you."

Before twisting off the water bottle cap, she examined the seal, twisting his heart in the process. Any trust she had in him was fragile, tentative. Still, she accepted the headache tablets and downed two with a long swig of warm water. It was a start.

"Can we talk?" She peered up at him.

He frowned. "Talk about what?" When women used those words, what followed generally made him squirm.

She waved a hand. "This room. It might be bugged."

Relief quirked the corners of his mouth. For a moment there he'd worried she planned to get personal. The thoughts intruding on his peace of mind, thoughts that involved the two of them rolling around naked, were already too personal for his comfort. "I swept the room with this nifty little gadget." He pulled a Swiss army knife out of his pocket. A quick maneuver and the case split apart lengthwise to reveal a tiny mechanism. "As sweepers go, it's not very powerful, but when placed next to the obvious hiding places, a bug activates this tiny light-emitting diode."

"Fill me in on what I missed then."

He shook his head. "Not tonight. We both need rest." Reaching over, he turned down the blankets. "Hop into bed."

"What are you going to do?" She frowned suspiciously over the top of the half empty water bottle.

He intended to strap her into the plane as soon as she recovered enough to travel safely out of reach of whoever drugged her. Then he'd be back to sort out this mess. He had tonight to impress upon her the danger of stubbornly remaining in camp. But he wasn't fool enough to tell her that straight out. He settled himself into the thinly padded easy chair and stretched his legs toward the bed. "I thought I'd keep you company until you fall asleep," he drawled.

Casting nervous glances his way, she plumped and piled the pillows before sliding long legs under the covers. Her curls fanned over the pillow, and long lashes drifting to rest on flushed cheeks extinguished the golden fire in her eyes. He began to relax. He could use a few hours of shuteye himself.

Seconds later her eyelids popped wide. "Did you lock the door?"

He struggled to keep the irritation out of his voice. "Of course. Go to sleep."

"I've had a seven-hour nap, remember."

"Well I haven't. I'm beat." He stood and stretched. "The chair is darned uncomfortable. Mind if I join you?"

"Yes, I do mind," Petra exclaimed with audible panic.

"I won't touch a hair on your pretty head. I'll lie on top of the blankets." When she began to protest further, he admitted, "My back will give out if I sleep in an awkward position."

Sympathy dimmed the agitated lights sparking her irises. "Back pain is the worst. I'm not keen to sleep sitting up myself." She made a decision. "Very well. We'll share the bed for tonight only, due to the extenuating circumstances. Tomorrow night we'll alternate."

There wouldn't be another night, but he didn't want to rile her. Regret tugged briefly that he'd never see her again after placing her on a commercial flight the next day. His line of work meant personal relationships warranted no place in his life. Too bad, though, in this instance. Petra, spirited and unaffectedly beautiful, lit an explosive chemical mix in his mind and belly that excited and occasionally frightened him. An undercover detective had no business allowing sexual attraction to interfere with his assignment. Petra's safety, not her curvy body, rated his attention. End of story.

Petra extracted one of the pillows and plumped it into place on his side of the double bed. After shucking his boots and jacket, he purposely ignored her deliberate effort to create distance and instead dropped heavily into a comfortable position on his back, shoulder to shoulder. As he anticipated, Petra squirmed away from the light contact. He deliberately readjusted his upper body, forcing her to withdraw to the very edge of the mattress where she remained rigidly quiet. To his pleased surprise she didn't insist he move over. It reassured him to feel her safe and close. Perhaps she experienced a similar comfort. After several minutes, a slight smile playing on his lips, he closed his eyes and relaxed in anticipation of a restful night.

"Who is Kate?"

The verbal jab convulsed his abdominal muscles. He'd never mentioned his ex-wife to anyone up north. His friends and co-workers back in British Columbia considered the divorce forbidden territory. No one dared raise the subject in his presence for fear of lighting a very short fuse. "What are you talking about?" he managed.

"Last night you called me Kate. Your exact words were, 'Kate, come to bed.'"

"I must have been dreaming." His firm statement broadcast a desire to end the discussion.

"Are you married?"

Dammit. He rolled onto his side away from her. "No."

"Girlfriend?"

"No. Go to sleep."

A small hand seared the flesh on his forearm. "Seth, in spite of my, ah, participation in this little romantic show we're staging, your girlfriend has nothing to worry about. A few kisses for appearances doesn't make you unfaithful."

Seth gripped the side of the mattress and ground out, "I'm not unfaithful. There is no girlfriend. Leave it alone, will you?"

"That's a relief. Men gossip, you know. Eventually word spreads to the—"

Seth reversed his body to pin Petra's chest with his. "I'm a single man. Got it? Kate is my ex-wife. We divorced two years ago. Three paroled drug smugglers I'd put away attempted to kidnap her. I couldn't guarantee her future safety, so she left. Satisfied?"

The tightly controlled admission belied the ugly truth. He'd failed at the most important job a man had—to protect his woman. He'd given her the divorce she'd asked for and thrown in the house and the car, but guilt ate a hole in his heart he refused to ever let another woman fill.

"But they didn't kidnap her, did they?" Petra persisted softly.

"No thanks to me." Bitterness shook his voice. "She escaped when their car stalled." He began to pull away. "She's alive today because the perps forgot to fill the gas tank."

"Wimp."

The insult stung like a slap. "Excuse me?"

"A woman who'd dump the man she loved due to an attempted kidnapping is a wimp. Marriage is a partnership."

"Our marriage put her life in danger. She did the smart thing by leaving."

"Cluck. Cluck. Cluck."

Dammit all to hell. He raised his upper body on one arm, rigid with a fierce anger that erupted from a dark place in his soul that didn't bear visiting. The woman insisted on pushing his buttons. Careful to rein in his temper, he replied evenly, "Any sane person in Kate's place would have done the same thing. I didn't protect her. Yes, she was scared. She had every right to be."

"I would have stayed."

The stalwart declaration speared his solar plexus like a needle into a balloon, allowing the anger to escape. A sheen of moisture glistened on serious burnt gold eyes staring up into his. She meant it.

He didn't know what to say.

Petra hooked a surprisingly strong arm around his neck and dragged him close in a hug. Her other arm tightened across his back, the hand soothing knotted muscles under his T-shirt. "You're a good man, Seth Cooper, or whatever your real name is. Kate's a fool to let you go."

Unfathomable emotion pinched his vocal chords. He didn't waste time attempting to figure out what he felt, or why. No, he did next what any testosterone-fueled man nestled against the full breasts of a desirable woman would do—he kissed her.

Swiftly, in a futile attempt to displace the gut-twisting guilt unleashed by his responsibility for the near loss of two women in his life, he descended to grind his mouth against hers. After a brief hesitation, Petra retaliated with matched fervor. Her lips parted to welcome access. Her tongue lashed out to tussle with his, engaging him in an erotic battle to wrestle their respective demons into submission. Liquid fire spilled from their incendiary kiss down his nerve pathways like lava.

His fingers fumbled of their own volition for the hem of her shirt, seeking, stretching, then sliding under the cotton camouflage and heading north across silky soft terrain. When his palm captured the firm, round breast he stilled his questing mouth and hand at the wonder of it. A man encountered perfection only once or twice in a lifetime. Reverently he smoothed a rough palm over the curvaceous contours. A thumb nuzzled the pebbled peak, eliciting a whimpering gasp. He took her breath into his mouth and kissed her deeply, a farewell of sorts, because he had another destination in mind.

Both hands now engaged, he liberated her luscious mounds in an efficient maneuver and repositioned to take full advantage of his conquest. His mouth descended to caress and nibble an exquisite nub hard at attention while a hand reconnoitered the next target. Panting breaths heaved Petra's ample breast deeper into his mouth, cycling against his laving tongue. As he massaged the sensitive tip of the other breast, an urgent hand clenched his wrist. Fingers on her other hand pawed restlessly through his hair.

He'd almost lost her today. The certainty of it spurred him on. He relished the quick intakes of breath, the pants of pleasure when he touched her in a way that pleased her, the tiny responsive moans that validated his efforts. At some level, feeling her luscious body pulse with arousal mitigated the churning fear overlaid with guilt that had consumed him when he'd discovered her missing. He needed the reminder that she lived. Not daring to examine the reasons too closely, he realized he needed her.

With the primal certainty born of his male sex, he knew that he'd find Petra slippery wet and swollen and ready for him. He in turn was as granite-hard and straight as that rock core she doted on. The day might not be a total disaster after all.

Then the cell phone in his jacket pocket warbled.

# CHAPTER SIX

Hell's bells. He'd forgotten the scheduled 23:00 call from his cover. Seth rolled off Petra's delectable body and scrabbled for the phone, all the while cursing the horrible timing.

As he punched the cell phone button, he watched annoyance supplant the passion glazing her expression. Man, could he empathize. "Cooper here."

Unlike regular satellite-hosted transmissions, the encrypted signal between these special-order RCMP satellite phones guaranteed a secure channel. The only person he had to worry about overhearing the call was Petra. He raised a shoulder to prop the phone against his ear while he tugged on his boots. "Right. Give me a minute, will you? I'm leaving the complex now."

Petra yanked the shirt down over her mouthwatering attributes and glowered as he crossed the room to the door.

"I won't be long," he apologized, one finger blocking the phone's mouthpiece. "Lock the door behind me."

At that, Petra grabbed his pillow and hurled it at him. He ducked and bailed out the door. Each step cost him, what with the zipper ridge on his jeans chafing an extreme hard-on. Somehow he doubted Petra would consider that sufficient punishment for abandoning her. She was steamed, all right. Yet a self-congratulatory smirk twisted his mouth. His assessment had been bang on—her fiery nature manifested into a fervently responsive bed partner.

Outside and a hundred yards from the nearest building, he spoke freely. "What have you got?"

Chuck Stanton, a new recruit saddled with the lonely overnight shift at Headquarters, reported on the results of background checks. "We dug a little deeper into the history of three mine employees as you requested. Other than a few parking tickets, Samson Smith is clean. He still hasn't paid his overdue child support, and there's no evidence of unusual activity in his bank account. Aaron Wintergate's file is a little more complicated. One of our hackers is tapping into his online gambling account. No results there yet. Wintergate doesn't own a thing—seems to have hocked all his worldly goods, and he owes five grand on last year's income tax. Keep an eye on him. Next—" Shuffling paper crackled in Seth's ear. "I found a file an inch thick on Bob Scott in the Records Room."

At Stanton's words, Seth's fingers tightened on the cell phone. A mechanic on his way to the truck maintenance complex cast a curious glance Seth's way. Anxious not to be noticed, he retreated farther out of earshot across the gravel a hundred feet beyond the water treatment plant. "Continue."

"On behalf of Excelsior, the RCMP went whole hog to investigate Scott. His grade school is listed, for cripe's sake. I'm surprised they didn't track down his teachers."

"Give me the details without the commentary," Seth bit out. Heat radiated from the metal cladding of buildings planted in the stark landscape under bright sun without shade or shelter. "I'm standing in the mine compound and sooner or later someone is going to wonder what business a pilot has outside this late at night."

"Right." More paper shuffling. "Scott has a business degree from a college in Vancouver, British Columbia." Stanton sounded surprised. "He joined the Vancouver Police Department after a stint as a shipping company manager, and worked his way up from constable to sergeant, no higher."

"Hold it." Seth pounced on the anomaly. Cops rarely had another career before joining the force. "What shipping company? What did he do there?"

"He worked for three years as the manager of shipping and receiving for a midsized import-export company named Takamura Cargo. It didn't own any ships. Takamura seems to have been a broker handling oceangoing as well as air freight."

"Why are you using the past tense?"

"Takamura changed ownership in the mid-seventies. Scott left then to join the police force." More shuffling. "Did very well on his exams. Made sergeant in less than twelve years. He's a bright guy."

"He worked the port beat along the way," Seth stated flatly.

"How'd you guess? Scott spent several years as an investigator in the Marine Squad and then in the Gang Crime Unit. He seems to have had a hand in joint RCMP-VPD investigations at the Vancouver port facilities."

"Including smuggling."

"Naturally. I know where you're going with this, but there's no evidence of corruption. His record is as clean as a whistle. He has a couple of commendations for exemplary service. He knows the tricks of the smuggling trade, but he apparently doesn't practice them."

"Why did he leave the VPD?"

"Good question." Stanton's voice faded then strengthened as he sorted through the stack of paper in front of him. "His wife died of cancer two years ago. He subsequently took a six-month medical leave of absence that turned into early retirement when Excelsior offered him the Chief, Security Services position at twice the pay. Scott's official reason was that he needed to make a fresh start."

Seth thought for a moment. "Where does he live off-rotation?"

"He owns a condo outright worth six hundred thousand dollars overlooking Vancouver's English Bay. That's not top end in Vancouver's pricey housing market by any stretch. He's got a small nest egg made up of blue-chip investments and a part-ownership in a sailboat. Nothing to raise suspicion."

"As you say, he's a smart man." Seth had another question. "Kids?"

"No. His wife battled cancer for twenty years. She'd undergone a hysterectomy at one time."

"The file is thorough."

"Yeah, and there's nothing to indicate Scott's not on the up-and-up. Grieving widower with no family decides to head north to earn an honest wad of money in the twilight of his career. Case closed."

"Maybe." Seth sifted the possibilities. Could Excelsior have asked the RCMP to investigate its prospective security chief to ensure he had a clean record? To guarantee he wouldn't be a suspect if smuggling out of Ptarmigan Lake came to light? Alternatively, Scott could be working for other interests, namely connections with the international crime rings operating back in his old stomping grounds. Seth's gut overrode the squeaky-clean paper record, told him Scott had a finger or two dipped in the Ptarmigan Lake smuggling operation.

"Dig up anything on Desirée Dumont?"

"Like all employees, she was fingerprinted as part of the security clearance before Excelsior allowed her on site. We matched the cook to the name on her passport, Gabrielle Dumont, Belgian citizen. She has a U.S. green card, believe it or not," Stanton returned. "She won the green card lottery approximately two years ago under her legal name. Worked in an expensive Las Vegas hotel restaurant as hostess for six months then seems to have fallen off the map. At least, Uncle Sam has no record of her employment since."

She likely found a sugar daddy in Vegas, Seth thought. Her legs rivaled those of any showgirl. "What about prior history?"

"We're still waiting to hear from the Belgium police. There's an eight-hour time difference. But she wouldn't have been allowed into the States or Canada with a record."

"Right." Seth exhaled, unreasonably disappointed. He knew better than to expect deep background searches to point the finger straight at the perp. Stanton's information generated more questions but no answers. Nothing about this case came easy. Seth then described the incident in the mine services office and the suspected drugging.

"It's serious, but if the RCMP launch an incident investigation, the smugglers will go to ground. It'll set back the undercover operation," Stanton said.

"That's the dilemma, and not for you nor I to decide. Pass my report up the line. I'll contact HQ tomorrow for instructions when I fly Petra back to Yellowknife. Thanks," he remembered to add as he signed off.

\* \* \* \* \*

Petra tossed restlessly in the too-empty bed, the thick cotton undershirt brushing against acutely sensitive nipples with every movement. She throbbed, blast it. The sexy cop had her more hot and bothered than she'd been in eons.

Maybe ever.

Angry embarrassment toasted her cheeks as she recalled how his devilishly wicked tongue reduced her to a squirming puddle of sensation with about as much backbone as a jellyfish. A minute later they'd have done the deed. Or maybe it would have been more than a minute. He seemed to delight in prolonging the torture. Perhaps his endurance matched the lengthy foreplay. Speaking of length, he certainly had more than his share.

Arggh! Why was she speculating? She threw back the blankets and surged to her feet. She had no time for sex, or even for thinking about sex. Especially with him.

She'd caved. She had ceded control after she'd vowed that would never happen. Once you succumbed to lust, your brain went into standby mode. She could not afford to be vulnerable to manipulation by someone she didn't trust. She couldn't trust anyone, she reminded herself. Not here. Not in her line of work. She had to stay sharp.

Tamping down the distracting thoughts, she pulled baggy overalls and a sweatshirt over fresh underwear. If Seth thought his attempted seduction put her in the palm of his hands, figuratively speaking, and that she'd be waiting for his return to finish what he'd started, he was wrong. As was her habit, she'd sublimate sexual tension into extra energy to tackle the monumental tasks of the next thirty-six hours.

Twenty minutes later, Seth tracked her down in Carter's office. When he spied her at the end of the room, anger chased unvarnished panic from his features. "What on earth do you think you're doing?" he yelled.

"Cleaning up. Isn't it obvious?" One arm swept a pile of rubble off the metal-topped table. The mess she encountered upon unlocking the door had stimulated her tear ducts—must have been the dust—but she'd quickly regrouped and begun to prepare for the drill crew's fresh batch of core. Seth interrupted before she'd had time to contact the night-shift crew boss. She scowled at him, hoping he'd take the hint and return to bed.

"Don't disappear on me like that." Rigid with a powerful tension, he stalked over to grab her shoulders. "A few hours ago someone drugged you unconscious. Do you think he's gonna sit back now and leave you alone to finish collecting and cataloging cores?" His extended arms vibrated with leashed fury.

She wrenched free and withdrew a safe distance. "There's no one but me to finish this job. I'm responsible."

"Is it worth your life?"

"You asked me that once already."

"You never answered."

She faced him, hands on hips. "I'm alive, aren't I? They're after the cores, not me personally."

"Why?" The question hung in the dusty air between them.

She maintained eye contact. Big mistake. Lost in the radiant depths that reminded her of Brazilian emeralds, her train of thought derailed. Who'd have ever thought she, the quintessential geologist, would be more bowled over by emerald eyes than by the mineral version? She shook herself. "That's my business."

"Who are 'they'?"

At that, she turned away. "I have no idea."

"You're lying."

"I'd tell you if I could. Don't you understand?"

"No. I don't understand." He threaded the fingers of one hand through his thick black hair and settled on a stool as if prepared to wait all night. "Explain it to me."

How did a woman explain that putting words to her fears, bringing them out for scrutiny by others, made them too real to bear? Besides, she'd never reveal her suspicions about her father until she was completely certain he'd cast his allegiance with Tony Athlone. And if she implicated Excelsior's chairman and CEO in a suspected stockmarket manipulation to gain control of the company, the trail led straight to the man who'd validated the original, possibly questionable, assay results—Edward Paris. Not for a fistful of diamonds would she be the one to set the RCMP's investigative machinery onto her own father.

She firmly believed that even if her father had a vested interest in the failure of her assignment, or worse, actually conspired with Athlone to ensure fresh cores never made it back to Colorado, he loved her and would never allow her to be physically hurt. However, she wasn't naïve. A ruthless man like Athlone wouldn't spare Seth or any other person unlucky enough to get his way. The less Seth, Carter and the drill crews knew, the safer they'd be.

"Go to bed, Seth. I have work to do."

He must have absorbed the stubborn will in her instruction and decided not to challenge it, because he tried another tactic. "I'm not leaving you alone."

"Oh for heaven's sake." She released a grunt of appreciation for his chivalry mixed with a liberal dose of exasperation. The cop had a "me man-you woman" protector complex. "I'll lock the door. When he merely glared, she amended, "Both doors."

"The perps could have an access card."

"Oh." She reviewed the possibilities, dismissing Carter, because he'd been drugged, and the drillers, because typically mine-office key cards were only issued to the occupants and the security staff. The geotechs had key cards, but according to Carter, both technologists had been temporarily reassigned. That left… "Bob Scott?"

Thick brows met in an angry vee and he cupped a hand over his ear. "Want to repeat that for the recording device no doubt planted in here?"

"Sorry." Rattled by the room's chaos and Seth's intensity, she'd forgotten to guard her tongue. So had he, apparently, or he wouldn't have questioned her after bursting into the room as frantic as a kid who'd lost his puppy. Perhaps Seth really did care. Nah. She dismissed the strangely stimulating thought. Like her, he had a job to do.

"Since we can't talk, and you insist on sticking to me like a burr, then make yourself useful. I want to clear out the debris before the drill crews arrive with the new batch of cores."

Seth crossed his arms. "I have a better idea. Let the cleaning staff do their thing while you rest in bed."

"With you?" Seth intended to take up where they'd left off. Distract her from the task at hand. Seduce her into blabbing her secrets. It's what she'd do, in his shoes.

"I haven't slept yet," he reminded her.

"I'll find a tech to help me." His clamped jaw and compressed lips broadcast that her suggestion had about as much appeal as sour milk. They had something in common after all—neither trusted a soul, not even each other. "I'm not leaving this room."

"After the close call this afternoon, I refuse to leave you alone until you're safely on a commercial flight." His eyes bored into hers. "Get used to it."

"You have a job, remember. Don't you have any charters scheduled for today?"

"The only flight on my agenda is the one to Yellowknife with you on board." He coughed. Perhaps it was the dust she'd stirred up. "I'll help you clean up until the cores arrive if you swear to come back to bed for the rest of the night. We'll get security to post a guard."

"Right." A shooting pain seared her temple. The painkiller had begun to wear off. She'd never admit it to Seth, but her energy level topped out conservatively at sixty percent. Truthfully, she welcomed another pair of hands and a strong back. She merely prayed his decision didn't get him killed.

\* \* \* \* \*

Two hours later, deep in the heart of an administration complex that never slept, a furtive cell phone conversation took place.

"She's stubborn. The drill crew dropped off more core, and it's under guard."

An obscenity sliced the miles between them. "You know what you have to do."

"She's too smart to fall for the same trick a second time. I can't approach the Geology Services office now without raising suspicion."

"We discussed contingency options," the voice on the other end stated with no inflection.

"Easy for you to say. Her bodyguard is capable of wringing my neck like a chicken."

Impatience stained his staccato response. "I never underestimated her. His presence is unexpected, but we can handle it. Everything is in place. However, if she's injured, I don't know you. Understood?"

Seth Cooper presented a triple obstacle. He inconveniently hovered, a sharp-eyed hawk. He never left the geologist's side when on site. And he intended to fly both the woman and her cases of rock back to civilization. "Does that apply to the bodyguard?" The ensuing silence stood in for an answer. "I may have to leave quickly."

"A plane is on standby. You have the number. Don't call me again." He disconnected.

\* \* \* \* \*

Seth slid an unopened bottle of water and a plate of scrambled eggs and buttered whole wheat toast across the desk. Petra's nose wrinkled and sniffed at his offering before raising a questioning glance to his.

"Fresh from the communal steam table," he confirmed. "I burnt the bread myself." To the unfamiliar young man sitting adjacent to the corridor door, a different man from the one he'd coerced into guarding the cores in the middle of the night, he said, "You can return to your duties now. I'm back."

"This is my duty, sir."

"Since when?"

"Since Scott paid a visit while you were drumming up grub in the cafeteria," Petra cut in. "His face turned eggplant purple when he found one of his night-shift men on guard without his authorization." Cheeks chipmunked with egg, she continued almost incomprehensibly, "Apoplectic pretty well describes his state of mind. If he's not careful, he's gonna burst a blood vessel. He wants you in his office at 07:15."

Seth checked his watch. He had three minutes. "If you're not careful, you're going to need the Heimlich Maneuver."

"I was a tad hungry after all."

"I see that. You're welcome."

She looked up from slathering raspberry jam from a sealed plastic packet onto her toast. "Yeah, thanks. How'd'ya know this jam's my favorite?"

"I'm beginning to get a feel for your…preferences."

Crimson appled her stuffed cheeks. Rendered speechless, she managed to incline her head toward the bored youth lounging in Carter's chair. Seth winked. She glowered.

"On my way to the cafeteria I stopped at the infirmary and roused Carter. He's fine," he responded to her unspoken question. "I told him to grab a bite and come directly here. Your orders."

Petra chewed frantically to clear her mouth to reply. "That'll put him in a great mood," she exploded. "Way to rally the troops, Cooper! Since I arrived Carter's been drugged and his office smashed to smithereens. I'll just bet he's anxious as hell to comply with my 'orders'. He's probably in his room packing at this very moment."

"You need his help if we're going to get out of here this morning."

His attempt to slip the departure time matter-of-factly into the conversation failed. Her entire upper body vibrated denial. "Tomorrow."

"Neither of us has a minute to waste arguing." He threw up his hands. "Fine. I'll compromise. At noon the rubber hits the runway." He surmised the RCMP Staff Sergeant in charge of the undercover operation would it shut down now that civilians were at risk. He felt comfortable leaving her under the watchful eyes of security. The departure delay gave him the morning to snoop around.

As she sputtered to her feet, he ducked into the corridor, a grin tugging the corners of his mouth. The grit and flash he admired had returned with a vengeance. Yet he'd feel *more* comfortable with Carter Lee at her elbow while he chatted with Bob Scott. Long rapid strides carried him on a detour to the cafeteria, certain he'd find Carter loading a plate with enough hot food to feed a man three times his size.

Half an hour ago tables in the cavernous room had groaned under elbows astride platefuls of bacon, sourdough pancakes and eggs. A few stragglers remained, lingering over coffee while uniformed kitchen staff wiped deserted tables preparatory to the influx of workers coming off shift. He scanned for Carter, came up empty, then sought out Desirée's hard-to-miss bodacious body behind the counter. Nada. He expected he'd find her at the grill whipping up a gargantuan mess of eggs, Carter at her side groveling for scraps of attention.

Outside the double swing doors to the kitchen, a tinny agitated male voice wafted through a ventilation grill above a door labeled Housekeeping. Muffled consoling words delivered in a French accent appeared to be having little calming effect. The knob turned easily.

Both occupants of the small storeroom presented startled faces to the intruder. Carter Lee, poker-stiff with anger, lashed out first. "Who the hell do you think you are, barging in on a private conversation?"

Seth discerned fear lurking behind Desirée Dumont's unadorned eyes before a coquettish expression fell like a theater backdrop. She smiled. "The cartoonist. I remember you."

"I overheard familiar voices."

Alarm pierced her outward calm. "Lovers' tiff," Desirée asserted on the defensive. "*Mon cheri* suffered yesterday, yes? He is not yet himself."

Carter's brows collided in a furious grimace. To Desirée he hissed, "We'll discuss this later. In private." Advancing, he pushed his nose under Seth's chin. "This is none of your business, Cooper. Get out of my way."

"Petra needs you."

"She sent her bloody messenger twice? Tell her to shove the frigging cores up her—"

"Carter!" Desirée exploded. "Do you want the entire camp to hear? *Mon amour,*" she added as an afterthought.

Carter slapped the door wide such that it slammed against the wall. "*Mon amour* my ass," he growled as he stomped down the corridor.

Seth turned to Desirée. "Are you okay?"

"Of course." She shrugged pretty shoulders. "Yesterday Carter saw me with another man. He is jealous. There are sixty men for every woman here. What does he expect? I am European. He must understand the others to me are only *hors d'oeuvres*. He is the *entrée*. The main course." Her wide full lips curved with invitation. "You could be dessert."

Seth retreated a step. "No thanks."

"A pity." She sashayed around him. "They will miss me in the kitchen. See you later." With a provocative wiggle of hips camouflaged under her oversized uniform, she disappeared through the swing doors.

Seth's eyes narrowed. He tagged Desirée as a predator, a she-wolf who culled vulnerable prey from the herd. But right now he was after the alpha male of the pack. His nose trailed a scent that led directly to Bob Scott.

* * * * *

The day-shift guard stationed at the camera surveillance monitors quickly shoved a portable game device under the desk. "You missed him by ten minutes," yet another of Scott's infant corps replied when Seth asked him where Scott had disappeared to. "He got a call and left in a hurry."

"Any idea where he went?" He indicated the tiled array of video feeds on the monitors.

"I think I saw him head toward the sewage treatment plant."

"You think?"

The boy, so new on the job that his shirt had its original creases fresh out of the packaging, flushed. "Hey, I just sat down a few minutes ago."

Seth grabbed the arm concealing the game device, palmed it, and flipped it into the air. "Save this for your off-duty hours," he said as the kid lunged for it.

Pink stained the tips of the kid's ears. "You can't tell me what to do. Who are you, anyway?"

Seth absently placed the game device on the desk as he scanned the monitors encircling the work station. Three of the exterior cameras showed at least a couple of dozen hard-hatted, identically clothed men strolling between structures like clones in a sci-fi film. Scott and his master key card had plenty of time to disappear anonymously into any of the buildings.

"Which monitor covers the sewage plant?"

"None of them," the guard admitted reluctantly. "It's a low-security area. I saw Mr. Scott walk toward the plant, out of range of the camera that sweeps the maintenance yard."

Seth's heartbeat shifted into first gear. "Did you see anyone else head in that direction?"

"No."

"Could you have missed someone?"

"Possibly." The boy powered off the game device with a surreptitious movement of his thumb.

"Who trained you?" Seth demanded, exasperated.

"Bob Scott, of course. I applied for the mine's on-the-job training program for new graduates."

"From high school?"

"Do I *look* like a college grad?"

Seth concealed his annoyance at the kid's attitude. He couldn't afford to waste any more time. His gut told him Scott wasn't on any routine shift change patrol. Before the front doors to the admin building swung closed behind him, he'd activated his cell phone and placed a protected call to Joe.

"Hang around the sewage treatment plant. Scott made a beeline for it a few minutes ago. I'm on my way."

"I've got your back," Joe responded before he broke the connection.

Avoiding the web of arctic corridors between each destination workplace, Seth strode the direct route across the maintenance staging yard, skirted the containment dike around the massive diesel oil storage tanks, and arrived at a long, thirty-foot-high windowless building located at the farthest end of the compound. Heat from the blazing, low-slung sun shimmered off exterior profiled metal panels. A side door opened easily, unlocked.

He stepped into the cavernous interior and closed the door behind him, willing his eyes to adjust quickly to the reduced illumination from pendant halogen lights high overhead. Humid, warm air clung to his skin, yet despite the fermenting contents of two enormous circular vats occupying most of the floor space, he inhaled without gagging. Much.

To his immediate right a computer and control panel station hugged the short wall. Sandwiched between it and the welded steel tank labeled "Aerator", a steep metal staircase accessed a catwalk running the length of the building. He stilled, listening. Pump hum masked any footfalls.

With swift strides he reconnoitered the ground level to the opposite end where it connected to the arctic corridor network. Glazing in the locked double doors allowed him to peer down the empty corridor as far as the maintenance complex. He swiveled to examine the gloom. Nothing moved. From his pre-deployment briefing, he recalled the sanitary engineers divided their time between the sewage treatment building, the fresh water supply pumphouse, and the process plant waste water reclamation facilities. This particular operation was left unattended for long periods.

Unease corkscrewed his gut. Scott or someone else had unlocked the side door without relocking it upon exiting as required by security procedures. Ergo that someone must still be in the building.

The catwalk twenty feet off the ground offered an aerial view of the crevices between the tanks. Metal grating rang under his boots as he walked above the sealed aerator tank to the narrow gap between it and the deep pool of the open clarifier tank. Far below, a swatch of familiar green cloth draped a pipe valve. Metal dug into his knees as he knelt to identify a Ptarmigan Lake Mine ball cap. Hundreds of them littered the complex. It could belong to anyone.

Slowly, hands gripping the railing, Seth inched on his knees toward the center of the clarifier. Black water swirled underneath in an almost imperceptible current generated by the slow movement of sewage from one tank to the other. He peered into the murk. And waited.

Long minutes later white hair floated funereally to the surface, the lower body dragged almost vertical by the weight of standard issue steel-toed boots.

# Chapter Seven

Petra stretched both arms overhead to relieve muscles tight from sweeping heavy chunks of stone into a metal garbage bin. With a few minutes until the delivery of fresh core by the crew coming off shift, she could spare a moment for Carter who was morosely poking at the entrails of his computer CPU.

"Did you run into Seth?"

Carter didn't bother to lift his head. "Yeah. We had words."

"What kinda words?"

He shrugged his shoulders. "I can't remember."

Petra marched over to his chair. "You feeling okay this morning?"

He didn't bother to look up. "Considering I was drugged unconscious, my office and computer files were trashed, and you're not telling me a bloody thing, sure, I'm hunky-dory."

She'd never seen Carter's spirits so low. Perched on a corner of his desk, she cajoled, "Come on. Give. It's more than that. I know you too well."

He shook his head. "You're unbelievable. Here's the deal. I'll tell you what's bothering me when you let me in on the reasons for the mysterious repeat core analysis exercise. Seems to me I have a right to know why I should stay a second longer in this hell hole. The next scheduled flight out is tomorrow, and I'm going to be on it."

"Fine. Leave." She slapped the top of the desk in a show of annoyance, raising a puff of dust. Relief skimmed a layer off the anxiety she'd attempted to dispel by sweeping out the debris in Carter's office. She'd been ready to suggest he fly to Yellowknife with her and Seth, but Carter's contrariness might have encouraged him to stick it out. Carter had been swept into this mess because of her, and she deeply regretted it. "I believe I'll wash up. Want some coffee?"

"Decaf. My head's still beating a tattoo," he admitted.

En route from the cafeteria, Petra detoured into the security area hoping to catch a glimpse of Seth. Scott had had sufficient time to grill him up, down and sideways.

Several tall young men in white shirts clustered around the red-haired clerk seated at the communications console. The thin youth raised his voice above the hubbub. "Cooper said to bring a rope."

"He can't give us orders."

"Where's Mr. Scott?"

Petra elbowed between two six footers. "What's this about Cooper?"

"That's none of your business, ma'am," squeaked the rangy youth towering over the seated clerk nervously twisting his headset cord.

Fear, excitement and confusion warred for supremacy on the other youths' faces and infected her like a virus. "Who's in charge?" she bit out.

"Craig Rudden's Deputy Chief, Security Services. He went off duty half an hour ago. We can't locate Chief Scott. He's not answering his cell."

She deduced Seth had called the security services office for help, an insane choice if he wanted to maintain his cover.

Unless he had no options.

Fear for his safety dragged her toward the emotional abyss where panic overpowered reason. She fought it. Her hands shook, sloshing coffee over the rims of the two cups she carried. She placed the mugs on the desk and stuffed fists into her jeans pockets.

"Find Rudden," she ordered two of the shorter youths in a low voice that brooked no argument. With a nod from the clerk, he loped away toward the cafeteria. You," she nodded at the seated clerk. "Repeat Cooper's instructions word for word."

The redhead's Adam's apple bobbed under a clenched jaw as he solicited each of his white-faced colleagues for direction, and received in return only panicked stares. To all, so as not to seem he was vesting Petra with authority, he said, "Cooper told me to send four men to the sewage treatment plant with rope and a stretcher, and to call in the RCMP homicide team."

Oh Lord. Her breakfast roiled, threatened to geyser. A murder. Yet Seth must be safe, and relief cleared her mind.

"You four. Go!" She pointed at well-built youths who appeared strong enough to carry a body. The redhead's freckles spotted parchment skin like ink. She feared he'd faint. "Make the call to the Yellowknife detachment," she instructed in a voice she fought to keep calm.

"Wh-what if he's not dead? I'll get in trouble for calling them out for nothing, without orders."

She inhaled, deep, to fill lungs with sufficient breath to sustain the effort to speak slowly, quietly. "The RCMP are three hundred miles away. They'll require at least half an hour to marshal a team and pilot and drive to the airport. If there's no…death, we'll know before their plane takes off, and you can request a medevac instead." She nudged a coffee cup across the melamine surface to within his grasp and tried to smile. "Drink up. Relax, you're doing great."

Inside, her composure dissolved like a cracker in soup. Seth might be wounded. She battled the dread storming her senses, suppressed the urge to run to him when responsibility dictated otherwise. First she needed to find a senior mine official to take charge. Swiftly she reviewed the options and butted up against the only potential candidate on site—her old buddy slumped in a blue funk in front of a busted computer. She grimaced. At the very least, she could trust Carter to contact Hank Horvath in time for the mine manager to catch a lift on the RCMP plane.

Ten minutes later Petra pounded across the compound and sidled between blue-coveralled, hard-hatted men jammed shoulder-to-shoulder inside the treatment plant, only to be blocked at the base of the metal stairs by one of the security staff. A foreman-type bellowed orders to clear the floor area, but no heretofore bored miner was willing to miss this show.

Blinking and vigorously rubbing eyes temporarily blind in the dim windowless interior after the bright daylight outside, Petra finally spied Seth high overhead crouched over the tank, precariously balanced with one foot on the tank lip and the other on the catwalk. She wasn't prepared for the emotion that swamped her senses—emotion that she didn't dare examine. She leaned against the tank wall for support. Gradually the thumping in her chest slowed enough to enable her to hear the conversation high above.

"Hand me the rope," she heard Seth demand.

Two young men on the catwalk grabbed for handholds on the body. Jabbering speculation behind her diminished to a murmur as the men pulled the sodden bulk sufficiently out of the water to allow Seth to pass a rope under the arms and knot it tight.

"Bob Scott." The name rumbled from the men on the catwalk, down the stairs and out to the men assembled in the compound. The Chief, Security Services, dead!

No accident, this. Seth's warnings sank home. Murder changed everything. She didn't have time to think through the implications, only recognized the urge to flee, to leave Ptarmigan Lake before she too was put out of commission permanently. But the crush of men pushing forward for a better view made immediate escape impossible.

A lean blond man slipped through the crowd toward the exit. With a tiny shock, she recognized him as Joe, the fuel tech. Close set eyes under the bill of his ball cap surveyed every upturned face. The visor of another ball cap incongruously peeked from between undone work shirt buttons.

Could Joe have killed Scott? No. She quickly dismissed the thought. Given the closeness she'd observed between Seth and Joe at the air strip, she had to believe Joe was RCMP. Joe would rather maintain his cover, she figured, than put himself in the spotlight by assisting with recovery of the body. She watched him until his glance slid over her, locked for a fraction of a second, and moved on to the next gawker in the crowd.

Who, then, killed Scott? Until now she hadn't wasted a minute speculating who exactly Athlone controlled here on site. When she discovered the rough hidden in the coffee tin she made the connection between the men who destroyed the drill core samples and the smugglers. Who else but smugglers would have access to loose rough? Seth had tried to warn her of the danger. But she'd been too intent on resolving whether her father had salted the original drill cores with commercial-quality diamonds.

She shuddered. It could have been her body in that tank. She'd underestimated how desperate Athlone's men might become. Her father, even if involved at a high level, would be unable to guarantee her safety if she got in the way. Seth was right all along. Until she hopped aboard a flight south to the U.S., her life was in danger. Hawaii or Arizona might be a safer bet than Colorado until the murderer was safely behind bars.

Another, happier, realization settled her stomach a little. Seth's new notoriety meant he'd no longer be able to nose around the camp unnoticed. His superiors would recall him to Yellowknife. He had become a target because of his role as her "bodyguard". Now he'd have no choice but to leave as well.

One of the bulked-up, young security guards pushed through the massed men, shouting for them to move back to preserve the scene. Carter and other reinforcements trailed in his wake. Petra was herded out of the building with the others, and found herself in the compound cut off from witnessing the action. Hundreds of the staff smoked and shuffled into chat groups, waiting for the stretcher to emerge, not caring that their shifts had started or that their post-shift meals congealed on cafeteria tables.

She peered into the workers' faces. One or more of these ordinary-looking employees killed a man. What was her father's connection? The answer, she intuited, lay back in Colorado in the office of Excelsior's CEO.

* * * * *

"Who are you?" Seth squatted to stretch the painful pulled muscles in his lower back.

A middle-aged man in a stained security golf shirt bent at his ample waist over the body lying face down on the narrow mesh catwalk. Eyes slitted under a furrowed brow remained fixed on his deceased boss. "Craig Rudden, Deputy Chief, Security Services. Who the frig are you?"

"Seth Cooper, pilot with Northern Lights Air."

At that, Rudden's head screwed on a neck thickened by a double chin to scrutinize him. "What are you doing here?" he growled.

To divert him, Seth indicated an ominous black patch on Scott's otherwise snowy wet skull. "He appears to have been whacked on the back of the head and then pushed over the railing into the tank."

"Who found him? You?" Rudden refused to be dissuaded.

"Yeah," Seth had to admit.

"So what's a pilot doing in the sewage treatment plant, eh?" Suspicion crimped the corners of eyes set deep in his ruddy flesh. "Never mind. You can tell your story to the RCMP when they arrive. Meantime, you're going with Reggie here to wait for them in the—" He motioned over one of the security guards. "Jeez, where will we put Cooper? I'm gonna need Bob Scott's office."

"How 'bout I lock him in his room?" the guard suggested.

"Do it. And station one of the kids outside his door."

\* \* \* \* \*

Too sore to bend to remove his boots, Seth reclined flat in the middle of the double bed to take the pressure off his painful lower back. Petra stepped forward to tug them off. The pain whitening his stubbled jaw twisted her heart. A small "ow" was all the big lug allowed himself.

"What else can I do?" she offered.

"I'd appreciate a glass of water for these muscle relaxants." He extracted a pill bottle from his jeans' pocket to place on the bedside table.

She eyed the half-empty plastic container. "How many have you taken?"

"Three."

"Any effect?"

"Not so's I'd notice." He attempted a grin. "I'll be fine."

"Then I'll get back to work."

"Oh no you won't." He pinned her with a hard stare. "The place is chaos, and with chaos comes opportunity. The perps might strike again. You're not going anywhere until the site is secure. I won't allow it." He waved her toward the easy chair. "Phone your drill crew or Carter. Do what you have to, but stay put until the RCMP arrive in an hour or so. Then you can get back to work." Eyelids blanked out dusky emerald as they slid closed. "If the investigating officer lets you."

"Why shouldn't he?" she bristled.

"You're a witness. They'll want to question you too."

"Oh right." She paced from one side of the small room to the other. "What will I tell them?" she wondered aloud.

"The truth would be nice. I intend to be around for that interview, even if it kills me."

She perched hands on hips. "What makes you think I'll tell them any more than I've told you?"

His eyes popped wide. "There's been a murder. It's your civic duty to help the cops."

She paced some more. "You keep bringing up my civic duty. What about my duty to my employers? To my famil—"

Seth struggled to prop himself up on an elbow. "What's your family have to do with this case?" Pain pinched his too-pale skin, alarming her.

"Who killed Scott?" she wondered aloud, pretending she hadn't heard his question.

"You know as much as I do. You eavesdropped on my cell phone conversation with Headquarters."

"You could have waited to phone until your 'girlfriend' left after assisting you to your room," she shot back.

"Couldn't wait. Besides, the whole camp knows the details by now. Sit, for heaven's sake, so I can relax." He lowered himself flat with a low moan designed to elicit sympathy.

Petra sighed. With Carter filling in until Hank arrived, her drilling crew ordered back to work with the rest of the duty shift, and the night shifts-worth of core locked up in the Geology Services office, time sat heavily on her hands.

"As long as I'm stuck here, I may as well make myself useful. Take your T-shirt off and turn over," Petra demanded. "I'm going to massage the knots in your lower back.

"What do you know about massage?"

"More than you know about diamonds. Hand lotion will have to do instead of oil." She dug around in her pack for the travel-size bottle while he removed his belt and gingerly complied with her instructions.

When he was settled on his stomach, she straddled his hips and rubbed her hands together to warm the lotion. His lean, hard-muscled body stretched before her, the arms and neck tanned at the T-shirt line, the rest pale and smooth. A pesky interior voice nattered that she'd offered the massage strictly for the excuse to touch him. *Not so*, she argued with herself. *The man's in pain.*

*It's the least I can do. So what if I take a little pleasure in the feel of his skin. Bonus.*

With long smooth strokes she slid the flat of her hands the length of his broad back, slowly and rhythmically seeking out the tender and cramped muscles causing the excruciating pain.

"You know what you're doing," Seth said into the pillow with some surprise.

"I train with weights. Sometimes I overdo it—"

"That's not a surprise," he mumbled.

"But fortunately a massage therapist at my club in Boulder works out the kinks. She taught me how to avoid muscle strain most of the time, and how to work it out when I've—"

"Ignored her advice?"

She paused. "Any more shots like that and I'll watch TV instead."

"I'll be good. Don't stop."

In fact, under the heels of her hands she felt the tightness release in the trapezius muscle radiating from his upper spine. However, the problem area lay lower down near his buttocks. She gently smoothed the surface with short flat strokes before probing deeper with her thumbs. He groaned but didn't flinch when she began working the contracted muscles with rolling movements and more pressure. The waistband of his jeans impeded her movements. "Mind if I lower your jeans?"

"Not at all. Pull them right off, why don't you."

She complied, yanking off his boots and jeans to expose his boxer shorts, today's version patterned with multiple cartoon images of cowboy Yosemite Sam, arms raised, guns blazing. She had to chuckle as she knee-walked into position astride his legs.

A complex man was Seth Cooper. Cop, artist, lover. Smart too. And handsome. Not to mention his superb torso. Her hands moved reverently over his ribcage, trailed down the taut skin defining a slim waist. Most women would kill to have sex with such a perfect specimen. The tips of her fingers bit into soft tissues until he protested. Kill. That was probably the wrong word to use.

She released the compression, probed gently for another too firm muscle, worked it with deft fingers. Other women, she amended, would trade their shoe collections for the opportunity to make love with Seth.

Why not her?

The audacious idea dried her mouth. Why not seduce Seth right now on her terms? Get him out of her system? He'd be leaving the site and she'd never see him again. Death moved a person. Life should be grabbed and savored. She wanted him, and this opportunity would never come again. So to speak. She grinned over the hint of desperation and need that gnawed at her insides.

Her alter ego protested. *You didn't want to get involved, for very good reasons. Give in to your baser instincts, and you lose control.*

*Pish*, she argued back. *I'm the one in control. I'm merely satisfying a biological urge, that's all. He started it last night. I'm finishing it. Then it'll be over, done, and we'll never see each other again. No complications, no consequences.*

Her inner voice taunted, *You're reacting to the fear of losing him earlier. You're letting your emotions rule. Bad things happen when emotions rule.* But the fingers of her left hand had already flown to the buttons on her flannel shirt.

Breaths quick and shallow in a chest now stripped of shirt and practical cotton bra, she bent low to curl lotion-slick fingers under the shorts' waistband, around Seth's hipbones and down far enough to encircle one rather flaccid muscle she'd thus far ignored.

"I am totally impressed by your talent," Seth said a minute or two later.

"How so?"

"Your miracle fingers can turn rigid muscles soft, and soft muscles rigid."

Petra grinned. "It's a gift." She paused, slightly insecure, wondering how sore he still might be. She didn't intend that he actually move to do the deed, just lie there while she bounced a little. Still, their present positions foiled that objective. "Are you able to turn over?"

With a minimum of groaning—only partially due to pain, Petra deduced from his expression when he caught sight of her breasts—Seth's long, gorgeous length soon stretched face-up. Meanwhile, she one-footed it out of her boots and jeans while scrabbling in a pocket of her pack for a small emergency kit that held waterproof matches, some medical supplies, and a solitary condom she'd added to cover all eventualities, no matter how improbable the odds. Now she congratulated herself for careful packing. Back in Boulder, she decided, she'd start buying lottery tickets.

Four seconds later, she braced fingers wide over Seth's shoulders and leaned in to kiss his amused mouth. Her tongue traced the bottom lip then darted inside like a hummingbird to sip and withdraw. He protested, raising his hands to cup her breasts, to entice her closer with sensuous kneading of the sensitive tips.

The previous night his movements had been insistent, hot, focused. With no choice now but to allow her to lead, still he cajoled with teasing fingertips that glided over her back in a playful imitation of hers on him earlier, until her skin sang with a high, fine sensitivity. His lips pleasured the delicate hollows in her soft neck and nipped her bare shoulders. His brilliant eyes glowed with invitation.

Heat rising from her core spiked desire into unknown territory. She plunged her tongue deep, lost in him, wanting him like she'd never wanted any other man, confident he wanted her and glorying in it. In this moment, only in this moment ever, she had the power to pull him into a mad ride, but also the power to render him helpless with the wanting until she herself couldn't bear it any longer. A satisfied smile betrayed her intentions as she stroked his manhood, watched his beautiful eyes darken until she could see her reflection in them, and held her breasts tantalizingly out of his reach.

Then to her consternation he attempted to sit up.

"You're supposed to be injured," she managed as his mouth enveloped one firm tip.

"Come to me then," he returned out of the corner of his mouth as he eased carefully onto his back, pulling her with him. "Don't hold yourself so far away."

She complied, not because he wished it, but because she gloried in the wet sucking kisses he bestowed on her full breasts, igniting nerves that sizzled their length to detonate short, sharp bursts in the tiny core between her legs, the core that held the promise of explosive pleasure she'd denied herself for so long.

"I want you now," she insisted, trembling with it, pushing his shoulders onto the mattress, crushing her breasts against his sculpted chest, aligning the requisite body parts.

He slid into her then, thick and slow, adjusting the angle to penetrate deep. She braced her knees, rising vertically, pleased.

"We fit!"

"No kidding." Seth's teeth gripped his bottom lip with the effort of holding back as she experimentally lifted up and forward, then back down to encase him once more. When she checked for his reaction, he appeared beyond words.

"Are you okay?"

"No, you're killing me," he ground out, his big hands grasping her hips, urging her to continue. "Faster."

She lifted her butt and leaned to capture his earlobe between her teeth. "Slower." She laughed, wicked and heady with the tart erotic scent arising from their mingled fluids.

Control freak, Carter called her. Ha. Seth wasn't complaining. His heavy-lidded eyes tracked hers, his hands busy cupping her breasts, smoothing her hips, now tangling in the curls at her apex. The hair on his chest electrified her nipples, shooting sparks to the area she slowly rubbed up and down his length.

Sensation built, a blossoming pressure that multiplied exponentially with every languid descent. She felt him thicken inside, and it excited her more. She had him where she wanted him, compliant, helpless, on the brink. He needed her to release him, to release them both. Shallow pants, urgent thrusts of his hips, his hands pressing her buttocks to him—she reveled in the all-consuming need straining his features.

When she herself could not bear it any longer, she sat erect, grabbed his hands and clutched them to extraordinarily sensitive breasts, and quickened her movements, deep and fast, and deeper still, until his thumbs tweaked both nipples and her body erupted in a blast of rippling pleasure that dimmed her sight and flashed to the tingling tips of her extremities. Inside, Seth's shaft throbbed with his own release, stimulating aftershocks that prolonged the exquisite sensations.

She fell to one side, numb with sensory overload. They lay side-by-side, panting and speechless, not moving for several minutes. Her brain cleared enough to archive the experience for future recall in the long lonely nights ahead. Without Seth.

He regained a modicum of strength first. One incredibly talented hand traced the curve of her hip.

"Petra—"

The bedroom door rattled under a sharp rat-tat-tat. "Cooper, the RCMP wants you in Scott's office."

She never did learn what Seth intended to say. Curses flew as they scrambled for clothes and boots.

# CHAPTER EIGHT

Down in the SAC, five uniformed RCMP officers—four male, one female—clustered in Bob Scott's office. Hank Horvath sat to one side, having hitched a ride back to the mine in the RCMP's Twin Otter. He'd ceding the chair behind the desk to a well-built, forty-ish RCMP uniformed officer with shaven head, sharp pale blue eyes, and dark mustache. Craig Rudden appeared to be briefing them. Petra gulped. Cops wanted answers. She fretted about how much to tell them.

Did Seth's cover still need to be maintained in front of the mine security staff? How forthcoming should she be concerning her relationship with him? Worse, she'd no idea what Seth had told his superiors of her purpose for being at the mine site.

The presence of their security guard escort had inhibited conversation during the march to the makeshift interview room. Seth had immediately blanked his features, shutting her out. He didn't seem worried, or he'd have given her instructions. A hurtful thought surfaced. Maybe, when he started to speak after she seduced him, he'd actually wanted to prepare her for the upcoming interview. Not that she'd expected mushy post-coital love talk. Theirs was a fling, nothing more. She should be happy he felt the same way. Ecstatic, even. Romance complicated life, and hers was complicated enough already.

Upon spotting them, the mustached officer rose and motioned them through the glass doors. "Sergeant Rick MacDougall, Major Crimes Unit," he nodded to the newcomers without a hint of recognition. "And you are…?"

At Seth's nudge, Petra stepped forward to shake the hand extended across the desk. "Petra Paris, geologist with Excelsior Mining and Exploration."

Seth followed. "Seth Cooper, pilot, Northern Lights Air."

"I understand from Mr. Rudden here that you discovered the body, Mr. Cooper." Sergeant MacDougall's statement held subtle censure.

"That's correct."

"I'd like to interview you immediately. Please take a seat." The sergeant pointed to one of the plastic chairs liberated from the cafeteria. "Corporal Sherry Parker here will take your statement in the mine manager's office, Ms. Paris."

Petra eyed the female cop—blonde, pretty with seen-it-all eyes in an ingénue face—relieved she'd escaped the hot seat in front of a panel of uniforms. Still, curiosity compelled her to speak up.

"Shouldn't you guys be crawling all over the treatment plant collecting evidence and such instead of wasting time interviewing me?"

The sergeant and Seth exchanged a glance before Sergeant MacDougall responded coldly, "Three investigators are crawling, as you put it, at the scene. I think it's best we stay out of their way, don't you, Ms. Paris?"

Unfortunately, she didn't have a choice.

\* \* \* \* \*

To Petra's dismay, Corporal Parker had the suspicious tenacity of a terrier circling a stranger's ankles, impossible to shake off. Frustration gritted Petra's teeth. Corporal Parker insisted she repeat her story again and again, presumably expecting her to trip up on a detail or two.

During ninety long minutes, Petra stuck to a factual description of the events since her arrival—discovery of diamonds stashed in the geologists' office coffee tin, the drugging incident and subsequent smashing of the drill core samples, her actions when the body was discovered. The officer recorded each detail in precise script in a notebook, her bright eyes simultaneously absorbing Petra's every nervous mannerism and uncomfortable squirm in Hank's hard visitor chair.

"Please." Petra protested the fourth time Corporal Parker requested she describe the discovery of loose rough diamonds in the coffee tin. "If I knew or suspected who put them there, I'd tell you."

The officer flipped through several pages of notes. "The day you met Seth Cooper, he revealed himself to be an undercover RCMP investigator."

"That is correct."

The corporal pursed her lips. "Within hours of meeting you."

"Yes."

The cop apparently found the concept difficult to accept, because she'd asked the question half a dozen times.

"How did you describe your relationship with Seth to the mine personnel?"

"I introduced Seth as my boyfriend." Petra fidgeted, twisting fingers in her lap. "At his request," she added.

Corporal Parker seemed way too interested in their "relationship". Clearly Petra would have been better off being interviewed by one of the men. Male cops might disapprove of Seth's breach of procedures and his unorthodox method of gaining access to the camp, but when Corporal Nosy ferreted out that she and Seth shared a room, her little nose twitched as if she'd caught a scent. Subsequent questions implied Petra had an ulterior motive, had purposely manipulated and distracted Seth to the detriment of his undercover assignment. Petra snorted at the image of herself as a femme fatale. In thermal underwear.

"I believe you said your colleague Carter Lee understands Seth Cooper to be your bodyguard."

Her cheeks burned. "Carter didn't believe I had acquired a boyfriend."

The officer curved a plucked brow but let that go for the moment. "Did you inform Carter Lee that Seth Cooper is your bodyguard before or after the cores were smashed?"

"Before. I told Carter Thursday at dinner, the day we arrived." Her stomach growled at the memory of the lasagna. She craned her neck to view the utilitarian wall clock opposite Hank's desk. Noon. Now that the shock of the security chief's death had worn off, her body craved food.

"But you maintained the illusion—" the corporal's head cocked in inquiry, "to the rest of the camp that Seth is your boyfriend?"

"Carter is a blabbermouth," came the reluctant admission. "Gossip spreads like the plague around camps. Everyone from the garage mechanics to the floor cleaners probably heard the rumor that Seth is my bodyguard."

"Let's review the forty-eight hours after your arrival in sequence."

Petra flushed to the roots of her hair. "Hour by hour?"

"It may twig your memory—"

Her memory didn't require twigging. The content of certain private hours with Seth was forever etched into her brain's pleasure center cells, and was nobody's business but her own.

A knock spared her.

Petra leapt to fling open the door. Hank Horvath stood outside with one fist raised, ready to tap a second time. Her savior.

"We're not finished yet." Corporal Parker's polite tone nevertheless sliced the stuffy air like a polished saber.

Hank, more haggard than when she'd said goodbye at the airstrip on his departure a few days before, stepped through the doorway and addressed the corporal.

"Sergeant MacDougall requested that I take you and Corporal Budinski on a tour of the plant operations. Here's an opportunity for cops from the Diamond Protection Unit to acquire a feel for the operation, maybe spot some security holes. He suggested Petra and her, ah, boyfriend tag along as well."

At Parker's frown, Hank elaborated, "MacDougall has a reason for sending Petra on the tour. MacDougall is hopeful Cooper's cover remains intact. Petra is an Excelsior employee, and her perceived personal relationship with Cooper gives him a valid reason for accompanying her on the tour, without raising suspicions that he's allied with the RCMP."

There they were, discussing her and Seth's "relationship" again. She'd be on a jet south to the U.S.A. in twenty-four hours. A "relationship" no longer existed. An idea elbowed its way through thoughts muddled at the recall of the "relations" part of their relationship.

She frowned at Hank. "Did the RCMP tell you that Seth was undercover?"

A rare smile lit his lined face. "I was aware the RCMP had assigned a couple of undercover cops to investigate out here at Ptarmigan Lake. When you introduced an NLA pilot as your boyfriend, I instantly knew he had to be one of them."

Heat bloomed on her cheeks. Apparently her little subterfuge of being gay had spread farther than she'd ever intended. It certainly explained why no men in the industry had asked her out on a date recently. Still, she'd play along with Hank so as to witness an industrial process that swallowed broken chunks of kimberlite at one end and spat diamonds out the other. Exploration geologists rarely saw the result of their discoveries in full blown production. That's why she eagerly agreed to the tour.

Not because she'd be with Seth for another precious hour.

\* \* \* \* \*

To Petra's disappointment, the keen RCMP officers didn't break for lunch. She managed to scarf a coffee and muffin from the cafeteria while Parker, Budinski and Cooper, similarly suited up in steel-toed boots, coveralls, safety glasses and hard hats with ear protectors, signed out access cards at the SAC reception desk.

Hank skipped the pit operation, starting the tour at the processing plant, an enormous eleven-story, one hundred and sixty-yard-long windowless building that sheltered a colossal spiderweb of conveyor belts feeding voracious computer-controlled rock crushers.

Individual access cards permitted each to step though a sliding exterior door into a narrow vestibule sized for one person. A security camera captured a frontal view, then another swipe of the key card opened the interior door. Petra stepped into disorienting cacophony. She quickly lowered her ear protectors.

Hank led the group along a pedestrian route defined by yellow lines painted on the concrete floor. They climbed stairs to a soundproofed room lined with computers, screens and control panels blinking colors and flashing digital numbers. It overlooked complex, oversized machinery in the brightly lit windowless cavern. Two men monitored video images of the nonstop crushing and screening of four thousand tons of ore per shift, two shifts per day, seven days per week.

Hank motioned the group toward the observation window and raised his voice above the muted thunder of heavy machinery. "No human hand touches the ore from the point at which it enters the processing plant to the recovery area at the far end where diamonds collect in a special bin."

Endless black tongues rolled broken rock into giant crushing and grinding maws. "In this facility the ore is ground to less than an inch in diameter, mixed with water, and conveyed though a centrifuge that separates mineral-rich concentrate from waste rock. The waste is diverted to the tailings area. The diamond-bearing concentrate moves into the recovery section."

They trailed him to the recovery area's observation station, Petra trotting at Seth's side, followed by Parker and sharp-eyed Corporal Roger Budinski, husky, dark blond, late thirties, bringing up the rear.

The ceiling dropped to six storys inside the adjoining fluorescent-lamp-lit recovery section of the plant Not a soul wandered the floor area between sloping conveyor belts. When Hank insisted no humans touched the fully automated operation, he wasn't kidding. Petra stepped close, keen to hear his explanation of how diamonds were separated from the pulverized worthless ore gliding continuously on conveyor belts far below.

"The ore concentrate that makes it this far passes through an x-ray device. The conveyor belt launches the pebbles and grit into the air within the x-ray zone. There, x-rays cause diamonds, no matter what grade or size, to fluoresce, that is, to light up," he said for the benefit of the cops. "Photocells detect the light and trigger thin jets of compressed air that deflect the diamonds, and only diamonds, into the recovery bin. It's clean and fast, and completely hands-off."

Responding to a question from Budinski, Hank revealed that the operation generated enough industrial and commercial diamonds each twenty-four-hour double shift to fill one coffee tin. Petra flinched at his choice of container to illustrate the volume.

Seth lifted a forefinger to catch Hank's attention. "What happens if the air jets miss one of the diamonds? Where does the rejected material go?"

"Good question. It's rare that a jet of air misses a fluoresced particle, but it can happen." He glanced at the two men staring at the monitors before indicating that the tour group leave the small room to continue the discussion elsewhere.

They descended the access staircase and shuffled along a catwalk to a metal deck outside the enormous x-ray unit. Two motion-activated security cameras tracked their approach.

"When commercial-grade diamond output fell off a month or so ago, I initially suspected the air jet controls had malfunctioned," Hank confided. "The jets tested out fine, but to be sure we'd recovered every diamond, the plant superintendent designed a procedure that rerouted the rejected x-rayed material through the recovery area again."

Deep bags hung under exhausted eyes. He continued, "It made no difference. We recovered the same quantity of industrial-grade diamonds and smaller gem-quality diamonds as we did during the first several months of production. Only commercial diamond output dropped a month ago, gems over a half carat, to be precise. The relative proportions of the rest of the output didn't change."

He waved a tired hand at Sergeant Budinski. "You know the rest. The first death confirmed diamond theft," he said in a reference Petra didn't comprehend.

First death. Another murder? Her world rocked. Death changed everything. If only she'd known. She'd been little Red Riding Hood, skipping along minding her own business, naïvely unaware of murderous wolves intent on grabbing the goodies. Chagrin heated her cheeks. Seth knew of the danger from the beginning. Why hadn't he told her about the first death? He'd held out on her. Though no more than she'd held out on him, she was forced to concede, and he had tried to warn her.

"That's when I began working with the RCMP. Unofficially, of course," Hank continued.

Petra grabbed Hank's elbow. "What did you mean by the first death? Did the Excelsior board know about this?" She'd assumed the board of directors had been straight with her, blast it. Trust no one, that was her motto, and she'd made an exception for the board. What a mistake.

Hank swiveled to drop a placating hand on Petra's shoulder. "I immediately informed Athlone that a man had died after swallowing rough diamonds. We hoped to clear this up without involving the other executives or the board. If the media got wind of it—"

He shoveled the other unsteady hand through thinning brown hair. His left eyelid twitched. "You know the implications. The stock price is already depressed. Fortunately the RCMP agreed to publicly attribute the first death to a ruptured ulcer, and gave us a month to root out the smugglers with the intention of capturing the head honchos, not just the runners."

Petra licked dry lips, pondering the implications. Athlone knew of the smuggling, but didn't tell the board. He encouraged the elderly gentlemen to believe the original assay results had been doctored, which sent them, and her, on a wild goose chase to procure fresh core for analysis. Yet when the assays turned out to match those of the original core, the board would immediately start digging deeper to find the reason for the shortfall. That's why Athlone's agents smashed her cores—to buy time.

It all fit, save for one loose thread. Her father performed the original assays. His forecasts for diamond grades and sizes were borne out in the first few months of production, but then suddenly quantities of diamonds over a half carat tumbled. The board suspected complicity to inflate the assay estimates, implicating her father. She had to know. "Is it possible someone salted early production with gem-quality diamonds to boost output?"

"Unlikely." Her former exploration boss barked his trademark guffaw. "Who has the dough to salt a new mine with more than three million dollars worth of high-grade rough? Initial production coincided with the assay predictions within the acceptable margin of error. No, we had 'em, and lost 'em. Under my watch."

Relief softened her knees, had her clutching the metal handrail for support. Her father was innocent. Hank's explanation meant the original assay performed by Edward Paris had to be valid. He might be an SOB, but he wasn't a crook after all. She blinked away moisture as she mentally rearranged the puzzle pieces. Athlone had implicated her dad to divert attention, and that meant Edward Paris wasn't in cahoots with the CEO. Didn't it? She needed to think.

When Seth moved forward to brace his arms on the metal railing beside her, Petra raised her eyes to link with hurt-clouded emerald. Recrimination bled from his white-knuckled fists gripping the horizontal bar. He'd read her well enough to ascertain she'd had suspicions and decided to keep them close to the vest instead of sharing with him. She lifted her chin, defiant. Well, he hadn't spilled his secrets and inside knowledge either.

He pulled away to refocus on the job. "How do the diamonds leave this building?"

"I'll show you." Hank advanced to a reinforced steel door with another controlled entry mechanism. "From this point on, we invested in a biometric security system. Only six people, three per two-week rotation, have clearance to enter the x-ray recovery section. Even the security guard escorts must wait outside this door. Once inside, left thumbprints from two of the six authorized personnel are required to mechanically empty the bin containing the recovered diamonds into an explosion-proof steel container. The machine automatically locks the container with another biometric-coded seal and shoots it out this slot for pickup. Two security guards escort the container and the two authorized transfer personnel a couple hundred feet to Diamond Sorting and Valuation."

"Whose thumbprints activate the seals?" Corporal Parker spoke up for the first time.

Hank's twisted grin didn't reach his eyes. "Currently four senior staff have access—me, Bob Scott, Craig Rudden, and another deputy chief of security off-shift in Yellowknife. I presume that puts Craig and me at the top of your list, eh?"

The three officers didn't crack a smile. He barked a laugh then got serious. "What saves me is our twenty-four-hour surveillance. The date and time to the second are imprinted on the digital video recording. I can vouch that no digital record or segment thereof is missing, right back to the day we commenced production, because security staff review them and I spot check before we batch a week's worth and send them via satellite uplink to Excelsior's head office in the States. There the IT specialists scan for inconsistencies again."

\* \* \* \* \*

Seth churned the operating procedures over in his mind and fitted them to what he already knew. The mine manager implied his tight security controls rendered the processing plant impenetrable to thieves. Employees other than senior management and security simply did not have access to the rough diamonds, so he claimed, at least until they reached the sorting and valuation facility. It made sense. If forensic analysis of mine production records confirmed Horvath's assertion that only top-end gem output had taken a dive, then skimming of the cream had to happen between sorting and shipping. The next stop on the tour should prove interesting.

Seth watched Petra tromp the short distance across the packed gravel to the sorting facility, rigidly erect, tight as a drum, avoiding his colleagues as if they had Ebola. Corporal Parker must have done a number on her. He grinned to himself. Served her right for holding out on him.

In the mental sense.

Physically, jeez, earlier she'd put it all out there, with gusto, and made him a very happy man. Then when they met up again at the security station to collect access cards for the tour, her freezing stare that screeched "back off" confused the hell out of him. A complicated woman, Petra Paris.

The main floor of the sorting and valuation building remained off-limits to all except three authorized employees per shift. Two security guards sat in an observation booth, one to watch the employees, the other to monitor output from video cameras trained on the tables and equipment from every angle.

"Each employee allowed in the sorting room must have the highest level of security clearance. The RCMP traced each of these men and women's employment records, associations with friends, hell, what they ate for breakfast ten years ago," the mine manager said as he ushered the small group into a corridor separated from the single classroom-sized room by a wall of reinforced glass. Only a domed skylight illuminated the workspace. Sorters at microscopes required diffused light to assess qualities such as clarity and color of the tiny, jagged stones.

Petra pressed her nose against the glass. Seth surmised her fascination mirrored his. Odds were someone in this room redirected gem-quality stones from the daily stream arriving and departing under guard.

"The diamonds are mechanically cleaned in an acid wash and weighed in bulk. Then these employees sort the rough into eleven sizes, weigh each stone, photograph it, and record its description on a manifest."

Corporal Budinski broke in. "The diamonds are weighed *after* they're cleaned?"

"Yes," Horvath confirmed. "No human hands touch the diamonds until after they are cleaned and weighed in bulk. The weights of each individual stone are totaled and compared to the incoming bulk weight. The weights match to within a tenth of a gram. It's a bloody mystery." Frustration tinged with embarrassment darkened weary features. This was his turf. His responsibility. His head on the chopping block. "Only production of gem-quality diamonds weighing half a carat or more dropped. We're getting the same quantity of industrial diamonds, more or less."

Corporal Parker quivered, snuffling the scent. "Who maintains the diamond-washing machine, and how often?"

"The maintenance superintendent can supply that information." Hank appeared to perk up at the possibility the machine was rigged, then deflated, shoulders rounded. "Even so, persons performing any maintenance in a secure area are required to strip to the buff, wear disposable coveralls, and be x-rayed before leaving the building. Even their tools are inspected and x-rayed. It's impossible to conceal any diamonds on their bodies, especially those over a carat in size."

"How big is a carat, anyway?" Seth asked.

"A fifth of a gram," Petra piped up.

"What's that in ounces?"

Hank explained in civilian terms. "A raisin weighs about a gram, or five carats."

"That small, eh? Should be easy to slip tiny stones into an orifice or two."

"X-rays will detect any foreign objects," Hank insisted.

Petra's delectable bottom lip sagged. Amber eyes sparked and flared into a familiar glazed glow. This time Seth doubted sex had anything to do with it.

Budinski seemed annoyed at the trivial side discussion. "Horvath, get me a list of all maintenance personnel with access to the sorting facility. I'm bringing in a forensic engineer to take apart the cleaning equipment."

"We can't halt production," Hank barked, alarmed.

"Two men are dead," Budinski snapped. "That cleaning machine may be the answer as to how diamonds disappear between the recovery operation and this sorting room. Stockpile the bulk diamonds in a vault for a day or two."

While they argued, Seth drew Petra aside. "You have an idea."

Petra swung her head between Corporal Parker and Seth, and obviously figured Seth to be the lesser of two pains in the butt. "Hank's right. X-rays detect foreign objects and unusual masses in tissue. That got me thinking—" She tugged at her delectably full bottom lip with two fingers. "Many folks do have foreign objects in their bodies, say surgical pins in joints or broken limbs. Most common of all—"

Seth pounced on her lead. "Dental fillings."

She smiled, and his stomach somersaulted. "Correct. It's possible for metal to mask the diamond when x-rayed."

Seth dragged her to him and kissed her soundly. "You doll. The maintenance guy slips diamonds into his mouth and tucks them inside a hollow set of false teeth lined with metal to throw off the x-ray. Brilliant. You're brilliant."

He kissed her again, because he enjoyed the rosy flush of her outrage, and because he plain old felt good. Terrific, in fact.

She pummeled his shoulders with small fists and hissed, "You're embarrassing me in front of your colleagues and mine. They think our relationship is pretense."

"Yeah? When I tell the others your theory, they'll want to kiss you too." He winked.

"The person monitoring the x-ray machine is probably in on the scam too." She stepped away. "Problem solved. That's enough for me. I'm leaving. I'm starving and I need to pack."

"Wait." He captured strong, talented fingers. He loved her fingers, especially loved what they could do slicked with lotion.

"Why? You wanna kiss me goodbye? Forget it." She yanked her hand free and aimed for the exit.

"Catch you later, babe," he called after her rigid back.

In response, she raised a middle finger high over one shoulder as she tromped through the scanner to exit the building.

He laughed. Ah, he'd make it up to her. Later. Alone. He liked his women feisty. Then he stilled, swallowed.

When had he begun to consider Petra as his woman?

\* \* \* \* \*

Carter sat alone nursing a coffee at a cafeteria table overlooking the main compound, chocolate cake crumbs on a plate in front of him. Tempted, Petra eyed the glass dessert cases. And regretfully resisted. Time was of the essence. Corporal Nosy Parker hadn't finished with her yet. She'd track Petra down any minute. Petra bit into an overstuffed tuna salad sandwich, filled a coffee cup and walked the few steps to Carter's table.

"You track me down to inquire about the drillers' progress?" Carter spared her a morose glance before resuming his perusal of activity in the compound. Strangers in city clothing spilled out of an extended cab pickup. One lugged camera gear. Another carried a black bag—a doctor or coroner, she surmised.

"I don't give a damn about the cores anymore."

Her emphatic assertion didn't shake him. He acted as though he hadn't heard.

"The drill crew dumped a new set in the office an hour ago," he said absently, continuing to track the newcomers approaching the main entrance.

"Carter." She nudged his shoulder with an elbow. "We have to talk."

Murder notwithstanding, the dining room had emptied after the noon meal, half to work, the other half to sleep. Still, even with Chief Scott dead, the bugs in the dining room might still be monitored. She and Carter needed to take a walk. "I have news. You wanted to know what's going on? Well, now's your chance."

Carter scowled, suspicious. "Why the big switch?"

"Come with me. Please." She gulped down her coffee and placed the cup in the dirty dish area on the way out.

Grumping, he dogged her out the back entrance to avoid the SAC, and quickened his short stride to keep up as she hurried across the compound toward the road leading to the open pit. Once hidden from view by the maintenance garage complex, she slowed to a walk, finished her sandwich.

"Carter, Excelsior is in deep trouble. Until Bob Scott's murder, I didn't understand the danger." Petra blinked back tears. Darn dust kicked up by the monster vehicles in the pit beyond.

Carter gaped when she scrubbed at her eyes. Well, death upsets a person. She'd been so naïve, so blindly focused on her own goals that she'd missed the signals, putting them both in mortal danger.

"By keeping you out of the loop, I thought I was protecting your career. But I was wrong. This is bigger than assay fraud and stock manipulation. This is—" She flung her arms wide. "Smuggling is major league criminal activity."

"Protecting my career? Smuggling? What?" Carter hopped in front of her, forcing her to halt. Rage chased confusion across his expressive face. "Tell me the truth, dammit, from the beginning."

She dragged in a tremulous breath. "You hear about an Excelsior employee dying from a ruptured ulcer?"

"The guy in the plane about a month ago?"

"He died when rough diamonds tore up his gut. He was smuggling, Carter."

His skin blanched beneath the tan. "Smuggling," he repeated. "No way. If I'd only known back then—"

Her voice rose over his, shuddering with guilt. "I was just a pawn sent here to obtain the fresh drill core for assays to divert the Excelsior board's attention. Meantime, persons unknown are ripping off millions of dollars worth of rough, and are willing to kill for it. I'm so sorry, Carter. I thought I was protecting you."

"Protecting me how exactly?" Sarcasm burned like acid.

She wondered which upset him more—the trashing of his office, or the drugging. "You pissed off Excelsior's VP of Exploration. You're darn lucky to still have a job. One more black mark, and it's the heave-ho for you. I didn't want your name associated with questionable core assays."

"I can take care of myself." His small hands clenched. "I'm the chief geologist. I had a right to know why you were sent here." His quick mind keyed onto a crucial question. "Why did the assays have to be redone? Initial production bore out the original assay results within a reasonable margin of error. We both know projected diamond output based on assay results is just an educated guess. It can swing up or down over the life of the mine."

Something in her face told him more than she wanted to.

"It's your father, isn't it," he exclaimed. "Your dad performed the original assays. You were afraid he'd falsified them."

"I thought he might be in on the scheme to manipulate the stock," she admitted.

"But why? Edward Paris has an excellent reputation. It doesn't compute." He shook his head, seriously disturbed. "Did you confront him with this?"

"We haven't had an easy relationship since—" Unshed tears clumped in her throat. Must be a delayed reaction to the murder.

She stopped to compose herself and brush some grit from the corner of her eye.

"Since when?" Carter prodded.

"Since he cheated on my mother with a twenty-two-year-old lab technician," she blurted. "I don't—I didn't trust him. He betrayed his wife and destroyed our family."

"Men's peckers get them in a damn lot of trouble," Carter said with a savage vehemence she didn't understand. "It doesn't make us criminals." His breath caught as he breathed deep and visibly changed gears. "But you're not off the hook. I am royally pissed that you didn't tell me why we had to redrill the cores."

"The board swore me to secrecy." And she hadn't trusted Carter one hundred percent, but wasn't going to admit that. The deaths changed everything. Her old friend's safety became paramount.

"Have the cops figured out who knocked us out?"

"Not yet. My theory is that the smugglers wanted to divert Security's attention from their operation and buy some time. They tried to frame us with stolen diamonds in the coffee tin, and when that didn't work, they drugged us and smashed the cores to occupy Security for at least another day."

"The smugglers did that to us?" His features crumpled as if she'd stolen his favorite toy. "Are you sure it's linked?"

"No, I'm not sure, Carter." Irritation needled. "But how many sets of villains wandering around a mine in the Barrens can there be? I didn't want to believe it either."

"So who killed Bob Scott?"

"The smugglers," she said simply. "He must have discovered something incriminating. These men working for Athlone, whoever they are, happen to be extremely dangerous."

His mouth gaped. "You think *Tony Athlone* is behind this? Our CEO?"

"He's been buying up Excelsior stock as its price drops. Could be that he's double-ending this. Right now his men are ripping off the best quality rough, and when they stop, production will rebound, the stock price will rise, and he'll clean up again. Not only that, he'll control the company."

"His men." Carter shook like a rattle. "Do you have proof Athlone's behind this?"

"Not a sliver. It's all speculation," she admitted.

"What are you going to do now?"

"Get the hell out of Ptarmigan Lake ASAP," she replied immediately.

"I meant, are you going to tell the RCMP what you suspect?"

She'd been tempted to pour out her theory to Seth, but loyalty to her employer took priority. "I need to report to the board and receive instructions from them. The board hasn't a clue what's happening on site. I left a message on a contact's voice mail to call me on my satellite phone. When I've apprised them of the situation, my responsibility ends."

"Seriously, you're leaving?" Carter's skin above the beard took on a waxy sheen.

"We're leaving," she corrected, "as soon as the RCMP gives the okay. I may have to submit to another interview." She grimaced. "There's a murderer wandering free. From the sounds of it, the smugglers are an organized group, and desperate. Not thinking straight. I don't intend to be caught in the middle. Come with me," she urged. "I'll pay for a charter out of my own pocket, if necessary."

Carter chewed the overlong ends of the hair on his upper lip, thinking. "I have things to do. My rotation ends tomorrow. I'll be on the scheduled flight to Yellowknife, guaranteed." His color improved and his next words held conviction. "The smugglers won't dare try anything with the RCMP in everyone's face."

"Let's hope not. Anyway, now that I've abandoned the cores, they, whoever they are, no longer have a motivation to go after either of us."

"If you say so." He didn't look convinced.

"What's worrying you, Carter?"

Before he could respond, the satellite phone hitched to her belt thrilled. "Petra Paris," she answered automatically. "It's one of the board directors," she mouthed to Carter, who jerked his head toward the camp complex, and then beetled off in that direction, a man on a mission.

The lengthy phone call pushed Carter out of her mind. He'd be safe now, she reasoned, and concentrated on stirring up a hornets' nest in an office tower thousands of miles away.

\* \* \* \* \*

Petra tracked Seth down in one of the TV lounges where he reclined in an easy chair, boots propped on a coffee table, a sketch pad balanced on his thighs. A charcoal pencil moved under deft fingers. She moved to peek at his work over his shoulder and recognized Craig Rudden standing over Bob Scott's wet, rotund body. "These pictures aren't caricatures," she said, surprised. "This is a real drawing."

Seth only laughed. "Caricatures are real drawings."

"You know what I mean. The figures are realistic."

"As opposed to abstract?"

He was playing with her. "I'm sorry. I bow to your talent. You're a genuine artist."

"As compared to a fake artist?"

"Oh for heaven's sake. Enough already." She pushed aside car magazines on the coffee table and sat to face him. "Seth, I'm leaving."

"Smart move. It's about time."

"Is that all you have to say?" Hurt slid down a throat tight with the words she daren't speak—*I'll miss you*. Silly her, she'd expected more from him after all they'd shared. A goodbye kiss, maybe. A modicum of regret at the parting. Something.

"I'm ready whenever you are," Seth said, interrupting her inner whimper.

"What do you mean?"

"After the plant tour Sergeant MacDougall cleared me to fly you back to Yellowknife. The RCMP has your statement. You didn't have to sneak around trying to avoid Sherry Parker." He chuckled. "Is Carter Lee joining us? I spied you two chatting out near the pit."

"You don't miss much, do you?" she said.

"Nope."

"Carter prefers to take the scheduled flight out tomorrow. You're a cop. Don't they require your assistance with the investigation?"

"My cover is relatively intact. When you leave, so does the boyfriend. I have no excuse to stay."

She made a decision. "Thank you for your offer. I don't want to spend another night here." That was a blatant lie. A night in Seth's arms held enormous appeal. Ever practical, however, she understood more nooky would lead to an even more painful wrench when they finally separated. Best to leave before she actually fell in love— Scratch that. Before she began to care about the man.

He stood and stretched. "We'll collect the bags upstairs. Do you need help with the aluminum cases?"

"I'm leaving them here. There's no point in hauling the few cores drilled today to Colorado."

He peered at her, a cop through and through. "Ready to tell me the story behind your little expedition to Ptarmigan Lake?"

She brushed loose tendrils of hair escaped from her pony tail off her forehead. "I gave my statement to Corporal Parker."

"My intuition tells me you left out a few key details." Exasperated, he shook his head.

\* \* \* \* \*

Shortly after 3 p.m., the administrative details of their departure taken care of, Seth tossed Petra's backpack and his duffel bag through the Beaver's cargo door into the area behind the rear seats. Drew Hamilton at Northern Lights Air would be very happy to see this plane, less happy to see him. Seth's explanation that he'd been detained for questioning by the RCMP hadn't washed. Drew had roared over the satellite phone that Seth should have been on his approach into the Yellowknife airport by 8 a.m., and of course he was right. Wildlife biologists had booked this tundra tire-equipped old Beaver for an aerial caribou herd count today. Presumably they'd be ticked. Drew probably had printed out his termination papers hours ago.

The thought depressed him. The murder blew the case into the public spotlight, meaning this particular assignment's days were numbered. Still, he guarded his cover, loath to return to a career chasing border-hopping drug runners and shutting down grow operations. He enjoyed flying in northern frontier country, the extra challenge to his skills, the lack of congestion in the skies, the passengers who each had a story to tell. The new start after Kate.

Awash in guilt, he'd paid a hefty emotional and financial price for loving and marrying a woman. He'd vowed to never again expose a life partner to the dangerous life he'd chosen. It made the time with Petra all the more special—a rare and wonderful interlude in his solitary existence.

A cool easterly wind ruffled the windsock adjacent to the runway. The temperature hovered around 70 degrees F, the blue sky was clear right up to the stratosphere. Perfect flying weather.

Today he paid particular attention to the preflight inspection. Joe had topped up all the fuel tanks after his arrival the previous evening. Still, he checked the levels. He inspected the two-blade propeller, the wheels, the wings and fuselage, opened the engine cowling to double-check connections between the mechanical components, climbed into the back of the plane and laid out the standard emergency equipment piece-by-piece on the floor, before repacking and storing it behind a cargo net.

"What's taking so long?" Petra called from the copilot seat.

A grim smile edged apart his lips. "How many planes leave Ptarmigan Lake?"

"Oh. You think the smugglers hid rough in this plane to retrieve at the other end?"

"That's what I'd do, in their hot shoes." He fished around under the seats and dipped fingers into every nook and cranny. "I'll alert the boys in Yellowknife to inspect the plane, but it appears to be clean."

That very fact unsettled him. Perps ruthless enough to murder a high-profile security chief must have a plan to transport the rough ice off-site before the RCMP discovered it during their searches. If not in his plane, then how? Intent on flying Petra to safety, he didn't waste any more time on the unanswerable.

He engaged the engine starter and, while the rebuilt old engine churned the single prop to a cranium-thrumming blur, focused on the preflight checklist, readied his charts, and planned the flight route. After testing the brakes and rudder pedals, ailerons, flaps and elevators on the taxi to the end of the runway, he ran through the pre-takeoff procedures twice. Temperature and pressure gauges, controls, lights, instruments all checked out.

"Is it my imagination, or are you spooked?" Petra asked through the headset microphone.

He didn't answer. He released the brakes, advanced the throttle to takeoff power, lifted off within thirty seconds and climbed into the wind. Once the plane reached a safe maneuvering altitude, the wings dipped in a shallow bank. Far below, dump trucks rolled like children's toys in a sandbox.

Petra exhaled heavily into her headset mic.

He spared a glance her way. "Relieved to be out of there?"

"No kidding."

He leveled off the plane at four thousand four hundred feet, their heading and one hundred thirty mph cruising airspeed consistent with a two and a quarter hour flight time. The reliable four hundred fifty horsepower piston engine droned through air as smooth as velvet. The tension cramping his shoulders and lower back eased. The hard knot twisting his gut since he spotted white hair floating on the dingy surface of the sewage tank loosened its grip. Soon he'd have Petra safely lodged in a Yellowknife hotel. His strategy included dinner at Yellowknife's fancy French restaurant, a bottle or two of wine, and, if the gods were smiling, dessert in her room.

He kept one eye on the horizon, the other on his instruments, with an occasional glance over to the uncharacteristically quiet woman in the copilot's seat. For several minutes she watched the landscape unroll below, lost in her own thoughts. Countless blue pools of water Swiss-cheesed the otherwise featureless tundra.

Petra's head lolled onto her chest about the time he became aware of pain building like a thundercloud between his temples. He gripped his window latch to slide the pane down for fresh air. It refused to budge. Dark suspicion thickened his tongue.

"Petra!" He shook her shoulder. When she didn't wake, he unbuckled his seat belt and reached across to open her window. Jammed also. He automatically lifted one hand toward the nearest ram air vent in the fuselage, but froze when he spied the steel plate screwed over the opening.

Terrible comprehension pierced the pain numbing his brain. Sabotage.

With effort, he searched his memory for the DHC-2 Beaver's engine specs. Pipes from the piston engine's nine cylinders funneled combustion products into one long exhaust pipe that passed under the cabin before emptying into the slipstream. A mechanic, and God knows the Ptarmigan Lake camp employed dozens, could easily have punctured that exhaust pipe and diverted combustion air into the adjacent heating duct that vented into the plane's cockpit.

He'd pulled Petra out of the death-tainted mine site to die trapped at four thousand feet in a plane filled with lethal carbon monoxide.

# CHAPTER NINE

Panic chomped at the edges of Seth's dulling awareness. Petra's lighter body mass made her the canary in the coal mine. Seth calculated he had roughly two minutes, maybe three, before the lethal gas knocked him out as well.

To buy time, he shouldered open the door a crack for fresh air. As a long-term solution it didn't work—the wind pressure from the plane's forward motion forced the door tight to the frame, unless he found some object to wedge the door open.

Petra's headset held his door ajar for a couple of minutes until an air pocket jarred the door wide and the headset became the first casualty of the flight.

Several deep breaths of fresh air temporarily staved off the encroaching brain fog, allowing him to examine his options. His first priority was fresh air for Petra. No telling how long she had before the carbon monoxide killed her, if it hadn't already. His heart stalled.

Seth tore his gaze from the instruments long enough to reassure himself she still breathed, agonizingly aware that with every shallow breath she inhaled deadly fumes spewing from the pipe under the cockpit. He shook his head. No. He'd save her. This time he would not fail his woman.

A tool box in the rear held a wrench heavy enough to smash the window, but he dared not leave the pilot's seat for fear of passing out. That left turning off the engine to halt the production of the CO. And that meant a forced landing. The balloon tires gave him a fighting chance to land safely, as long as he remained conscious.

Sweat trickled down the side of his face. His previous rough landing on the tundra hadn't gone well, and that was in optimal conditions on flat terrain. Here, two hundred miles from civilization, blue water filled hollows between brush-covered hilly glacial deposits. His head split with mind-befuddling pain.

He'd cut the engine and then attempt a dead-stick landing. It was her only hope, and his.

The Beaver's thick wings had been designed to provide maximum possible lift for a high payload. Unfortunately, this made it a relatively poor glider. The only power-off forced landing he'd performed was during flight training ten years earlier. He'd have one chance to land, and God help him if the wheels slammed a boulder or sank into a hole in the uneven ground.

With rapidly depleting strength, he shoved a shoulder hard against the door, fighting the powerful pressure of the slipstream for less than a precious minute, but long enough to drag in four lungfuls of fresh air.

Engine off.

The eerie silence further unnerved him. Petra's life depended on his rusty skills. Yet again he'd put a woman he loved in life-threatening danger. He groaned. After Kate, he'd sworn to never allow this to happen.

Seth corralled his drifting thoughts and tilted the nose ten degrees below horizontal to maintain the airspeed recommended in the manual he'd memorized when he hired on. He trimmed the ailerons with fingers that slipped and fumbled on the controls. Tense seconds slipped by. Seth fought the toxic lethargy that softened his muscles and leadened his eyelids.

To hell with the recommended airspeed. He pushed the nose down and adjusted the flaps to increase the angle and speed of descent. Still too slow. Pain blurred his vision, affecting his depth perception to such a degree that the brush covering the terrain fast approaching below might be ground-hugging or six feet high for all he knew. He squinted at the altimeter and prayed for smooth turf between the two lakes dead ahead.

Petra's head hung unmoving, her breathing imperceptible. If he lost her— A great black wall of tangled emotions threatened to destroy his concentration. It was now or never.

At two thousand feet, he remembered to try the radio. With luck he might be within radio transmission range of the Yellowknife tower. He pushed the switch on the control yoke to "transmit" and reported the Beaver's position to a disembodied voice at Air Traffic Control. In turn, the specialist acknowledged the coordinates and reassured him a search and rescue helicopter would be mobilized. Seth slurred thanks and signed off. They didn't have to tell him paramedics would be onboard. He merely crossed his fingers that neither he nor Petra would require the services of the coroner.

Seth aligned the plane with the widest, most promising green and brown blur, and lifted the nose to make his final approach. The motley smudge of color filling the cockpit window grayed as he adjusted the pitch, lowered the flaps, checked the airspeed, and waited for the two wheels under him to touch *terra firma*.

Then the lights went out.

# CHAPTER TEN

Cold water lapped Petra's face. She lifted her head, sputtering, and immediately regretted the movement. A ferocious headache had her gasping. Petra blinked to clear the water from her lashes and found her torso suspended by the shoulder harness over a pool of water, her legs submerged.

Seth!

She twisted to see Seth out cold, cheek pressed against the control panel. She unsnapped her harness and stretched a hand to feel the pulse under his right ear, fear snatching her breath. Blood thrummed slow and strong under her numb fingertips. Thank the Lord.

She relaxed enough to survey their situation. Ahead, the plane's nose had disappeared underwater. To her right, beyond the window, waves rippled the surface of a small lake. On the other side, blue sky over solid ground was visible through Seth's open door.

"Seth." She slapped his cheek. "Wake up."

Several more pats and shoves and scoops of cool water splashed across his face had no effect. An adrenaline rush borne of alarm sharpened her muzzy wits. She tried the radio. Nothing. Not even static. The battery must be waterlogged.

The plane had come to rest tilted at an angle with her door partially underwater. She crawled between the pilot and copilot seats into the rear, shoved open the left cargo hatch, and dropped onto coarse glacial deposit. Her knees wobbled. Dizzy, she sat down until burgeoning nausea subsided.

After a couple of dry heaves and several chest-expanding deep breaths of the cool sub-arctic air, she forced herself to stagger twenty feet from the plane, turn around and take stock. The Beaver had apparently veered off a wide strip of uneven moraine material and taken a dive into the lake. The small tail wheel dangled in the air. They'd need a chopper to haul the plane out. It appeared Seth had made another unscheduled stop on the tundra, this time with disastrous consequences. She seethed and stomped in her wet steel-toed boots, and seethed some more. Once she dragged him onto dry ground and revived him, she'd kill him.

The effort took fifteen minutes. A wet, one hundred eighty-pound RCMP cop was not easy to maneuver. Her rubber arms refused to cooperate, compounding the difficulty. She regretted the bruises on his legs he'd wake up to.

If he woke up.

She vaguely recalled from a first aid course that the longer someone remained unconscious, the more serious his condition. She crouched beside Seth flat on his back on the sleeping bag she'd retrieved from the cargo hold, a fresh, fierce alarm clanging at her ribcage. Gentle breathing raised that fabulous chest, but his flushed, cold skin tore her heart. He needed more care than she could provide. He needed a doctor.

Stark terrain undulated to the horizon, black ravens, assorted brown rodents, and several million mosquitoes her only companions. No doctor out there. Attempting to clear her head of the debilitating pain so she could think, she sucked in several more deep breaths of the clean air. Painkillers were in order. And her satellite phone.

A large metal box stored behind a cargo net yielded a treasure trove of supplies—food in airtight packets, water purification tablets, matches, a first-aid kit and flares. From her own pack she retrieved bottled water and pain tablets. Gratefully she gulped down three.

"Seth, a doctor will be here in no time," she said, trying to believe it, trying to convince herself he'd be okay, choking down the dread clutching her throat at the sight of him lying perfectly still, his wet jeans steaming slightly under the warm sun.

She called the Ptarmigan Lake camp and apprised Hank Horvath, then Sergeant MacDougall of their situation. The sergeant communicated with the Search and Rescue service on another line and gave her the welcome news that a helicopter had been mobilized half an hour earlier with an ETA of fifty-five minutes.

"Seth radioed an emergency landing?"

The sergeant briefly provided the pertinent details. "Cooper said the plane had been sabotaged. He managed to supply your coordinates before the cra— Before the radio cut out. Glad to hear you aren't injured. What's Cooper's condition?"

"He won't wake up." Her voice broke. *Good grief, girl. Pull yourself together.*

A gruff voice said in a cool, professional tone intended to quell panic, "He's been unconscious for less than half an hour, but he may be in shock. Keep him warm. I'll have the camp nurse call you." The sergeant signed off.

After relaying to the nurse Seth's pulse rate and lack of obvious bumps or wounds, other than the ones she'd caused hauling his limp body out of the plane and over the loose stones, she covered

Seth with another sleeping bag and applied mosquito repellant from the bottomless emergency kit to his exposed skin and hers.

Then she waited.

Without even the flies to distract her, several very unwelcome thoughts pushed to the surface, elbowing for attention. According to Seth, the plane had been sabotaged, meaning someone was trying to kill her. She'd abandoned the cores. What more could they want? Why her?

For a few minutes she speculated as to how the plane was sabotaged, before discarding that line of thought. Her scant knowledge of the inner workings of planes left her pretty much in the dark on the reason for the emergency landing. The only accurate deduction possible with the information available was that someone had tried to kill her, and Seth had saved her life.

She brushed a palm across his red, cool skin. Dear Seth. Emotion welled from an overfull heart. She'd nearly lost him in the crash. He might be mortally damaged. She cradled one limp hand between both of hers, pushed back terror and grief that had her groping for sanity, and prayed. *Wake up, Seth.*

Seth's brush with death, not her own, not Scott's murder, had great tears rolling down her cheeks, had mighty sobs shaking her frame for the first time since her parents' divorce when she was thirteen. She could no longer deny even to herself what Seth meant to her.

She'd fallen in love with the man, blast it.

* * * * *

Seth pried open one eye to a gray nothingness, then the other. Oh hell, he'd gone blind.

A memory swam to the surface of ground rushing toward him, of Petra slumped in the copilot's seat out cold, then nothing. Sweat prickled his skin. If this wasn't hell, it sure was damn hot. He moved his limbs under a thick blanket.

Suddenly the blackness was snatched away and strong sunlight lasered his eyeballs. "Ow."

"You're awake!" A dark shadow passed between him and the blazing sun.

When his blurred vision adjusted, he saw a beautiful angel haloed in brilliant light smiling down at him.

"Heaven," he croaked out of a dry throat. "For a moment there, I thought I'd landed in the other place."

The angel morphed into Petra, still beautiful, but in a white T-shirt with an Excelsior logo above one luscious breast and with a ball cap clenched in her fist.

"What other place?" she asked.

"The hot place. I'm sweating to death." He peered down his nose at the double thickness of arctic sleeping bag covering his body from the neck down. "This bag's good to fifty below zero!"

"The nurse instructed me to keep you warm in case of shock."

"What nurse?" He flung the cover aside, sat up and looked around. The Barren Lands lay barren as far as the eye could see.

Petra barely paused to point out the satellite phone beside her pack before crouching to fling her arms around his neck. "You're alive!"

"So far," Seth returned, pushing her away to inspect her from auburn curls to leather boot-shod feet. Her facial skin was blotchy, which he attributed to a side effect of the carbon monoxide. Otherwise, to his unspoken relief, she appeared to be all in one piece, including the attitude. "Where's the plane?"

She helped him to his feet. "The plane's not going anywhere.

When he caught sight of the Beaver's short nose taking a long drink, he stumbled. Not one of his best landings, he had to admit. Yet by some miracle the plane appeared intact, and so were they.

"We're alive," Petra said, echoing his thoughts. "What happened anyway? Sergeant MacDougall said you reported sabotage."

Seth decided he needed to sit down again. Petra tossed him a bottle of water, and he gratefully drank. "I remember radioing our position before the final approach. A chopper should be here any minute."

Petra checked her watch. "In twenty-six minutes, so they tell me. How's your head? Mine was splitting when I came to."

"It feels like the worst hangover of my ill-spent youth, coupled with nausea. How can you be perky and…vertical, when I'm so wiped?"

"Vitamins and clean living," she shot back. Taking pity, she retrieved the bottle of painkillers from an outside pocket on her pack and tossed it to him, then settled cross-legged on the sleeping bag beside him. "Engine problems?"

It would do no harm to tell her, he supposed. "Carbon monoxide poisoning."

She ran the answer through the circuits in that scientific brain of hers, then pronounced, "CO gas is odorless. Very clever of them. At first glance, investigators would attribute our deaths to the crash, not the gas, because we'd still be alive at impact. Let me see if I've got it right… I passed out first, you noticed, switched off the engine then glided in." She crossed her arms and frowned. "Why didn't you open a window?"

He glared at her. "I tried. The windows and outdoor air vents were sealed shut."

"You saved my life." It wasn't a question.

"I suppose I did, and my own in the bargain," Seth admitted. "It was close. I lost consciousness before the wheels touched down. By the time I switched off the engine, I must have already absorbed too much CO into my system."

"My hero." She raised a hand to smooth his hair, sharing a shy grin with him. Secretly, he allowed a shard of pride to co-mingle with the pleasure of her gentle touch. This time he hadn't screwed up. This time he'd saved his woman.

He bent to kiss her, sip a little nectar of the gods as a reward, but she ducked, slid away and upright, and began to pace.

"We can rule out the idea the smugglers hid stolen rough in your plane." She whirled. "But why do they want to kill me?"

"Or me," he said, slightly peeved at her reaction to the attempted kiss and not understanding why. "Tell me how they could possibly know you'd be flying back to Yellowknife with me today?"

"Oh." The agile mind behind golden darting eyes clicked through the implications. "They're on to you?"

"Possibly. I figure persons unknown tinkered with the Beaver during the night shift, well before I'd normally leave in the a.m. to fly charters all day. If so, they targeted me, not you."

"Oh. They tried to kill you." Worry quenched the glowing amber to a dull brown. "I got you into this. I'm sorry."

"It's my job. So you'll do what I say from now on?"

"I'm not that sorry." A weak grin rewarded his effort to lighten the mood. "Seth, since I'm leaving the north, there are certain facts you should know."

"About time." He had a primal urge to tuck her safe and close to his body, and now was as good an opportunity as any. He patted the sleeping bag. "Sit and tell the good cop all about it."

She wavered, an arm's length out of reach. "Carter's still on site. I'm worried—"

A distant whir from a black speck on the horizon forestalled any revelations.

"The flares," they yelled simultaneously.

Seth forced himself upright onto unsteady legs and went to retrieve the flare gun. A scant minute later an arching crimson streak announced their location to the searchers.

\* \* \* \* \*

"You're a very lucky woman," the nurse said. "Both of you." With a toss of her short curls, she indicated the person behind the adjacent curtain.

"We know," Petra, propped up on three pillows on the narrow emergency room cubicle gurney, agreed. "Seth's a good pilot, or we wouldn't be here." She grabbed the nurse's arm as she took her pulse. "He was affected worse than me by the CO poisoning. Will he be all right?"

"Nothing that a good night's rest won't cure. The doctor wants to keep you under observation tonight, and then after morning rounds you'll be free to leave."

At that, a strong arm abruptly swept aside the cotton curtain.

"Hold it. Stop right there." Seth's six feet towered over the petite nurse. "If Petra's feeling fine, we're leaving. No way we're spending the night in the hospital."

"The cops want to interview us as soon as we get out. Frankly, I've had enough for one day. If avoiding the cops means staying here overnight, I'm willing."

"Well I'm not." Seth elbowed aside the nurse, leaned over, and pinned Petra's body under the thin blanket between two muscled arms. "I have a better idea."

She quirked a brow. Seth had the air of a man on a mission, and no doubt he had another bed in mind for her last night in town. His. She didn't want to spend the night with him. She did but she didn't. She didn't trust herself to hold it together. He might discover how she felt about him. He'd made it crystal clear his top priority was to get her on a plane and out of his life. Still, the prospect of one last night together might be worth the risk. And risk hadn't ever stopped her before.

"Such as?"

"Dinner. With me."

"Dinner," she repeated without much enthusiasm. "You want to feed me?" Ever the cop, what he really wanted was the dirt on Excelsior she'd been about to dish out a few hours ago on the tundra, she realized, not her. She'd have to gaze across the table into precious eyes muddied by fatigue and the lingering effects of CO poisoning, loving him and hating him at the same time for not loving her in return, for not wanting her so bad that dinner was the very last thing on his mind.

"Sure," he cajoled. "You've been eating cafeteria food for days. I know a great restaurant where we can talk for a few hours."

"What sort of food's served at the restaurant?" she stalled.

"Your choices are Arctic char for the fish entrée or what they call country meat up here—caribou, bison and muskox," Seth ground out, irritated. "Whiskey-flavored chocolate mousse for dessert."

"No alcohol tonight," the nurse warned.

"Oysters Rockefeller for an appetizer," Seth threw in.

"I do enjoy oysters." Petra tapped a finger against her bottom lip. He glowered but held his tongue. Served him right. Finally she patted his arm. Dinner would give her time to plan another seduction. Hey, if he could use her to get what he wanted, so could she, on her own terms.

"Very well, I accept your invitation on one condition."

"I think you're gonna drive me into another kind of hospital," Seth muttered under his breath for her ears alone. "The kind with the rubber rooms." Aloud he said, "Name it."

"We share a hotel room."

"Not a problem." A grin lightened his features. "I was going to suggest the same thing myself. Until you're safely on the plane tomorrow I'd rather not let you out of my sight."

\* \* \* \* \*

An hour later, Petra sipped tomato juice across from a showered-and-shaved Seth in Yellowknife's most expensive restaurant. A waiter in black cords and long-sleeved white shirt swiftly removed the empty appetizer plates and replenished a woven basket filled with warm multigrain rolls.

"The oysters were delicious," Petra admitted. "I made the right choice in accepting your invitation." She eyed him over the rim of her glass. He did not appear to be amused.

"What was that little scene in the hospital all about?" Seth blurted. "You no more wanted to stay there overnight than I did."

"Seth, I know what you want." She plastered half of a fragrant flax seed roll with a thick pat of butter, too hungry to wait until the waiter finished placing the fondue pot of aromatic broth simmering over a flame alongside a plateful of raw meat chunks. "Quiz me. I'm ready."

Seth leaned forward in his wooden chair. "We almost died today. Staring the Grim Reaper in the face gives a man the heebie-jeebies. I want to know who is behind this. Can you blame me?"

She lifted her chin and stretched the corners of her mouth into a smile. "I'm sorry I've been…difficult. I'm starved and tired and cranky."

She resented feeling like her heart was being fed through a paper shredder because this was their last night together, and he wanted to talk, and she wanted to crawl into his arms, wrap her arms around his waist and never let go. She didn't want to need him, and she did, blast it. Defiantly, she skewered raw meat onto four fondue forks and dunked them into the broth to cook.

While their dinner simmered, she told Seth about the shortfall in diamond output that led to instructions from Excelsior's board of directors for new assays. She described her father's role, and her unfounded suspicions that he was involved in salting the original cores. As they dipped the morsels of tender meat into savory sauces, she revealed her gut feeling that the Excelsior CEO, Tony Athlone, was both attempting to manipulate the stock price to take control of the company, and was the brains behind the smuggling operation. But, she had to admit, she had no proof.

Seth chewed silently for several minutes, presumably slotting the new information into what he already knew. Meanwhile Petra savored the gamey flavor of wild muskox, a distant cousin to cattle. He had what he wanted from her now. Her eyes teared. Must be the cigar smoke wafting from the bar.

He put more meat in the pot to cook and noticed her bent head. "What's wrong?"

She breathed deep and went for it, with nothing left to lose. "Is your life still in danger? Can you guarantee that after I leave tomorrow, the RCMP will capture the bad guys so that I can sleep at night, knowing you're safe?"

"You're worried about me?" His surprise appeared genuine. "This is my job. After these perps are locked up, there will others to take their place."

"I was afraid of that."

His faced hardened. "This is why, much as I'd like to spend more time with you, a relationship can't work. Once you're safe, I'll be able to sleep at night."

*But I won't.* She didn't understand where these protective feelings had sprung from. She'd been drugged unconscious, interviewed in a murder investigation, almost died from carbon monoxide poisoning, crawled out of a wrecked plane, and poked by doctors in a hospital, yet her thoughts centered on the danger Seth was in. They'd tried to sabotage his plane. They might try again to kill him.

"Are you returning to Ptarmigan Lake tomorrow?"

He squinted at her over the candles. "You mean after I put you on the plane?"

She resented his lack of trust. She'd meet the scheduled flight from Ptarmigan Lake to ensure Carter arrived safely and they'd travel together on the jet home to Colorado. Seth didn't have to babysit her.

Without waiting for her answer, he continued in a matter-of-fact tone, "The Transportation Safety Board investigators are flying up from Edmonton to interview me tomorrow morning about the crash." He waved a broad hand. "It's standard procedure. I'll be tied up for a few hours but should finish in time to join you for lunch and drive you to the airport for the 2 p.m. flight."

She pushed her plate away, no longer hungry. This was it then. The end. Only twelve short hours of alone time lay ahead, and she could barely keep her eyes open, this time from fatigue. Every muscle ached, including her heart.

He leaned toward her, his clouded eyes concerned. "No chocolate mousse? Tea?"

She shook her head. "I'm beat. I think I'll turn in."

After Seth paid the bill, they walked across the street to the hotel they'd checked into earlier. She needed this last night together, at some primitive level. Needed him in her arms and in her body. While he showered, she'd slipped out to the drug store across the street to purchase a small box of protection. They didn't come in quantities less than twelve. It seemed wasteful. With a pang of regret, she doubted she'd ever have the occasion to use the remaining eight or nine.

Their bags remained untouched where they'd left them on the double bed. Seth swept the room for listening devices with his gizmo, and declared himself satisfied.

While Seth brushed his teeth, Petra stripped, turned off all but the bedside light, and crawled naked between the covers. She yawned. He seemed to be taking forever. She'd just close her burning eyes for a minute.

\* \* \* \* \*

Seth emerged from the bathroom stiff with anticipation under his boxer shorts. A shallow snort greeted him. Petra lay flat on her back, rich dark hair splayed over the white pillow, mouth agape. Even asleep she was extraordinarily beautiful.

As he flicked off the lamp, he ruefully noted the four foil packets arranged on the bedside table. An optimist, his Petra.

His Petra. He shook his head. Not possible.

He crawled in beside her and gently kissed her cheek, then one white, smooth shoulder. She moved, turning her back to him. He wrapped one arm around her waist and drew himself close, spoon-style against her tush and knees, a palm cupping a full breast, his nose buried in herbal shampoo-scented thick hair. Heaven.

Gradually his heartbeat slowed, and he gave in to the exhaustion he'd fought for an eternity. With Petra safe in his arms he could finally relax. The heat from her body warmed the cold in his at the prospect of living without her after tomorrow.

He'd love her tonight in the only way possible—by enfolding her in a caring embrace. He'd felt this way for only one other woman, the wife he'd failed to protect. Oh, Petra was different from Kate—less passive, braver, with an inner strength that rivaled his own. Petra challenged his decisions. Her reactions to danger often astounded him. Yet still and all, she was a fragile woman to cherish and safeguard.

And because he loved Petra, her safety was paramount. He had to put away the perps who drugged her at Ptarmigan Lake. He must insulate her from the criminals he dealt with every day.

She twitched and sighed under his arm. He'd walked away from one woman and survived. But Petra had infiltrated deeper into his guarded heart than he'd ever thought possible. His need for her prickly companionship, her sharp mind and her luscious body consumed him.

Sending her out of his life forever would twist his very soul.

* * * * *

The next morning Petra woke with a kink in her neck. She rubbed the locked muscle and carefully moved her head to scan the small hotel room. Empty. The bathroom door hung ajar. One bleary eye fell on the clock radio on the nightstand. Pale green numbers announced 9:20 a.m. She groaned.

A folded sheet of hotel stationary covered the foil packets she'd positioned the previous night. Stretching across the bed, she pinched the paper between two fingers.

*Petra*, she read in a tidy script. *I will be tied up with the crash investigators all morning. Stay put. I'll be back to check out and take you to lunch before your flight. S.*

Bitterly disappointed, Petra let her arm fall to the bed. He could have woken her an hour before duty dragged him off. Then again, she thought as she struggled to sit up, maybe he felt as rotten as she did this morning. Her mind was alert and the thudding headache had faded, but her muscles were as fatigued as after a punishing workout in the gym.

She threw her legs over the edge of the bed and, after the room stopped whirling, staggered to the bathroom. A few minutes later, while scrounging for a T-shirt to cover her nakedness, she spied Seth's sketch pad protruding from the end pocket of his duffle bag. Perhaps another hour in bed wasn't such a bad idea. She snagged the pad, retreated back to bed and arranged the pillows to support her sore neck.

The first dozen or so pages contained a series of caricatures of Ptarmigan Lake employees in their work clothes, most of whom she didn't recognize. She quickly caught onto the rhythm of his quick line drawings. Seth seemed to draw sketches as a form of note-taking and memory aid, his charcoal pencil capturing the most recognizable features of each person.

She flipped the page to discover his impression of her—shadowed eyes, full, sensuous lips, and enormous boobs. Her cheeks heated. Peering closer, she realized he'd captured a quality of stubbornness in the head tilt and shoulder alignment. Above those 36-D breasts. He indeed had a fascination with them, she recalled, and the heat in her cheeks slipped lower.

The next page had Carter's furry visage gazing adoringly up at a woman with a knock-out figure in a white uniform, a chef's hat over her fair hair. Her teeth were bared in a gleaming, predatory smile. Her fingers ended in long talons, with the right hand clutching a leash attached to a studded collar around Carter's neck.

The drawing was labeled with their names—Carter Lee and Desirée Dumont. She frowned. Although she had not met Carter's new love, the sketch of the statuesque dominatrix stirred a memory. Where had she seen that smile, those nails? Leaning back with eyes closed, she allowed her mind to drift in hopes of making a connection.

Women in her profession did not sport fingernails sharp enough to slice leather. Geologists' nails were blunt, cut short and ruthlessly scrubbed to remove grit from the stone and earth of their trade. Who else in her world, then? She recalled the female staff in Excelsior's Colorado headquarters from memory one by one, then widened that scope to include the wives and girlfriends of male employees, starting at the top.

A divorced Tony Athlone had paraded several gorgeous women on his arm to corporate and social events over the years. She'd paid little attention. She vaguely recalled a newspaper color photo taken at a Boulder art auction the previous winter that showcased one such girlfriend who managed to hang on to him longer than the rest. Literally hang on. At the time Petra couldn't help but notice the fingernails possessively curled around Athlone's arm, a triumphant smile creasing the perfection of the woman's oval face.

Petra sat upright to stare at the likeness Seth had sketched. There was a resemblance. But the girlfriend had been called Gabrielle Dumont. After dating a rich, powerful man, why was Gabrielle-Desirée slumming with a dweeb like Carter?

A dreadful certainty squeezed her heart. Unless Gabrielle had an ulterior motive.

She had to warn Carter. Throwing aside the bed coverings, she grabbed the hotel landline. Rapid calls to Carter's office, room and the security desk produced no results. Carter seemed to have disappeared. Worse, the desk clerk told her the RCMP had cancelled the rotation change. No employee would be leaving for at least another week. Carter, the world's biggest sucker, was trapped there with the murderer and a girlfriend on the wrong side.

Oh gawd. Petra pressed forefingers to throbbing temples. She had to think. Could Carter be in cahoots with Athlone's gang? She didn't want to believe it. Yet the whole camp knew Carter and Desirée were an item.

Maybe she'd jumped to a conclusion too fast. Carter wasn't involved with the processing operation. He didn't have much to offer the smugglers in the way of inside information. Maybe Desirée or Gabrielle or whatever her real name was hadn't manipulated an unsuspecting Carter after all. Doubt had her reaching for the phone book to find the RCMP's local phone number. Then she remembered what Carter had insisted when they last spoke by the open pit—"Men's peckers get them in a damn lot of trouble. It doesn't make us criminals."

Too late, she realized he'd known then he was in bad trouble. Carter had figured out his supposed girlfriend was using him. Desirée certainly had access to his office. She likely drugged the coffee, maybe even planted the rough in the coffee tin. But was Desirée aware that Carter had cottoned on to her role in the smuggling operation? If so, he was in terrible danger. These criminals had already demonstrated they'd resort to murder to buy themselves some time.

She dialed Hank Horvath's office number out at the Ptarmigan Lake site. Hank listened carefully to her theory linking one of his cooks to the smugglers and ultimately to Athlone.

"I'll advise the RCMP to question Carter and Desirée Dumont," Hank interjected when Petra ran out of breath. "Athlone is already on their radar. He's nowhere to be found. The FBI have been alerted. Take my advice, Petra, and go home to Colorado and lock your door until the murderer is behind bars. It's not safe here for anyone connected to Ptarmigan Lake Mine."

"Wait!" Petra didn't want him to hang up yet. "There's more. Carter seems to be missing. But if you mobilize the RCMP to search for him, that could tip off the smugglers. They might kill him straight away." She left unsaid what they both were thinking—if they hadn't already killed him to shut him up like they had Bob Scott.

"Sorry, I can't spare any security officers for a search. They're watching for any unusual activity in the compound or in the recovery area. The murder investigation is a distraction that makes us vulnerable. MacDougall warned me they may attempt sabotage or another disruption to give them a chance to get away. And because I'm not sure who I can trust on the security team, I have to pair the boys up. I can't spare anyone. If the RCMP want to question Carter, they'll have to find him themselves. I'll suggest to MacDougall that he send in more cops on the next charter."

"Carter's life might be at stake." Panic thickened her voice.

"All I can do is tell my security staff to keep a lookout for him on their rounds. It's the best I can do."

"Then let me come back there to look for him," she blurted.

"Absolutely not," he roared. "You stay out of this. Let me handle it. Go home. That's an order." He disconnected.

She clutched her sore neck and flipped through her options. The most obvious? Go home and forget about Carter. Abandon her friend. She jammed a thumb into the painful muscle and twisted. Not gonna happen. She believed he'd been seduced by that woman. Carter was as susceptible as her own father had been when temptation tangled with lust. Carter had recently been dumped by his wife, she recalled. He was a sitting duck for an ego-boosting affair. She'd made the mistake of rejecting her father for his weakness, but damned if she'd repeat that mistake with Carter.

Next up? Tell Seth and let him handle it. But she didn't have a clue where Seth's interview was taking place. Carter could be bleeding to death at this very minute. She could call the local RCMP and have Seth paged.

Without any better ideas, she dialed the local detachment on the hotel room phone, only to be told to leave a message. Petra described her suspicions about the cook and her concerns about Carter Lee and slammed the phone back into its cradle. Her glance fell on her backpack propped on a chair. The side pocket contained her plane ticket and wallet. She had one more card up her sleeve. The company credit card.

\* \* \* \* \*

Seth emerged from the airport staff lunchroom onto the parking lot asphalt and blinked in the midday sunlight. The federal investigators from the Transportation Safety Board had taken over the lunchroom for interviews of Air Traffic Control staff on duty at the time of the forced landing, the plane mechanics, Drew Hamilton, part-owner and Operations Manager for Northern Lights Air, and of course Seth himself.

His stomach growled, his muscles screamed, and his head pounded. The physical uproar left a man's brain struggling to remember details needed to satisfy the technical analysts investigating the crash. CO poisoning was not pleasant. From now on he'd add window and air vent operation verification to his preflight checklist.

Beyond the chain link fence, a Northern Lights Air twin otter taxied off the main runway and drew alongside the arrivals apron. After the props stopped whirling, the passenger door airstair swung down and out spilled several uniformed officers. Although Seth could not recognize individual officers from this distance, the woman had to be Corporal Sherry Parker.

When he first arrived in Yellowknife, she'd offered to show him around, cook him dinner. He'd declined, citing his undercover status. Truth was, he didn't believe it wise to date colleagues, especially when he had no intention of entering a committed relationship. There was only one thing that scared him more than a pissed-off woman, and that was a pissed-off woman who packed a gun.

He ducked back into the building, flashed his pilot ID at the security guard, and strode out to intercept the RCMP contingent.

Sergeant MacDougall wasn't among the weary cops. Sherry Parker paused with a surprised grin as the others trudged past toward well-earned time off.

"Hey, Seth. You look like hell," she said cheerfully. "How many lives have you used up now? Six? Seven? You are one lucky SOB."

Seth pulled her aside, too tired for social chit-chat. "Any breaks in the case?"

"Two hours ago your girlfriend," she said, raising one thin eyebrow, "tipped us to the cook, Desirée Dumont. Says she's really the Excelsior CEO's girl."

"Desirée is Anthony Athlone's girl?"

"Desirée, aka Gabrielle Dumont, aka Jeanne Coté. She's Belgian, all right, at least according to two of her numerous passports. The background check on the cook that you requested came through soon after Petra Paris' phone call. Interpol had a few tidbits that made MacDougall sit up. She's been photographed by the pool at a Portuguese villa owned by a dealer in blood diamonds smuggled out of African mines. She has the connections to fence the rough."

Seth tried to ignore the jackhammer rat-tat-tatting behind his eyes so as to concentrate. "Desirée was sleeping with Carter Lee."

"We know. The two of them have disappeared. Not that they can get far."

"Carter is a suspect?"

Sherry laughed and shook her head. "What do you think? They're all suspects out at Ptarmigan Lake. Get some sleep. You're no help to anyone right now," she said over her shoulder.

Seth advanced toward another friendly face, Jason White, the NLA pilot with whom he'd flown the scheduled flights into various communities and mine sites. Jason and his copilot for that flight tossed baggage from the Twin Otter's rear cargo door onto a flat trolley. Jason kept his eyes open, overheard gossip here and there. Maybe he had more news.

Jason scanned him briefly before accepting a box from the copilot bent double inside the plane. "Not a scratch on you from the crash yesterday. What are you, invincible?"

"Nah, just lucky. Need a hand?" He peered into the gloom of the hold at boxes stacked three high. "Seems like a lot of cargo for passengers who barely had time to gather forensic equipment before they left for Ptarmigan Lake."

"Some of this was scheduled to come back on the jet at the rotation change. You heard it was cancelled?" At Seth's nod, he continued, "The jets might not get in for another week. Drew thought we might as well pick up some extra business hauling stuff on the RCMP charter flights in and out."

He handed Seth a cardboard box labeled as containing a familiar brand of pickles. "What is this? Food?"

"Overstock from the kitchen, apparently, to be returned to the supplier," Jason said.

Kitchen. Seth dropped the box to the tarmac and ripped off the top. Ignoring Jason's reprimand, he lifted one jar out of the box, opened it, dumped the sliced pickles back into the box, and then selected other jars at random to do the same.

Jason swore at him. "Hey, you can't do that! Drew will have your ass, if he hasn't fired you already."

"Listen," Seth grunted as he lifted a taped box of pickled pearl onions from the baggage cart and sliced it open using his pocket knife. "Food goes into Ptarmigan Lake Mine. It doesn't come out. The miners have the waistlines to prove it."

He unscrewed the top off a jar, shook four marble-sized white onions into his palm, and squeezed the hard round balls between his forefinger and his thumb. Nothing. He tossed them and tried again.

One of the onions split on one side. Bingo. He squeezed it until the hard pit dropped into his palm.

A greasy glass-like pebble winked up at him.

# CHAPTER ELEVEN

Petra hopped lightly from the pontoon to the dock, her backpack over one shoulder. When she was clear, the engine in the Cessna 185 she'd chartered at the float plane base in Yellowknife revved. Minutes later the TransArctic Air pilot accelerated into the wind down the length of Ptarmigan Lake, lifted the bush plane up and over the small island in the centre, and tipped its wing in farewell.

Turning, she spied a plume of dust rising from the gravel road that led to the mine complex. Uh-oh. Here came the cavalry. She bit her lip. Skulking doubt that her plan would work nibbled at the edge of her resolve. Maybe she'd been the tiniest bit hasty in coming to Carter's rescue, after all.

A dirty pickup lurched to a halt, both doors opened, and two white knit shirts spilled from the cab. "This is private property," the taller youth, the driver, shouted. "You are trespassing."

She spun a one-eighty so they could read "Excelsior Exploration & Mining Co." printed on her jacket.

"It's Ms. Paris, you idiot," the youth with a severe case of acne and gelled blond hair hissed to his partner. She recognized him—he'd guarded Carter's office after she discovered the rough in the coffee tin. Unfortunately the guards didn't wear nametags. It'd be easier to sweet-talk him and his friend if she knew names.

Spiked Hair approached. "What are you doing here? We heard your plane crash-landed yesterday."

"You got some kinda death wish?" the other security guard added. "This place isn't safe, especially for you."

Petra thought fast. "Carter Lee, the chief geologist, is missing. I'm here to do his job. I'm a geologist too, you know, and the mine is still operating. They need me."

Spiked Hair didn't buy her explanation. "If I may be frank, ma'am, you gotta be nuts to return here. The killer is still at large. Does the mine manager know about this?"

"Sure." She forced a grin to allay their suspicions.

"Then he'll expect you to report to him immediately," Spiked Hair asserted.

The grin slipped a fraction. "Uh, of course. Thanks for picking me up, guys. I appreciate the lift. What are your names, by the way?"

"Just doing our jobs, ma'am." Spiked Hair slung her pack over one shoulder and threw it into the box behind the pickup cab. "I'm Christopher, and he's Darren. We'll take you to the SAC first, as usual."

Petra scrambled into the vehicle, angled her knees away from the stick shift, and laced her fingers to still the trembling. During the flight she'd drafted a sketchy plan of action, but meeting Hank first thing didn't figure in it. Her mood took a dive. Hank was going to blow a gasket. After chewing her out, that paternalistic old goat would no doubt lock her away in a residence room for her own safety until the next RCMP charter left. She'd never get the opportunity to search for Carter.

As the pickup bounced over the rough track back to camp and crossed the compound to the administration and residential complex, she scanned the outbuildings. Employees hustled between them as if everything were normal. The difficulty lay in determining where a body—a person—might be hidden without being observed, where no employee would stumble across it accidentally. The only roads led to the pit, lake or airstrip. Anyone fool enough to attempt a land-based escape would be visible for five miles on the rolling tundra in any direction.

During the flight she'd analyzed the possibilities, knowing Carter to be a brilliant yet socially immature lovesick wuss. Not a recipe for smart decisions. Men in love didn't think with their brains. He'd told her that. Was it a warning? An excuse?

Either he knew of Desirée Dumont's connection with Athlone or he didn't. Courage certainly wasn't Carter's strong suit. In danger, he'd hide. The fundamental question was whether he'd hide from the cops or from the smugglers.

He might be holed up with his so-called girlfriend, also missing. But Petra didn't believe it. Knowing he'd be furious at being played for a sucker, the more plausible scenario was that Desirée Dumont seduced Carter, kept him distracted, for reasons he'd finally figured out. Then his big mouth landed him in trouble. Again.

Oh Lord, he might not be hiding. The smugglers could have perceived him as a threat, eliminated him like they did Bob Scott. Carter at this very moment might be inside one of the buildings, out cold, bleeding to death, or worse. She was Carter's only hope. Her resolve to search the buildings stiffened.

She'd need a master key card. Or an ally. Her gaze sidled to Darren, the driver on her left, then Christopher on her right, speculative.

Twenty minutes later, thoroughly searched and even more thoroughly chastised by the acting head of security, Craig Rudden, for her rash decision to return, she marched down a hall sandwiched between two different escorts and up the stairs to Hank's second-floor office overlooking the compound.

"What were you thinking?" Hank exploded the instant she crossed his threshold. At Hank's dismissal of the security staff, the door snicked closed, leaving her to face the music alone.

"Nice to see you again too, Hank." She strode across the room to where he'd risen behind his desk and shook his hand.

"Not three hours ago I ordered you to return home," he reminded her in a tone that straddled a fine line between control and outrage. "Next thing I hear, you've arrived to replace Carter."

"See, Hank, here's the thing," she interrupted before he had a chance to decide what to do with her. "Carter is missing, and no one is searching for him. I came back to do just that."

After scanning her expression, he lowered himself into his chair. "I do believe you are serious," he said at last. "I think you are certifiable, myself. Did it occur to you that the RCMP might have a strong reason to talk to Carter? You told me he's screwing Athlone's girlfriend." Hank's voice rose on the last, but he did his best to ease up before continuing. "I don't have the staff to mount a search as well as maintain production, but of course the RCMP are looking for him and Desirée Dumont." His eyelid did a fast rumba. "Every bloody employee on site is on the alert. We don't need you to search."

"Mind if I look around anyway?" she ventured.

"Yes!" Hank's bloodshot eyes bore down into hers. "Yes I mind. Stay out of the way and let the RCMP do their job. I'd order your charter back here to pick you up, but this site is locked down after the plane sabotage that almost killed you and that boyfriend of yours. No employee is allowed to leave Ptarmigan Lake until the RCMP give the go ahead. Could be days."

"Then I—" She shut up quick as his brow knit into one thunderous line.

He tip-tapped the top of his desk with a pen in time with the nervous twitch in his eyelid. "I have a mine to run. Production targets to meet. Since you're here, and getting paid to boot, I may as well put you to work. Seeing as how Carter's alternate is stuck in Yellowknife waiting for the rotation change, we're short a geologist. The crew is ready to drill a new grid for the next blast and needs confirmation of the drilling pattern coordinates. Carter estimated them weeks ahead based on pit dimension survey input married to haul truck production quantities. But that data was lost when Carter's computer was smashed to smithereens."

Hank glared at her as if it were her fault. She grimaced back. Another layer of guilt at involving Carter, and indirectly his computer, settled over her shoulders.

"You can make yourself useful by downloading the backup pit data into another computer. Once you've retrieved the backup data off the Colorado server, locate the pattern coordinates in one of the pit operations folders. Input today's survey results, verify the pre-calculated grid layout, and don't forget to compare the current pit depth to the drill hole depth. Too shallow, and the face won't break to grade. Got that?"

Petra nodded. "When's the next blast scheduled?"

"Tomorrow, if all goes well," he said.

Come to think of it, casual observation at the pit the previous day showed a limited quantity of broken granite and kimberlite blasted from the pit floor remained to be scooped up by the excavators and loaded into the haul trucks. Her heart skipped a beat. No employee would have had a reason to enter the highly secure explosives storage building since the crew loaded the drill holes for the previous blast.

Hank wasn't finished. "Then I want you to prepare an equipment order to resupply the Mine Planning and Geology Services office. This way we can fly the goods in with the next rotation. Bring me the requisition before 4 p.m. Got it?"

"Yes sir," she said, glancing at her watch. Her stomach protested the lack of fuel since dinner the previous evening. The cafeteria quit serving lunch in twenty minutes. With luck she'd run into an RCMP officer there, and have the opportunity to ask if they'd thoroughly searched the explosives storage area.

"Don't leave this building," Hank warned. "I'm posting one of the guards to stay with you on and off duty."

"Hey!" She fisted her hands on her hips. "I thought you had no guards to spare for a search for Carter."

Hank slapped a palm flat on his desk, making her jump. "There's a criminal investigation going on, dammit. The cops are handling Carter's disappearance. I'm counting on my own security staff to make sure you don't disappear too."

"A guard it is." She forced an agreeable smile. No biggie. At least she'd be free to move around, talk to people, maybe wangle key cards—the magic rectangles of plastic that unlocked doors to all the hidden spaces—from her new best buddy, the assigned security guard.

Unfortunately Hank, through long association, read her like a book. "Don't try anything," he warned. "Until that pilot arrived on the scene, I'd never have pegged you for a Mata Hari, but you sure are full of surprises this trip."

Cheeks flaming, she thumped a palm over her aggrieved heart. "I'd never seduce a kid. How could you even suggest—"

A reluctant smile hinted at the old Hank. "Of course you wouldn't. I meant don't try to manipulate the guard. I'll learn about it, one way or another. Stay in the building," he repeated. "I mean it. You are not authorized to set foot outside."

When Hank picked up the phone to call the security desk to request a twenty-four-hour bodyguard, she occupied herself with dreaming up ploys to fake out the very same assigned guard. Ever focused, the search for Carter was her top priority.

Before the guard arrived, Hank had one more message, an announcement that magnetized her steel-toed boots to the cheap carpet. "Your father heard about the plane incident. He wants to talk to you."

\* \* \* \* \*

Seated alone in the RCMP Headquarters visitors' waiting area, recovering from yet another interview, suffering from a wicked CO poisoning-induced headache, Seth lifted an aching wrist to check his watch and swore blue under his breath. It was nearly 13:15 and he'd promised Petra lunch. Her plane to Edmonton left in forty-five minutes. He hadn't even checked out of the Yellowknife Inn yet.

His colleagues from the Diamond Protection Unit, buzzing with excitement, had swarmed the Twin Otter and carried off everything loose in the cargo hold. He'd had to file a report under the guise of being interviewed. By some miracle his cover remained intact, and he intended to talk his way out of the order for a week's leave to recover.

He crumpled an empty paper coffee cup, tossed it into the waste basket beside his chair. Not that the sludge that passed for coffee had reenergized his brain. He was too far gone for that.

With creaks and groans foreign to a man his age, he rocked upright and tried to remember if he'd driven to HQ or caught a ride from the airport.

Outside in the parking lot the sun blazed in a sky bisected with a contrail from a jet taking the short cut over the North Pole to Europe. He sniffed the light breeze blowing off Frame Lake a few hundred yards away. Perfect flying weather. He scanned the lot. No black SUV. Not his, at any rate. Ah well, a brisk two-block walk to the hotel might loosen cramped leg muscles. He quickened his pace, keen to be with Petra for the duration of the taxi ride to the airport since lunch was a wash, anxious to apologize, frustrated that he'd lost an hour with her.

Five minutes later he tapped on the hotel room door, used his key, pushed the door open to unaccountable disappointment. His chick had flown the coop. One piece of baggage—his—rested on the unmade bed. He'd join her at the airport, he decided. For his own peace of mind, he needed to watch her walk onto that jet, watch the take-off.

He grabbed his duffle bag and in his haste almost missed the folded page torn from his sketch pad and tucked into the end pocket.

*Seth*, he read. *By the time you find this I will be in Ptarmigan Lake. Carter is missing and I'm going to search for him. I, or actually Excelsior, paid for the room for another night. Get some rest this afternoon. I'll call you tonight at the hotel since I don't know your cell number. xo Petra*

He sank onto the double bed, shock crowding disbelief. Why the hell couldn't the woman stay rescued? Then it occurred to him that the logistics didn't compute. The RCMP hadn't taken her in on their charter. No way any other plane or chopper had permission to land at Ptarmigan Lake mine. She'd be on her way back to Yellowknife, might even make the flight south. He unclenched one fist to punch a number into the RCMP-issue encrypted cell phone, only to connect with his cover man's voice mail. With no other option, he waited, tension contracting every muscle.

Ten minutes later his cell vibrated in his palm.

"A TransArctic Air float plane landed at the mine an hour ago? She gave him how much?" He snorted. Good luck slipping an expense claim with that thousand dollar bribe past Excelsior's accountants.

He disconnected. Horvath had put her to work, with a bodyguard dogging her heels. She was safe. At the moment. He raked both hands over his throbbing skull, frustrated to the bone that she'd spun out from under his watch when his back was turned, and returned to the hornet's nest for no logical reason that he could fathom. Women.

He reviewed his options. Not that he had any. He wasn't medically cleared to pilot a plane, and the return RCMP charter to Ptarmigan Lake didn't leave until the next day. Much as it galled him, he was no damn good to anyone at the moment. He decided against retrieving his vehicle until he'd snatched some shuteye. His basement apartment in a residential subdivision near the airport beckoned, but by leaving he might miss Petra's call.

He swallowed three pain killers dry and passed out fully clothed as soon as the comfort of a pillow faintly scented with Petra's herbal shampoo cradled his head.

\* \* \* \* \*

Seth probably had her note in hand by now, Petra considered as she munched a chicken sandwich and watched the screen of a monitor she'd liberated from the heavy equipment depot. Backup pit data files slowly downloaded from the Boulder server via satellite uplink to the internet.

None of the mine's computers were networked—that'd make it too easy for someone to hack into those with confidential production information. A robust firewall protected every computer from unauthorized access through the encrypted internet connection. It occurred to her that this computer's hard drive had not been reformatted prior to its temporary deployment to Mine Planning and Geology Services, giving her rare access to another division's data.

With nothing better to do while she waited, she clicked on an equipment maintenance spreadsheet and skimmed through columns of repair costs organized by month. As the figures scrolled down the screen, she stopped chewing. Man, who'd have guessed the twelve-foot diameter truck tires cost twenty-five grand a pop to replace.

She scanned the bottom line. Monthly totals crept up a steady eighteen to twenty percent over the past six months. Replacement tires were one reason. It cost a small fortune to fly them in on a Hercules aircraft. It was either that or wait until they could be trucked in over the winter ice road from Yellowknife, but ore truck downtime was not an option.

Another repair item jumped out at her. Truck engines, big as a room, required a very expensive part. Its order number peppered the month-by-month lists with unsettling frequency. She set the sandwich aside, frowning. A suspicious person might detect a pattern of systematic sabotage. She didn't need to be an accountant to understand rising costs inevitably led to plummeting profitability, especially when the finest quality production rough were simultaneously being skimmed off the top.

Since she'd been given access to the Excelsior server, she decided to try using the same password to snoop through backup records from other operational divisions. An over-the-shoulder glance reassured that Jeremy, her short, sturdy Inuit bodyguard, diligently thumbed a handheld game device in a comfortable chair swiped from the SAC.

Soon she'd scrolled though the water and waste management records, which showed pumps being rebuilt or replaced with perplexing frequency, pumps commissioned less than a year ago, for heaven's sake. The drilling and blasting records told a similar story—drill rig repairs escalated incrementally every month. Denied access to the Finance Division's accounting and financial statements, she nevertheless projected the operation was drenched in red ink, with bankruptcy a viable threat.

But why?

She respected Hank, knew him to be a competent manager. He'd racked up an MBA after his undergraduate degree in geology. He was conservative, detail-oriented, and he meticulously tracked every line item in budgets under his control. He'd have identified problems and taken action to stem the flow of red ink immediately. Bankruptcy did not correlate with his character.

What else did she know about him? His wife divorced him a decade or more ago, she recalled, divorce being an occupational hazard due to long absences from loved ones. No kids, no ties. He vacationed in Brazil every winter, after becoming enamored with South America during a two-year stint as head exploration geologist on an Excelsior copper property down there. His salary as mine manager topped out at two hundred fifty grand per annum plus bonus, she estimated. He wasn't hurting for money. Nothing pointed to any involvement in the crime bedeviling Ptarmigan Lake Mine. He'd been in Yellowknife at the time of the murder.

Still, she wondered. Only Hank had signing authority for expenditures over five thousand dollars. He had to be aware of the mounting maintenance costs. Doubt churned the mistrust she automatically harbored for just about every man on the planet but him and Carter. They were family. She didn't want to believe either colluded with Athlone.

Forty-five minutes later Charlie Wha Ti, the drilling crew boss on the day shift, arrived for the drill pattern reference coordinates Petra had ready on a topographical survey map. Jeremy took advantage of the burly aboriginal's presence to slip out for a bathroom break.

While the driller rolled up the map, Petra dropped a casual question into the silence. "How are things going? I hear you've experienced a few equipment breakdowns."

"Not a problem. We use the auxiliary drill rig until the problem's fixed. Production is right on target."

"Must be expensive to fly the parts in."

He raised serious but not unfriendly brown eyes to hers. "Maintenance is not my concern. We here at Ptarmigan Lake do fine as long as we don't stick our noses into other people's business. Take my advice, Ms. Paris, and do the same."

Jeremy returned before she could dig anything more out of Charlie. Reluctantly she acknowledged his nod of farewell and settled to Google e-commerce sites for scientific equipment.

She spent the next couple of hours surfing for a petrographic microscope and accessories, a rock saw, grinder and other sample preparation tools, a powerful laptop complete with high-end video and sound cards and speakers for Carter's games—it was the least she could do, a thirty-inch LCD monitor, specialized software, and the most essential item, a quality twelve-cup coffee maker.

After dropping off the requisition form filled out with supplier and order details for Hank's signature and action by the Contracts and Procurement Unit, she and Jeremy headed to dinner. The RCMP contingent had commandeered several tables in the corner by the cafeteria window. She recognized Sergeant MacDougall, shoulders drooping over his steak and fries. Corporal Parker, she was relieved to note, was not among the unfamiliar officers who must have flown in that morning.

Jeremy disliked small talk, or perhaps he'd been ordered to blow off her questions. He'd been raised in Inuvik, a small community located on the shore of the Arctic Ocean, she discovered while sirloin steak, salad, three glasses of milk and two pieces of apple pie disappeared into the growing teen's stomach.

Unlike Charlie, an aboriginal of Indian heritage from the southern part of the territory, Jeremy shared his ancestry with the Alaskan Inuit of the high Arctic. However the Inuit of the western Arctic called themselves "Inuvialuit", meaning "the real people", similar to "Inuit", which translated to "the people". Otherwise, Jeremy kept his mouth too full to answer questions. Who was she kidding? Maybe if she were ten years younger she'd have more than a snowball's chance of persuading him to lend her a master key card. Some Mata Hari. She blew out an exasperated breath, and Jeremy threw her a quizzical look as he wiped his mouth with a napkin. As far as bodyguards went, Seth ruled, with benefits.

Alien loneliness smothered her driving urge to find Carter. Petra picked at her maple-glazed salmon and broccoli. Seth had been an ally, a back-up. Too late she twigged to an uncomfortable truth—his protection gave her the confidence to plow full steam toward her goals. She'd believed she needed him to quench sexual craving, not for himself.

She'd been wrong.

Squirming, she admitted she'd been wrong about a lot of things. Her dad, for example. Yes, he'd fallen in love and ruptured her family. Her mother, betrayed, blamed Edward Paris for ruining her life, then taught her only child to distrust all men, to be independent and self-sufficient.

Petra rebuffed her father's overtures post-separation, sent him thank-you cards for gifts and for funding her college degree, continued to avoid him and his new wife both professionally and in her personal life. But at thirteen she'd no awareness of the state of her parents' marriage. Her mother, bitter to this day, had closed herself off to loving another, had never remarried.

A man had a right to love and be loved, a right to an emotionally satisfying life. Seth showed her what she'd rejected for too many years. He had awakened her capacity to love. It didn't matter that he didn't love her in return, or that he'd tried to push her out of his life as quickly as possible. Her heart had opened with the giving, as her father's generous heart had been open all along, loving the daughter who refused to accept that love.

Tomorrow she'd scrape up the courage to phone her father at his lab. Her immediate priority, to pass on information to the investigators, took precedence. Or so she told herself.

She angled a glance over to the RCMP in the corner, hesitant to report the drain on the mine's finances in Jeremy's presence. Word might wend its way to the wrong ears. She longed to shake her shadow for the privacy to call Seth, but she wasn't permitted outside to use her satellite phone, and without Seth's fancy gizmo, she couldn't be certain her room wasn't bugged.

A coded message, then.

Shortly after, Jeremy escorted her to a residence room on the third floor. Petra frowned at the shiny deadbolt installed on the corridor side of the bedroom door, seriously annoyed at this new obstacle to her plans to sneak out and search for Carter.

"There's a show I want to watch on television in the lounge." Petra had nothing to lose by trying. "I'll return to my room and lock myself in from the inside the second it's over."

"There's TV in your room," Jeremy reassured her. "You won't be bored. My shift starts at 7 a.m. I'll come by then to take you to breakfast."

Hand wrapping the edge of the door, Petra made another stab at freedom. "Locking a bedroom from the outside contravenes the Fire Code. I'd be trapped in the event of a fire. Don't worry, Jeremy, I'm so tired I'll sleep for hours."

"Sorry, Ms. Paris. Orders. It's for your own protection. If the fire alarm sounds, I'll rescue you."

"Sure you will." She sighed as the bolt shot home.

\* \* \* \* \*

The persistent *briiing* of the hotel room phone roused Seth from a dream in which his face snuggled between Petra's soft breasts. He raised his head from the foam pillows and reached for the receiver.

"Lunden here," he croaked, shaking his head to clear the drowsiness.

"Who? Oh, sorry, I must have the wrong room."

He recognized Petra's voice. "No, wait. Petra, it's me, Seth."

"London? You're kidding, right?" She laughed.

He sat upright, immediately alert, rubbing the crusty sleep from the corners of his eyes. "Of course I'm kidding. London. Paris. Ha-ha." Inside he cringed. *Way to blow your cover, Seth Lunden.* Was her line secure? "Where are you calling from?"

"I'm on my satellite cell in a room in the mine residence. Security's locked me in for the night, so don't worry about me," Petra said too brightly, adding "sweetheart" after a heartbeat.

"You'd be in Boulder right this minute, *honey*, if you'd listened to me," he said, unable to keep the frustration out of his voice. He cleared his throat, eased up. "What are you doing out at Ptarmigan Lake?"

"Oh, I'm filling in for Carter since he went AWOL. There's no *accounting* for what happened to him. I mean, he doesn't have a *record* of this sort of behavior. It's going to *cost* him big time. *Hank is number* one in my books, but he doesn't seem to care about Carter."

"Really," Seth replied, swift on the uptake. He scribbled her words in shorthand on the hotel stationary. "Carter's in trouble, you think?"

"Definitely. He's still missing. I don't understand it. Maybe he's getting *a charge* out of scaring us all silly, but it's going to *blow up* in his face." She paused for breath. "So how are you, sweetheart? How's your headache?"

"Fine, now that I've heard your voice," he said, and realized the truth of it. Her current situation, ideal to his mind, irksome to hers, loosened the anxiety clamping his gut. For another eight hours minimum she'd be safely confined to her room. "Listen, take down my home phone and cell numbers. I'm heading to my own place right now."

They exchanged numbers and signed off with a few more endearments for the bug that, at least on his side, honestly reflected his sentiments. Her "sleep well, sweetheart" warmed a corner of his cold, shriveled heart.

On the job seconds later, he flipped open his cell, speed dialed his cover man, and relayed instructions to assign a forensic accountant to the mine's financial records, and to send a team to search the explosives shed.

He stood and paced. Petra pointed to the man at the top of the mine management hierarchy, the only man in Ptarmigan Lake with an alibi for the murder. If Horvath suspected… If his security staff indeed bugged her room, interpreted her rather obvious message…

His instincts shrieked a warning that the moment she left the safety of her temporary prison in the morning, Petra's life would be in danger yet again. He needed an antacid.

\* \* \* \* \*

A knock at Petra's door roused her shortly after midnight, according to the bedside clock radio. She stumbled across the floor clad only in a T-shirt and cotton underpants.

"Who is it?"

"Security, ma'am," said a deep male voice, low. "We need to talk to you. It's about Carter Lee."

They found him! "One moment." She snagged a flannel shirt and jeans draped over the armchair and pulled them over sleep-soft limbs.

"Okay, I'm ready."

The lock clicked and the door swung inward to reveal Craig Rudden, the acting chief of security, alone in the hallway. Perspiration glistened on his jowls from the climb to the third floor. Behind him, a housekeeping cart blocked the corridor. He slid his master key card and the key for the deadbolt lock into a pants pocket.

"You have news about Carter?" she asked.

"Sure do. The RCMP found him safe and sound, tied up in the rear of the explosives shed behind some barrels. I understand you supplied the tip." A grin slashed his round face. "Smart girl. If you'll come with me downstairs to the SAC, you can talk to him yourself."

Wait a darn second. The RCMP wouldn't reveal who tipped them, not to the Ptarmigan Lake security team, not to anyone. She sidled over to the nightstand, reaching for the telephone. "I'll call Jeremy. When he finds me gone, he'll worry."

"No need." Rudden's grin widened to reveal nicotine-stained teeth in the sunlight pouring from the unshaded window. "He's off-shift, sleeping like a baby."

When her hand touched the receiver, Rudden kicked the door closed behind him, reached into his back pocket, and extracted a white pad from a plastic freezer bag.

Oh jeez, she thought. This was bad, bad, triple bad.

He braced his legs wide to block the exit. She'd never make it past him. Her gaze slid to the window, three stories above hard-packed gravel.

Petra swallowed. "I don't think—"

"That's the problem, Ms. Paris. You think too much." He advanced, taking his time, watching her as he unfolded and draped the pad over his palm, releasing the sweet odor of an ether-based chemical.

Uh-oh. A thin squawk escaped her throat. She tried again, and screamed to save her life. This time they'd kill her. They'd killed at least once, had nothing left to lose.

Rudden swung his head from side-to-side, chuckling. "The staff assigned to this floor are on-shift. Scream all you want."

She gasped a lungful of air as he reached for her, determined to fight unconsciousness, then wasted precious oxygen on an accusation. "You killed Bob Scott." For the hidden microphone to pick up, she yelled, "Craig Rudden did it, and now he's after me."

"Who do you think bugged this room, lady? Me, no one else." He eliminated the distance between them. A thick arm encircled her back, pinning her to his belly, the hand corkscrewing into her loose hair to yank her head backward. She kicked with her bare feet, scrabbled with her unrestrained arm to knock away the soaked white pad snaking inexorably toward her face, held her breath as it clamped over nose and mouth.

Rudden moved fast for a big guy, using martial arts techniques to reposition her body, then shoved one fat knee into her stomach to force an exhalation. An involuntary breath drew the foul chemical deep into her lungs, and then…oblivion.

# CHAPTER TWELVE

Petra awoke on her stomach, head twisted to one side, choking on material stuffed in her mouth that uncomfortably propped her jaws apart and, worse, blocked air flow. Disoriented, she inhaled nostril-burning air a tiny breath at a time.

Either she'd been blinded or the space was unremittingly dark, the deep blackness incongruous at a time of year when the sun never set. She became aware of crossed wrists tied behind her back with a thin strip that bit painfully into her skin. Pain was good. Pain indicated she was alive.

Her head ached, and she'd trade her investment portfolio for a fix of caffeine to clear her head. The acrid fumes churned her stomach, but the gag precluded emptying it. She forced down the nausea. Her arms were out of commission, the wrists possibly broken, going by the intensity of the pain shooting to her shoulders. Fortunately her legs functioned. Her bare ankles rotated freely.

Fighting dizziness, she attempted to maneuver into a sitting position on a hard floor slippery with a thin liquid film. Gasoline, she recognized. Her hair dripped with it, her clothes stank of it.

To the left in the narrow space, her bare foot struck a hard metal surface, and she wiggled her toes over a round, horizontal metal flange studded with spiky bolts attaching it at regular intervals to the floor. Lifting her foot higher she explored the shape of an upright, curved object connected to cool round tubes—two-inch piping, she surmised. They'd tossed her into a mechanical room somewhere on the property, leaving her alive for the moment. Gasoline everywhere, evaporating and filling the room with explosive fumes, didn't bode well for long-term survival. One match, or one spark from a motor in the room, and kaboom…

Stilling, she listened. A whirring hum emanated from above and to the left, a sound she recognized as an exhaust fan efficiently sucking fumes from the room. Without its clearing effect, she might never have regained consciousness.

Given a respite, resolve fired to determine what she dealt with. Rooms had doors and light fixtures. She knelt in the greasy spilled gas, slithered until finding her footing, and blindly advanced the perimeter of the space, pausing to balance on one foot while the other explored the smooth metal wall on one side and a mysterious conglomeration of pipes and odd shapes cool to the touch of her toes on the other.

After ten steps a tentatively extended foot stubbed against an end wall, so she turned a ninety and advanced in the new direction until abruptly colliding with horizontal piping at knee height. The pipes penetrated the wall, but no light glimmered. This room was exceptionally well sealed. She wondered where fresh air entered.

Sitting on the parallel pipes and lifting her legs over, she then advanced eight short steps to the next corner, continuously feeling for a vertical break, a door, in the metal-clad wall. Where there's a door, there's a light switch.

Three feet from the corner her forward toes butted against a softer object covered in wet fabric. The balls of her foot traced a familiar shape perpendicular to the passage. A leg with a boot on the end. Her heart hammered. Carter maybe. Or Desirée. She leaned a shoulder against the wall for balance, toed a path in the opposite direction to the hip and up. The body seemed to be lying in an L-shaped position, unmoving. She'd never touched a dead body before, and had no intention of exploring it further in the dark. Bravery had limits.

She stepped over the legs to continue onward. Four paces, and her big toe brushed over a significant vertical crack in the wall. Success. Her arm slid across the wall surface to a protrusion at waist height—the door handle. Next she nosed around for a light switch and was rewarded when the tip bumped up against a small surface-mounted rectangular box. Flipping the tiny lever merely required a chin swipe upward.

Light from a ceiling fixture flooded the space, effectively blinding her for an endless minute until blinking, smarting eyes adjusted.

To her left Carter lay stretched between the wall and a pump, gagged, pasty above the beard, hair plastered to his head, jeans and sweatshirt similarly saturated with gasoline. A fondness for Carter welled. His very presence indicated he wasn't in league with the smugglers after all. She didn't think they put men in jail for being duped by a beautiful criminal. If he indeed lived.

He looked dead, but who could tell. Carter had looked that bad plenty of times in summer field camp after weeks without a shower and adequate sleep. His closed eyes were a good sign. Had they been open, there'd be no doubt. She crouched close, wishing for a free finger to check his pulse. Her nose would have to fill in again. She inhaled, leaned forward to press her nose against his neck, and off-balance, toppled over sideways.

Oh, for heaven's sake. She scrambled to her feet, prodded his rear with one foot, initially gentle, then with oomph born of distress. *Carter, if you're alive, wake up.*

The body shook, twitched. A rumble in the back of the throat reminded her of a small angry bear roused from hibernation. Relief, gratitude, eased pain-laced tension in her shoulders.

She prodded him again. His eyes popped open then, and he blinked up at her. Strangled, panicked sounds gargled from the back of his throat until his sight adjusted to the light. He tried to sit up on the metal-sheeted flooring. She wobbled her head, gag-speak for "pay attention", then swiveled to waggle fingers at him. He understood, repositioning on his knees to give her access to the knot at the back of his neck. Fingers numbed by restricted blood flow worked the knot side to side, up and down, picking at the tight knot until the fabric loosened enough to allow Carter to retract his lower jaw and use the back of his tongue to push the gag out of his mouth.

She scooted out of the way as he coughed, hacked, and threw up bile.

"Thanks," he croaked, drawing gulping breaths. "I'm okay. Your turn."

With his teeth he twisted and jerked at the knot at her nape, yanked, and the gag fell away.

Petra worked her aching jaw, dredged up some saliva, swallowed several times, wished for water. The improvement in physical comfort provided emotional room for anger to flash. "That rat bastard Rudden is gonna pay for this."

"Craig Rudden? That's who put you in here? When?"

"No idea." She walked around, bent, and read the digital numbers on his wrist watch. "It's 4:35 a.m. He abducted me from my room over four hours ago." A thin plastic strip bound Carter's wrists, the type with a jagged reverse slip lock. Forget teeth, they needed a knife or a sharp edge to saw through it.

She raised her head to search for possibilities. Two pumps, motors and meters occupied the center of the small, windowless room. Supply and return pipes connected to each pump penetrated the wall at one end. The pump room walls were bare save for standard explosion-proof electrical boxes and conduit typical in industrial facilities. A sensor-activated exhaust fan whirred near the roof line, out of reach. "Where are we?"

"I believe we are in the fuel dispenser shed at the float plane wharf. It's a prefab freezer building, and normally padlocked." Carter slammed his weight against the door's interior push rod, but the door didn't budge.

Petra nosed wide the cover on an electrical panel and read the labels beside the breakers. "Someone will eventually notice if I turn off the power to the fuel pumps."

"Are float planes allowed to land yet? No? Well, pilots won't be refueling their planes any time soon, then, will they?"

"Carter, you're such a downer." She flipped the breakers with her chin, cutting power to all circuits except the ones for the lights and the fan.

"Why the hell did you return to Ptarmigan Lake? Are you insane?"

"People keep asking me that." She shrugged, and winced when the plastic strips bit deeper into throbbing wrists. "I returned to search for you, Carter. Hank told me that you and Desirée went missing, and here I am."

"Desirée." Disgust rolled off his tongue. "She used me."

"For what, exactly?"

"Not for sex, that's for damn sure. Turns out she wasn't exclusive with me after all. The other day when you sent me for coffee I surprised her and Craig Rudden together in the store room. The store room was *our* rendezvous!" Outrage pinked skin above his beard. "That's when I started thinking, what's a knockout like her doing with a schmuck like me? Unless—"

"Unless?"

"I plead the fifth."

"Carter."

"Okay, okay, odds are we'll never leave this place alive."

"Spit it out."

"Rudden made some lame excuse about doing inventory. I wanted to trust Desirée 'cause he didn't have his hands all over her, or anything, so accepted the coffee tin she handed me. When I woke up in the infirmary hours after drinking that laced coffee, I knew for sure I'd been had."

"What did you give her?" she asked, dead inside.

He refused to meet her eyes. "This mine is supposed to last twenty years, right?"

"Yeah, at least, given the depth of the kimberlite pipe. So?"

"In open pit mining, you have to continuously widen the bowl, removing the waste rock around the sides, so that as the pit gets deeper over the years the trucks can spiral down roads cut into the sides to the bottom. The normal ratio at Ptarmigan Lake is one ton of kimberlite ore excavated per nine tons of granite. For two months we've been excavating straight down the pipe in a 1:2 ratio."

"Oh Carter. I cannot believe you accelerated diamond extraction for that woman."

When the walls eventually became too steep, the miners would be forced to blast and excavate worthless rock to widen the pit instead of diamond-bearing kimberlite in the middle for unprofitable weeks or even months. The mine might go bankrupt, but by that time the smugglers would be long gone. And Carter was responsible, his reputation in the mining industry ruined if word got out. She sagged under crushing disappointment. Until this moment, she'd believed in her old buddy. "But your alternate and Hank *must* have known about this? Every mine manager scrutinizes production data. Hank in particular is as sharp as they come."

He glowered. "My alternate is a mining engineer a year out of college. He did what I told him to do. But the boss never questioned my calculations or what I assumed would be a higher yield of diamonds as we mined pure pipe these past few weeks. I was so relieved, I didn't clue in to the possibility Hank let me off the hook because he was in on the scheme."

"And now do you believe Hank is involved?" She dreaded the confirmation. Not Hank, her mentor and friend. He'd replaced the father she cut out of her life, Carter the half brother. In this nightmare she lost her entire substitute family.

"I wonder," he mumbled. "Each processed ton is projected to yield five carats of diamonds. Lately the yield should have been in the order of seven, eight carats per ton. I couldn't figure out why the stock price tumbled. Profit for those two months should have been through the roof. But it makes sense that if someone skimmed off the gem-quality rough there wasn't any increase in reported profit—"

"Hank must be involved at a high level," Petra interrupted, shivering as her blood ran cold. "Otherwise he would have been on your case as soon as the yield dropped, to investigate the cause." Another thought stuck her. "With so many diamonds rolling in, the smugglers apparently had a few to spare for a coffee tin. Was that you?"

He shook his shaggy head. "I didn't know about the smuggling, I swear."

She didn't believe him. He'd certainly been shocked and frightened by the discovery of loose rough hidden in the office, but she only had his word that he'd disposed of them by tossing them away. More likely he'd handed them off to his girlfriend once out of Petra's sight. She tried for the truth from another angle. "Who smashed the cores?"

Carter studied the floor, but with Petra in his face silently waiting, infinitely patient, he decided to clear his conscience. "When you arrived to reconfirm the assays, I worried it was because diamond production exceeded estimates, and I'd be found out," he confessed. "My mistake was telling Desirée about your assignment. Her people, she never told me who, tried to frame us with the rough. They smashed the cores. I felt terrible. I never intended for you, for us, to be drugged or hurt. I just wanted you to leave."

"Why'd you do it, Carter?" The angry words flew from a heart crushed into a pulpy mess of hurt. She'd cared for him and Hank.

He avoided her eyes. "I did it to hold on to Desirée. She had her pick of three hundred men. I didn't ask questions or know who else was involved in the scam. Honest."

"Oh Carter." His weakness had led to poor decisions, criminal behavior, fatal results. "Desirée is Tony Athlone's girl. I recognized her from a picture in the newspaper."

"No way." Carter looked stricken. "She just used me."

"She used her body to manipulate every man useful to her, Carter," Petra scoffed. "She played on Athlone's power-hungry quest for control of the company, your fragile ego after the wife dumped you, maybe Hank's, what? Greed? He makes good money, but not enough for a luxurious retirement. Continue. What happened next?"

"After you took off with Cooper, like an idiot I confronted Desirée about the smashed samples, the rough in the coffee tin, the drugged coffee, all of it. I insisted she tell me about her connection to the smuggling, pretending I wanted a cut."

"Pretending?" Petra flung him a challenge, her illusions shattered. Why else would he have stayed behind after she offered him a ride to Yellowknife?

He lifted his bushy chin. "Okay, maybe I did want a cut. I was in too deep already to ever work again in this business. I wanted compensation. She invited me to take a walk with her down to the lake to discuss it, and next thing I knew, something hard smashed me on the back of the head and I woke up in here a day later."

"Two days later," Petra corrected. "That was one hell of a wallop. Let me see." He bent, angled, to allow her to inspect the back of his dark head. "Your hair is matted with blood, not gasoline."

Sapped of strength and hope by Carter's admitted involvement, overwhelmed by the scale of the fraudulent activities that encompassed diamond production from ore excavation through processing, she sank to sit cross-legged on the floor. "Horvath, Security, perhaps a dozen other employees must be in on the fraud. These smugglers covered all the angles. They will never let us live. We are so screwed."

"Didn't you notice the AN/FO over there?"

She followed the direction of his nod to a fifty-five-pound sack wedged between two pumps, the label indicating the trade name of an ammonium nitrate blasting agent. A wave of dizziness had her chin dipping to her chest. The smugglers planned one mother of an explosion. Ignited, the dispenser building and its fuel storage tanks outside would erupt into a cataclysmic fireball.

A white ignition cord dangled from a hole poked into the side of the packaging. When the white flashes behind her eyeballs faded, she knee-walked over to the sack, and with her teeth yanked out the cord and metal blasting cap on its buried tip with the intention of gently depositing it on the floor in a far corner.

"A lot of good that'll do. They don't have to enter this room to start a fire. They'll open an exterior valve to flood the ground with fuel, or drop a match into a tank, or—"

"Enough, Carter! I need to think." Why plan a massive explosion? If eliminating her and Carter were the objective, why wait? A small fire lit at the time they were dumped in the building would have killed them quickly. "They intend to create a major diversion," she said slowly, "to give them time to escape in the confusion."

Morose, he agreed. "Makes sense. The RCMP made things too hot. The lake is the farthest point from the airstrip. Attract everyone away from the camp, and a plane or chopper can pick them up without interference."

"When, do you think, they'll blow this place, literally?"

"If I were them, I'd time it for when half the camp is still asleep off-shift, including the cops, and the other half is exhausted."

Her stomach somersaulted. "That's now, Carter! People will be waking for breakfast in less than an hour."

He nodded. "We are so screwed."

\* \* \* \*

Seth paced the length of the basement room that comprised his bachelor apartment, unable to settle. The television screen, habitually set to The Weather Network, indicated 1:50 a.m. local time. Through the basement walk-out patio door he'd watched the sun sink to the horizon, hover for ten minutes and gradually rise again. Yellowknife's sky, three hundred miles southwest of Ptarmigan Lake, already hinted at dusky nights ahead. By late December, only three or four hours of daylight relieved the -40 degree nights, or so he'd heard. Many left on holidays or risked cabin fever during that dark stretch. He'd built up several weeks leave. When he saw Petra again on her way through Yellowknife, he'd mention a January visit to Boulder, see how she reacted.

A disturbing thought popped into his mind. Maybe she had a guy waiting back home. Maybe she'd hook up with someone by January. Nah. He shook his head. He understood her character enough to know her loyalty was selective and hard won. She'd permitted him into her inner circle, confided in him at last. He'd been the one to make no promises.

He dropped to a recliner and picked up his sketch pad. Earlier he'd drawn for a couple of hours. Often when he disconnected his rational mind and liberated his charcoal pencil to fly over a clean white sheet, it extracted and recorded subconscious perceptions from his memory. The insights had proved invaluable in a case or two.

He leafed through various sketches, searching for something he might have missed—Bob Scott's body on the catwalk, the Beaver crash site, the boxes offloaded from the Twin Otter that contained smuggled rough, the interior of Diamond Sorting and Valuation, the cafeteria, the Mine Planning and Geology Services office, the bedroom he shared with Petra—

Petra. He flipped to the caricature he'd drawn around midnight, after he woke from a nap slouched in the recliner. A buxom bride stared up at him, veil lifted by a breeze to reveal a smug smile.

Petra in a dress—a dream image, for sure. Man oh man, she was gorgeous, with a double helping of courage. He smiled, remembering her soft, yielding behavior under his ministrations the first time they made love, then the reversal the second time when she seized control to give more than she got, a surprise that had made his heart flip. He loved her assertiveness in bed, not so much out of it, when her unpredictable next moves left him anxious instead of eager.

Beside Petra he'd drawn himself in a penguin suit and added a ring to his left hand. He squirmed, decidedly uncomfortable. He'd sworn never again to marry, to put a woman at risk due to his job. He cared for Petra, he'd admit. Maybe, if pressed under oath, he'd reluctantly confirm the love word had inadvertently slipped into his mind once or twice before he booted it out. All the more reason why he had to keep Petra out of his life for her own safety and continued survival. For her own protection.

He peered closer. Gray circles linked her left wrist with his right. Handcuffs. Why handcuffs? He studied Petra's smug smile, the defiant lift of her chin, the determined set of her shoulders. Her goal-oriented, no-thought-to-consequences attitude placed her in jeopardy on a regular basis.

Then it hit him with the force of a boxer going down for the count. The only possible guarantee of Petra's ongoing safety was for him to be at her side 24/7. Joined for life.

In fact, the separation had him on edge all evening. Subconsciously he'd registered that she was not safe locked in a bedroom at Ptarmigan Lake, not safe without his protection. A bead of sweat tracked down his right temple.

He reached for his cell, punched in the phone number Petra provided earlier. No answer. He let it ring six times, dread massing in his heart, then speed-dialed Joe's cell.

Joe promised to check her room.

Twenty-seven minutes later, according to *The Weather Network's* clock, and an eon according to his nerves, his cell vibrated in his palm.

"I found her room locked up tight," Joe reported. "But Petra didn't answer my knock, so to preserve my cover I woke the sergeant and had him arrange with security to unlock the deadbolt and door locks." He paused. "To all appearances she escaped, Seth. We found bed sheets and blankets knotted together and hanging from the third floor window."

Oh hell. Petra and her harebrained goal to find Carter. He cursed her independent spirit. Loved it, but cursed it.

"You still there?" Joe inquired.

"Yeah."

"The ruse woulda worked, except those first into the room smelled a lingering odor of chloroform. Despite the open window there was no cross draft to clear out the odor, and the perps forgot to turn on the bathroom fan."

The bottom dropped out of his world. "She was abducted?" he yelled.

"Calm down. The RCMP officers are being roused out of bed as we speak. We'll find her."

"You find Carter Lee yet? Desirée Dumont?"

"Not yet," Joe was compelled to admit.

"I'm coming out there."

"You can't. If MacDougall overrides his own orders to make an exception to allow you on site, your cover will be blown."

His gaze landed on the book fallen open to his sketch of the murdered Bob Scott, and he imagined the horror of finding Petra in similar circumstances. He'd broken a non-negotiable rule to remain emotionally detached or risk making poor decisions. His professional training urged him to wise up. The emotional corner of his brain told it to go to hell. His woman was missing. Nothing else mattered. "Expect me in a couple of hours. Warn Sergeant MacDougall."

"Your pilot's license is suspended."

"I'll think of something." He disconnected and dialed the home number of Drew Hamilton, the operations manager for Northern Lights Air and part owner of the company.

"It's 2:30 in the morning," Drew bellowed after Seth identified himself and stated his request. "You want to borrow a plane? After crash landing a Beaver and costing me thousands in lost business? You want an answer right away? Here's your answer. I fired you yesterday morning when you didn't show up for work." He hung up.

Seth redialed. "I'll charter the plane," Seth said quickly when Drew answered.

"On what I paid you, you can't afford it," he snapped.

"Wait." Seth sucked in a deep breath. Oh hell. He was out of options. Icy fear that he'd arrive too late to save Petra stiffened his spine, drove him to say words that spelled disgrace and demotion or worse.

"I'm an undercover RCMP officer."

"You a cop? Gimme a break."

"I'll prove it. Expect a call from RCMP Headquarters to confirm my identity." He grimaced. Hell and damnation. If someone had bet him two weeks ago that Seth, a cop's cop, would compromise an assignment for the sake of a woman, he'd have laughed and tripled the bet.

"The RCMP is gonna pay for the charter? Then let them arrange it the usual way in the morning." Drew sounded pissed.

"No time. I gotta leave for Ptarmigan Lake immediately. I'll pay by credit card."

"The Yellowknife airport is closed. I can't access the Northern Lights hanger until 6:00."

Seth slapped a hand to his forehead. He'd forgotten. Unfortunately he'd have to charter a slower float plane with its higher drag. Time meant everything. "I'll take the 185 on floats."

"And your license is suspended. You can't pilot," Drew stated as if that ended the discussion.

Oh damn. The man followed the rules to the letter, treating his license to operate like gold. No compromise possible there. "You have your pilot's license. I'll meet you at the Back Bay Float Base." Seth disconnected to forestall more arguments.

His cover man, surly from being woken at home in bed, ranted that he wasn't senior enough to validate an ID, especially for an unauthorized op. Seth lost precious minutes on another call to Ptarmigan Lake to secure authorization from Sergeant MacDougall.

"You realize the consequences, Seth?" MacDougall's voice was rough from fatigue and suppressed frustration. "With your cover blown, there will no longer be a place for you at the Yellowknife detachment. I don't want to lose a good man."

"I have to do this," Seth insisted.

His superior's sigh rippled a shiver through Seth's body. What MacDougall didn't say but they both understood was that the

RCMP had no place for undercover cops who acted independently of orders through the chain of command.

"Permission granted. I'll have a detective telephone Drew Hamilton."

That was all Seth needed to hear. He snatched his wallet and badge off the kitchen counter. He'd left his standard issue Glock hidden under the Beaver's seat while on-site at Ptarmigan Lake, and it had been returned to him during his interview at HQ. He now retrieved it from a locked case under the bed. Quickly he loaded it, donned his shoulder harness, and strapped the weapon in tight. To hell with the Ptarmigan Lake security rules. With his leather jacket zipped, he was good to go.

* * * * *

Drew Hamilton no longer trusted Seth Cooper. The remote north attracted three types of men he privately labeled "renegades"—freedom-seekers who didn't fit into conventional society and didn't wish to be bound by its rules, "gold diggers"—short-term workers after the big bucks in the natural gas and mineral resource industries, and "escapees"—men who had ducked out of facing their obligations to family or had other reasons for disappearing. Fifteen years in the northern territory taught him to recognize the difference between a law-abiding citizen and a renegade. In his estimation Seth had crossed the line from one to the other, and that made him dangerous.

Hamilton, always hungry for business, wanted to hold onto the lucrative RCMP charters. That was the only reason he reluctantly hauled his big-boned five-foot ten-inch frame out of a warm bed and down to the float plane dock after receiving official confirmation of Seth's identity. For insurance, he'd telephoned an RCMP officer who played on his hockey team, and the buddy promised to alert his superiors to the charter's imminent arrival at Ptarmigan Lake. Hamilton didn't want to show up unannounced and risk the wrath of the commanding officer.

Nor did he want to risk losing another plane. Rather than wake another of the young, less experienced NLA pilots, he chose to fly Seth into Ptarmigan Lake himself.

It was a decision he'd soon regret.

# CHAPTER THIRTEEN

"There's a twin engine at three o'clock about two miles away at approximately five thousand feet," Seth in the copilot seat of the C-185 announced to his former boss via the headset microphone, an hour out of Yellowknife. "What's it doing in the middle of nowhere at 4 a.m.?"

"Obviously it's flying to the same place we are," a grumpy, tousle-haired Drew shot back. "There's nothing below but caribou and muskox on this heading until the Ptarmigan Lake mine."

Wrong answer.

Apprehension shrouded the anxiety tensing Seth's jaw. He pressed the radio transmit button and attempted to contact the other pilot on the air-to-air frequency. After three attempts he conceded to the other's failure to acknowledge. No surprise, there. The mystery plane had no business being in the vicinity. Seth checked the airspeed of the NLA Cessna—one hundred twenty-five knots, or about one hundred forty-five miles per hour thanks to a boost from a slight tail wind. Not bad considering the drag from the floats. He checked the satellite navigation system for the distance to the way point, Ptarmigan Lake—one hundred fifty-five miles.

Restless energy had him squirming in the cage of the cockpit. Seth reached into an inside pocket in his leather jacket for his encrypted satellite phone and removed his radio headset to prevent Drew from overhearing the conversation. He pressed buttons and connected with his cover man in the Diamond Protection Unit at RCMP HQ.

"An unidentified plane is on a heading to Ptarmigan Lake," he reported, pressing a forefinger into his free ear to block the deafening drone of the single engine. "Alert Sergeant MacDougall that the perps may be preparing to pull out."

He listened for a moment to an update on the status of the investigation and then broke in harshly, "Petra?" Still missing, came the reply.

Frustrated by his colleagues' by-the-book, plodding investigative approach, and by the delay before he could search the camp himself, Seth bit out, "Our ETA is 5:05." Grabbing a pen, he copied MacDougall's satellite cell number onto the corner of a map.

The mystery plane altered course, allowing the little Cessna float plane to press on until the larger twin engine plane shrank into a pinpoint on the horizon. Seth worried about that. Either the NLA Cessna spooked the other pilot such that he aborted the retrieval, or the pilot slowed to maintain a scheduled ETA, or maybe with its greater speed and fuel capacity the pilot decided to take a circuitous route to avoid the C-185.

He phoned MacDougall's cell and was redirected to the detective coordinating communications on the scene.

"Any developments?" Seth inquired after a brief report on his situation and ETA.

"We arrested one of the mechanics. His prints matched those lifted off the exhaust system on the Beaver you piloted the other day."

"That was quick." And lucky for the mechanic, because if Seth had been the arresting officer, he'd never have been able to control his fists. Petra nearly died. He clenched his jaw to suppress bubbling rage.

"Gotta love computer analysis—no wait for the forensic lab fingerprint analysis results," the detective continued. "This particular mechanic was already on our suspect list because he did maintenance on the diamond-cleaning machine in the sorting and valuation building."

Seth remembered the suggestion Petra fed them as to how the thief might conceal stolen rough from the x-ray security system. "False teeth?"

"A full set," the detective confirmed. "Big honking cavities in the molars. The maintenance records provided a picture of the frequency of his visits. We calculated he personally skimmed off fifty carats per twelve-hour shift, or about seven hundred every two weeks."

"You arrested the other three mechanics servicing that machine on the other shift and rotations?"

"They are being questioned. They had an ingenious scam going."

Seth did the math. Three thousand top-quality carats per month skimmed off the top would be worth what uncut? Three million bucks at least, because they stole only the most valuable stones a half carat or more in size. Cut and polished, he guessed three thousand carats retailed for fifteen million dollars or more. Men had been murdered for far less.

Yet he was under no illusion the mechanics masterminded the thefts. The rot in the Excelsior organization reached to the top. As-yet unidentified gang members on site would be feeling enormous pressure about now as the RCMP picked off the lower-level minions. Skittish thieves desperate for a way out became ruthless. Emotion, not reason, controlled behavior. The only escape option was potentially the twin engine plane en route. But the Ptarmigan Lake smugglers had one crucial advantage—hostages.

He prayed they intended to trade Petra for the opportunity to leave on the mystery plane, because otherwise they'd have no use for her. They eliminated liabilities, as Bob Scott's murder demonstrated. He shook off the thought. Petra lived. For his own sanity and capacity to reason, he had to believe it, had to stay cool and focused.

Seth mentally mapped the circumstances which entrapped Petra. The shift changed in three hours at 7:00 according to his wristwatch. Employees woke about 5:30 to workout, shower, eat. He figured the perps planned their departure for the quiet lull before half the camp rose for their shift, and anticipated they'd have ordered a charter to arrive between 5:00 and 5:30 at the latest.

Despite excellent visibility under wispy cirrus cloud cover at thirty thousand feet, there was no sign of the twin-engine plane. Still, he took no chances. At his request, Drew shaved another five minutes off the flight time, the best he could do.

During the rest of the flight Seth mentally prepared by running through possible scenarios. He patted the holster under his jacket. Drug smugglers backed into a corner inevitably resorted to violence, and diamond smugglers were no different.

In Seth's Scenario A, the smugglers would expect the first plane to arrive to be their plane, and would approach the pilot accordingly. He conferred with MacDougall. Horvath was to be kept in the dark.

"You've gotta be kidding," Drew exclaimed when Seth outlined the RCMP's strategy. "You want me to pretend to be the smugglers' charter?"

"We're hoping to draw the perps out of the camp and down to the lake. The RCMP will meet the plane. You're safe."

"I never agreed to be part of any take-down." The muscles in Drew's broad jaw bunched. "I shoulda hung up on you this morning." He slammed a fist against the cockpit door.

"You did."

"Not the second time you called." The normally unflappable operations manager cursed Seth up, down and sideways. "You're not setting foot in one of my planes ever again."

Seth lifted a shoulder and didn't bother to answer. The chances of him piloting a plane for NLA, or any other aviation outfit in the Northwest Territories for that matter, evaporated the instant he blew his cover.

The Cessna circled the camp before making its final approach. Far below, haul trucks kicked up dust en route to the processing plant. The wind sock at the airstrip fluttered in a light breeze. No small plane sat beside the runway. They'd arrived first.

Seth asked Drew to make another pass over the compound, buzzing low, to smoke out the perps. Two figures, likely the security officers assigned to meet every plane, emerged from the accommodation complex and ran to a pickup parked outside.

From his aerial perspective Seth was able to identify two strategically positioned pickup trucks ready to follow any vehicles the quarter mile to the lake with the intention of boxing them in, per the RCMP plan. He spotted one pickup parked near the wharf where a sole figure he knew to be Joe, undercover as a fuel technician, waited alone so as not to tip off the smugglers to the RCMP's presence.

Nothing moved along the dirt road to the lake, human or vehicular. Disappointed, he concluded the perps expected a wheeled plane, not one on floats, and remained holed up. He reported to Sergeant MacDougall on the secure channel who agreed another pass would appear suspicious and ordered them in.

Drew diligently proceeded through the requisite checklist in preparation for landing into a light headwind on Ptarmigan Lake. As the floats skimmed small whitecaps, Seth unbuckled and crawled into the rear seats to cover himself with a sleeping bag.

With practiced skill Drew maneuvered the plane alongside the wharf and killed the engine. Joe, wearing the mine uniform of blue coveralls and peaked ball cap over his bleached hair, caught hold of a rope to secure the plane to the wharf.

"I can't pretend to refuel," Joe said loud enough for Seth to overhear through the open cockpit door. "The pumps are shut off, and someone changed the padlock on the dispenser shed door. My key no longer works."

A vehicle door slammed. "Here's Craig Rudden, the acting chief of security. He's heading that way now," Joe announced.

"What way?" Seth demanded from his hiding place.

"Toward the shed."

The hairs rose on the back of Seth's neck. Wrong move. Duty dictated that Rudden immediately approach the unannounced plane to perform a search. There was no reason for security to go directly to the building instead, unless something inside was more important to Rudden than his job. Unless Rudden assumed the NLA plane to be his charter, and he needed to retrieve something before taking off.

Seth swiftly processed the possibilities. Fuel pumps had filters. Maybe Rudden had hidden the stolen rough in them. Or maybe he hid the hostages inside the building. Either way, he'd have changed the padlock to restrict access to the pump shed, which he figured wouldn't be needed for the duration of the RCMP's ban on incoming flights.

"Is Rudden alone?"

"Someone, I can't tell who, is in the pickup's passenger seat," Joe reported.

Oh shit. His worst case scenario, murderers loaded with diamonds jump into the C-185 piloted by a civilian, zipped to the front of the line.

"Cast off," Seth ordered Joe. To Drew he said while scrambling into the copilot's seat, "Be ready to get the hell out of here immediately if anyone tries to climb aboard." Knowing the older pilot's propensity to be obsessive about preflight procedures, he spared precious seconds to reinforce the order. "I'm talking immediately, Drew. Screw the checklist. Start the engine now and move away from shore if I signal with a wave."

Seth pulled out his gun and disengaged the safety. "Where is our backup? Joe, tell them not to wait for another vehicle. I think we've got our perps."

Joe crouched over the line he'd lashed to the metal hitch and fumbled for his cell phone.

From a couple of hundred feet away, through the cockpit window, Seth observed the driver's-side pickup door left wide open. An overweight male in a red Security jacket had already reached the small, white, trailer-sized building, his hand digging into his pocket, presumably for the padlock key.

He squinted. From the size of the guy, he agreed with Joe it had to be Craig Rudden, the deputy chief of security. Rudden, whose biometric thumbprint was necessary to release the diamonds collected in the processing plant. Rudden, conveniently one of the first on the scene after Seth discovered Bob Scott's body. It didn't take much of a leap to figure Rudden had opportunity and motive to eliminate his boss.

Now Rudden wanted inside that building, and Seth's instincts obliged him to prevent that from happening.

Seth reversed out of the cockpit onto the pontoon and leapt from there to the dock, his gun out of sight in his right pocket. At a quick pace down the wharf and onto the pebbled shore, he approached Rudden, who'd dropped the key and, swearing, scrabbled for it in the dirt.

Seth stopped twenty feet away at the crest of the four-foot-high ridge that formed the fuel spill containment dike around two fuel storage tanks and the small white building. "Hey, Rudden," he threw out, assuming a nonchalant stance, both hands in jacket pockets.

Rudden recognized him. The guy's florid face blanched. Rudden glanced at the float plane adrift offshore, and then over his shoulder as the distant growl of approaching vehicles reached him. The drone of a small plane on an approach to the airstrip intruded, setting off a string of filthy curses when he realized he'd been tricked. He turned the key in the lock, wrenched it open, and tossed the padlock aside.

"I wouldn't do that if I were you." Seth raised his left arm and brought it down in a backward wave in the agreed signal while drawing his weapon with the right. "Stop right there. RCMP."

Rudden moved fast for a big man. With one hand he swung the door open, and with the other he pulled a pistol from inside his jacket. "Stay back," he shouted, and fired.

Seth dropped flat behind the containment dike, still an easy target, but the other man's single-handed grip fortunately sent the shot wide.

A metallic ping worried Seth. Behind him a man's yelp and a splash followed in seconds by a rushing, thunderous explosion telegraphed that one of the plane's fuel tanks had been hit. Let Joe deal with it. Seth didn't dare take his eyes off Rudden.

Instead of retreating to hide behind the open door, Rudden brazenly stood outlined against the dark interior as if daring Seth to return fire. He aimed and got off three more shots at Seth, one hand incongruously fumbling in his pocket instead of bracing the gun in a more accurate double-handed straight-armed stance.

Seth sniffed, catching the stench of gasoline on the breeze fanning the entrance. A white cigarette lighter appeared in Rudden's fist, the tiny flame a deadly clue that his goal lay not in retrieving stolen rough, but rather in blowing up the facility.

Why?

Seth accurately read Rudden's intention to create a diversion, then make a run for the airstrip. Fear pooled in his lower regions. What better location to hide hostages, or bodies, than in a rarely used outbuilding?

A shout from inside distracted Rudden, giving Seth the opening he needed. Joyful hope that Petra might be alive after all propelled him forward. He refused to allow Rudden to incinerate her.

Ditching caution with his gun, he launched from a crouched position into a sprint and tackled the obese six-footer at the waist. They fell together, rolled, and Seth groped for the weapon, too easily prying the gun from sausage-sized fingers gripping it like C-clamps. He threw it out of reach, breathing hard.

But Seth miscalculated. It wasn't the gun that Rudden protected. The cigarette lighter remained firmly gripped in Rudden's other fist. Seth avoided the generously padded stomach, instead attempting to land a disabling punch to the head, but the heavier man leveraged his weight to pin Seth's neck to the ground with a forearm the size of a tree limb.

Two figures stumbled through the doorway.

"Seth!" Petra's hoarse voice screamed.

He twisted to track the welcome sound and took a fist in the eye for his trouble. Instead of retreating to safety, Petra stuck close to kick at Rudden's vulnerable kidney with one bare foot. The other figure lurched out of range of Seth's peripheral vision.

Acrid fumes clogged Seth's nostrils, the danger clear. Yet Petra lingered, hovering above the struggling pair and ineffectually slamming a foot into the soft mattress that was Rudden. Cold fury consumed Seth. Here he was rescuing the woman he loved, and again she refused to escape to safety.

"Run," Seth gasped despite his crushed throat.

Rudden elevated an arm skyward to throw the object through the entrance. Seth took advantage of the small adjustment in his opponent's balance to shove the three hundred-pound dead weight upward, creating sufficient space to slam a knee into Rudden's crotch. Howling, the big man accordioned into a fetal position.

"Stay back," Joe's familiar voice ordered Petra as he stamped one heavy boot on Rudden's fist to extinguish the tiny yet deadly flame.

Moments later Seth's colleagues, guns drawn, subdued and cuffed Rudden. Two uniforms hoisted Seth to his feet where he swayed, a hand clutching his aching throat, his full attention on the bedraggled woman relegated to the rear of the men surrounding a sullen Rudden. She offered a triumphant smile that plucked his heart strings.

He couldn't decide whether to praise her bravery or shoot her for intentionally returning to Ptarmigan Lake with a murderer still on the loose. His heart eased off the gas, the blood flow in the arteries decelerated. She was safe. Again. He frowned. For the moment. The woman needed a keeper.

"Are you okay?" Seth and Petra asked simultaneously. They inspected each other for damage. Petra's hair hung limp to her shoulders, her skin pale, her irises a dull mud within red spider webs mottling the whites of her eyes. She reeked of gasoline. Despite the ruin, he contrarily decided she was a beautiful sight to behold. Overcome by emotion he couldn't name, he moved to hug her, to kiss the shock-whitened tremble from her lips.

"I think my wrists are broken." Petra swiveled to show him her bound wrists.

Purpled skin had swelled over thin plastic strips sunk into bloody welts. She'd endured excruciating pain in a determined attempt to escape the bindings. He marveled at her endurance as he unsnapped his Swiss Army knife, unfolded a thin blade and contemplated how to slice the plastic without hurting her further. Petra's breath hitched. "I knew you'd come," she said for a distraction, as he, of necessity, gently maneuvered the sharp tool under the thin strip and into the wound.

"You did not," Carter Lee inserted, approaching from Seth's left. "You were prepared to die, as I was." He rubbed bruised wrists to restore the circulation, having had them freed by another officer.

When Seth learned of Petra's abduction, the prospect—no likelihood—of finding her dead instilled a bone-deep fear guaranteed to give him nightmares for the rest of his life. He didn't appreciate the chief geologist's blunt reminder of the close call.

He balefully examined the man Petra risked her life to find. Carter Lee appeared to be fully functional after the ordeal. The man's emotional state was another matter. He shook so hard his teeth rattled.

"I'm taking you both to the infirmary," Seth asserted.

A scowling, red-faced Drew limped toward Sergeant MacDougall dripping lake water. Uh-oh. Seth sought out the Cessna floating seventy-five feet off shore and winced. Its snout housing the engine burned merrily. A blaring alarm announced the fire pumper cresting the hill, the cavalry to the rescue, but odds were Drew's C-185 was a total write-off.

Seth herded Petra and Carter Lee to a vacant pickup. Joe, soaked to the skin, trotted up the rear. "Sorry, Seth, this vehicle is off limits until a forensic team finishes with it. Rudden and the other woman drove it down here."

"Other woman?"

Joe gestured at three officers encircling Desirée, blonde head tossed back, lips pursed in a pout.

Ah, the cook. The curvy blonde had good reason to pout. The RCMP had seized the rough ice stuffed into pearl onions, and it so happened it was her signature scrawled on the shipping manifest. As she protested her innocence to this lot, other detectives back in Yellowknife traced two other shipments of food from the mine site.

A big mistake made that task relatively simple. She'd arranged to air-freight these particular boxes on from Yellowknife to Edmonton, the closest major city. Back at HQ during the interview the previous day, he'd shared his theory that the trail ended at a location such as a rented storage locker or private house, a safe place until she and her partners in crime had the opportunity to assemble in the relative anonymity of the city and divvy up the rough. An opportunity that would never come.

Joe broke into his thoughts. "Sorry I took so long to pry Craig Rudden off you. The civilian pilot sank like a rock and I had to haul him out of the lake."

Carter Lee's face crimped with anguish. A thin sheen of moisture glistened on dilated black pupils. He'd loved the woman, Seth realized without sympathy. MacDougall would find that useful in Carter's interrogation.

Petra too had trained her gaze on Desirée. Unlike the men attracted to yards of skin revealed by the flowered blue dress with plunging neckline, Petra's attention fixed on a lower portion of her anatomy—the feet encased in chunky, thick-soled black shoes.

"Check her shoes," Petra croaked in a voice that scratched like sandpaper.

"Does anybody have a bottle of water?" Seth called out.

"Her lace-up shoes," Petra insisted. "No woman wears ugly shoes like that with a dress."

She swayed. He reached for her, clutched her to his chest as Petra crumpled in a dead faint.

\* \* \* \* \*

Petra labored through dense gooey mud up to her waist away from a sky-high round tank labeled AN/FO. Her feet refused to advance, though she strained forward, writhing and sweating with the effort.

A horn blared. She recognized the warning signal. The explosive charge was about to be detonated. In a frenzy she struggled to escape certain death, to no avail. A thundering colossal blast jostled her body.

She woke with a small cry.

Seth gripped the fingertips of one hand. "It's okay," he soothed. "They're blasting at the pit."

"I'm alive," she breathed.

"You're safe," he agreed. "You're in the mine infirmary."

Her wrists throbbed. She lifted one arm to inspect the white gauze encasing the hand and lower arm. A plastic splint peeked out from underneath the bandages.

"Are they broken?"

"The nurse isn't certain. He's made arrangements to have them x-rayed at the Yellowknife hospital."

"Carter—" She half rose.

"He's fine." He pushed her down into the pillows. "He's singing like a canary upstairs in Horvath's office."

"Poor Carter."

"He almost got you killed." Seth's harsh tone explicitly expressed his opinion of Carter. "Horvath is under arrest, by the way."

She nodded, not surprised. "Were Hank and Desirée—?"

"Don't talk." He fondled the tips of her fingers as if his equilibrium depended on maintaining physical contact. "The detectives will take your statement after you've received medical attention in Yellowknife. A medevac team will arrive in an hour."

She sniffed and choked, newly aware of the fumes emanating from her clothing under the cotton blanket. "I stink of gasoline. Under normal circumstances they'd classify me as a hazardous substance and refuse to transport me. I'm not going anywhere until I shower and change."

He hesitated. "Are you sure you're up to it? You fainted and were unconscious for thirty minutes."

"I'll need assistance," she said, rotating one arm at the elbow. "You offering?"

He swallowed, and a familiar grin displaced the grim lines bracketing his mouth. "If the nurse gives permission, I do indeed volunteer."

* * * * *

Seth arranged for housekeeping to retrieve Petra's belongings from her assigned third floor room and deliver them to a vacant bedroom on the first floor. Ignoring protests that she was perfectly capable of walking, he scooped her into his arms and carried her to the room.

Forearms waterproofed in plastic wrap by the obliging male nurse practitioner bounced on her chest as Seth lurched through the corridors. Amused, Petra decided she rather enjoyed the sensation of being carried off and cared for by a handsome single-minded male.

He set her down outside a bedroom door and swiped a key card through the lock. A young native woman trotted down the hall laden with Petra's backpack and boots. Once inside, the door locked, Seth removed his jacket, shoulder harness, navy T-shirt, boots and jeans to stand before her clad only in fighter jet-themed boxer shorts.

She laughed at his eagerness. "My shampoo is in the side pocket of the backpack," she suggested.

"Right." He placed it on the edge of the sink.

"My clothes." She held out her arms. The nurse had rolled up the sleeves of her plaid bush shirt, but the bulky splint and bandages obstructed its removal. "You'll need your knife again."

"Right." He unbuttoned her flannel shirt and carefully cut the fabric off her body.

"Now my T-shirt." She raised her arms above her head. "It's oversized. You don't have to cut it off."

He squinted at the Northern Lights Air logo above her left breast. "Hey, you're wearing my shirt!"

She wiggled her shoulders, guilty as sin. "I wanted a memento, okay? I didn't think you'd mind."

"When—" he began, and then halted abruptly as he tugged the fabric over her head. She recalled she wasn't wearing a bra.

After he discarded the shirt, her breasts attracted his hands like homing beacons.

"The medevac," she reminded him. "We have thirty minutes."

"Right," he agreed, the word somewhat garbled. With commendable efficiency he unzipped her jeans and pushed them to her ankles, then her panties.

Unable to resist the temptation, she lowered her gaze to his shorts and grinned. One fighter jet aggressively led the rest of the wing on cotton stretched tight to his butt. "Someone's ready for take-off," she teased.

Blushing, Seth hustled her into the bathroom and adjusted the temperature of the water spurting from the shower nozzle into the narrow shower stall. After giving her privacy to use the facilities, he stripped off his shorts and squeezed in to join her.

His lean muscular body, intimately familiar, dominated the small space. She glimpsed the size of his enormous erection and swallowed. Twice. Knees buckled, compelling her to sag against the wall for support.

Seth slid his hands under her armpits to prop her upright. "Do you feel faint?" Concern etched grooves between his brows.

She groped for an explanation, and settled on one close to the truth. "Hungry," she breathed. Hungry for his lips on hers, his palms cupping her breasts. Curling need bloomed. A slight adjustment, and the thickened member inches away could slide between slippery thighs...

To her extreme aggravation, he eschewed any funny business, awkwardly lathering her hair twice in the tight space while she luxuriated under the stream of wonderfully hot water. The pummeling heat loosened tight shoulders and strained neck muscles.

She yearned to press her body the length of his, yet understood his reticence. He fought an internal battle to resist the attraction, to resist making love to avoid becoming further enmeshed in a relationship he'd forsworn. Poor guy. She reconsidered her plan to make it more difficult for him to sever their connection. After he put her on a flight to the States in a day or so, sending her out of his life forever, at least she'd have memories to sustain her in the lonely years to come.

A snicker escaped her throat. Who was she kidding? Petra pressed the stop button on the martyr music playing in her head. The north was a hotbed of exploration. Jobs for geologists abounded. She'd be back sooner rather than later, under new management, and had every intention of "accidentally" crossing Seth's path in Yellowknife. Let him enjoy his little fantasy that she'd docilely succumb to an uneventful life in Colorado out of harm's way.

He wanted to play it platonic naked in the shower, telescoped member at 100x magnification betraying how much he desired her, gritted teeth broadcasting a superhero effort at control? So be it. There'd be other opportunities to ravish and be ravished once she bounced back from her injuries. She'd make sure of it.

She overestimated Seth's willpower.

# Chapter Fourteen

As water sluiced the remnants of shampoo from Petra's hair, Seth soaped a wash cloth and scrubbed her torso, rear and limbs until skin tingled. Her breasts, saved for last, apparently required particular attention. The rough cloth abraded sensitive nipples, evoking such pleasure that she moaned aloud.

It was Seth's undoing.

He closed the infinitely small gap he'd maintained between their slick bodies and lowered his lips to encase hers in a hot, open-mouthed kiss. His tongue sought the depths as she opened to him with equal fervor.

"I'll never have enough of you." His lips sought her nipple, licked, tugged, ignited a fiery path straight to the tiny mound under his thumb. She put her busy thoughts on hold when his hands roamed past her butt, sought sensitive crevasses, massaged and dipped into the tunnel that ached for him with a lust so powerful, awareness of her surroundings faded.

Husky words penetrated the haze of sensation clouding her senses. "I almost lost my mind when I thought you were dead. I adore you."

Her heart stopped. She jerked her head to drain waterlogged ear canals. "Pardon me?"

"I love you, God help me. You drive me crazy, but I can't imagine life without you."

He loved her. Her throat closed. Joy set eyelids blinking madly, and not because of the water cascading from overhead. Evidently it wouldn't be too difficult to convince him she belonged in his life after all. She met solemn emerald jewels glowing in the dim stall. "I love you more," she burbled.

"It's not just the sex?"

"It's not just—" She inhaled deeply as he slid a finger inside and rubbed a soapy thumb over the hypersensitive nub. "The sex." Her insides flowed, liquid energy, her legs melted. He encircled her midsection with a muscled arm to brace her spread-eagled against his body. His skilled fingers continued with a creative exploration that left her limp as exquisite pressure built.

"However," she qualified with sharp exhalations. "The sex would be reason enough to love you. It's so intense, I practically pass out every time we—"

"It won't always be this intense." He nipped at the sensitive spot under her ear, torched nerve endings. "Danger and its aftermath heighten sensation. This is extreme sex, not regular sex."

"I'll manage," she said, her tone wry. "Shut up and kiss me."

The instant their tongues tangled, her core exploded, shattering into a thousand rhythmical waves that rippled to the edges of her soul.

\* \* \* \* \*

Seth and Detective Tag Rumford, the official RCMP escort, accompanied Carter and Petra on the twin-engine Piper that flew them to Yellowknife.

Seth hovered as a nurse arranged a pillow to support Petra's splinted wrists and buckled her in, then took the adjacent seat across the aisle from her. The cafeteria had supplied bagged food and beverages for the passengers. After the plane reached cruising altitude, he unwrapped a bacon, egg and cheese sandwich and lifted it to her lips. Ravenous, she devoured it in healthy bites.

As the others munched their makeshift meal and sipped bottled water, Petra's natural curiosity revived and demanded answers.

"Did anyone check Desirée's shoes?" she asked over the droning hum of the engines.

Detective Rumford leaned around the forward seat. "Yes, ma'am. We found rough diamonds hidden in cavities in the soles just as you suspected."

"Did Craig Rudden kill Bob Scott?"

The detective's eyes shifted to the nurse listening avidly a row behind Petra. "The investigation is ongoing."

"Can you tell me any more?" she beseeched.

Seth reached the short distance to touch her upper arm. "Later," was all he would say.

\* \* \* \* \*

But it was her father who eventually filled in the missing pieces of the puzzle for her.

A husky but fit fifty-five, russet hair graying at the temples, Edward Paris strode into the small private hospital room where Petra lay propped on pillows. He shucked off a casual blue summer-weight blazer to reveal a taupe golf shirt with a country club insignia, and dragged a visitor's chair close to the bed.

"Daddy!" Her mouth gaped. He was the very last person she expected to walk into her room. She'd mentally and emotionally prepared for Seth, for the cops, but not for her father.

Throat working, he stared down at her splinted wrists. X-rays had revealed a hairline fracture in one tiny bone. The other wrist escaped with pulled tendons. Amber eyes flecked with green traveled up to her face. "When I heard you were in the hospital I flew up here only to discover you'd chartered a plane back to Ptarmigan Lake, and that you were missing." He paused. "Your mother is sick with worry. She's having trouble getting a seat on a flight."

"I called her," Petra said, and took a moment to recover from astonishment at his presence before asking, "What are you doing here? Who told you I was in the hospital?"

"Brent Switzer," he said, naming a member of Excelsior's board of directors. With a small smile that didn't reach his eyes, he admitted, "I've been keeping tabs on you."

"Since when?"

"Since—" He waved the hand with the gold wedding band from his second marriage. "Since whenever," he finished lamely.

His bulk blurred, and she blinked to clear her vision. "I'm sorry, Dad. For everything."

He squeezed her shoulder. "We'll talk about that later. Tomorrow we start over. A clean slate." He hesitated. "I'm glad to have my daughter back."

As he rose to his full six feet she suddenly felt bereft. "Are you leaving?"

"You need sleep, and I have some calls to make. I'll be in to see you later." He brushed her forehead with a quick kiss and was gone.

Her heart stretched to bursting. She filled lungs with a shaky breath. Her lids slid closed for a moment to lubricate dry eyes that burned with unshed tears.

\* \* \* \* \*

The creak of the door roused her. Outside Stanton Yellowknife Hospital the day remained bright with the constant sunshine. She had no idea whether minutes or hours had passed.

Her father entered, held high a sub sandwich. "When you were a little girl you liked tuna," he said.

"I still do." She smiled. He'd packed her school lunches when she was very young, she remembered with a pang. So many years lost.

"This is tastier than hospital food," he said as he unwrapped the roll.

She lifted bandaged wrists to prop the long roll awkwardly between her palms. "The splints will be replaced with wrist supports tomorrow when I get out of here. I'll only need to wear them for a few weeks."

He laughed. "It already is tomorrow. You slept for hours."

"No kidding?" Come to think of it, her mind was free of the debilitating fog of fatigue, though muscles through shoulders and back ached abominably.

"No kidding. It's 8:30 in the morning."

As her empty stomach filled with the most delicious tuna sandwich ever, her father settled into a chair, crossed his chino-clad legs, and proceeded to entertain her while she ate.

He'd acquired several disparate pieces of information from industry contacts which he'd shared with the RCMP in a long interview the previous evening. Now he was ready to share with her.

He launched into a description of international trade in blood diamonds, otherwise known as conflict diamonds. Diamonds stolen from certain African mines or skimmed off the official production were smuggled out of Africa. Insurgents in small African countries relied on the sale of these illegal diamonds to buy weapons and fund their bloody civil wars.

Then gem-quality diamonds were discovered in Canada's far north and several diamond mines went into production. Canada quickly became a major producer, supplying one third of the world's diamonds. With a new, clean source of high-quality rough, demand for diamonds of dubious origin plummeted. The smugglers couldn't find buyers. The cash flow to the rebel armies began to dry up and they became desperate. Guns sales in turn took a nosedive, and weapon suppliers became desperate. Enormous amounts of money were at stake.

"How did Hank Horvath fit into this," Petra mumbled around a mouthful of bread.

"The arms dealers and diamond smugglers needed to cut off the source of new diamonds flooding the market. They partnered to shut down the North American diamond mines. Desirée Dumont, legal name Gabrielle Dumont, is the trilingual Belgian mistress of a Portuguese millionaire in the business of supplying weapons to African militants. She tracked down and seduced Hank Horvath when he was on holiday in Brazil."

Of course. Hank learned to speak Portuguese in Brazil, Petra recalled. When the cook and Carter disappeared, no doubt Desirée hid in Hank's room—the only place no one would search.

"Horvath orchestrated the attempt to sabotage the mine's life and destroy it as a viable business. He hired Desirée into a cook position and staffed as many key mine jobs with inexperienced young employees as he could get away with under the absentee supervision of a VP far away in Boulder. Bob Scott twigged to the scam and had to be eliminated. Craig Rudden has been arrested for his murder."

Her old friend and boss, a criminal. She'd so misjudged the characters of the men in her life. "What was Hank's motivation?"

"A cut of the stolen rough. He was promised millions."

"What about Athlone?"

"Horvath initially set Desirée up with Tony Athlone to get financial intel on the Excelsior organization. She convinced Athlone to send the stock price into a free fall." Her dad laughed shortly. "She had him believing it was the only way he could gain control of the company and make a bundle in the process when the stock price rebounded."

Petra nodded. "I suspected Athlone artificially manipulated the stock price so he could buy it up cheap."

"Desirée and her cohorts were very clever. They wanted investors to dump the stock, thereby crippling the company financially and forcing it into bankruptcy. Once that plan was in motion, Horvath brought her north.

"As for Athlone, in a sworn statement to the FBI he insists he didn't know about the strategy to destroy the mine. You know, I actually believe him. Athlone wanted to wrest control of the company. Bankruptcy would have left him holding a lot of worthless stock, ruining him. He did admit he knew about Horvath's smuggling scheme at Ptarmigan Lake, and went along with it as a means to an end, but he never touched a single stolen rock."

Her brows hiked. "And you believe that?"

"Not a chance. The missing rough has to be somewhere. The FBI is searching Athlone's residences in Colorado, California and Hawaii as we speak."

She lay back on the pillows, pleasantly replete, to mull over the information.

Her father stood. "I should let you sleep."

"I'm not tired," she insisted, but a yawn belied her words. "How many mine workers were in on the scheme?"

"Investigations are on-going, but every mechanic, on and off shift, who worked in the sorting facility was hauled in for questioning. Rumor has it the lock-up in Yellowknife hasn't room for everyone who's been charged. Many were shipped out to the Edmonton RCMP." He bent to bus her cheek. "I'll be back in a couple of hours."

Her lids drifted south. A short nap was all she needed. Then she'd phone Seth. It occurred to her that he hadn't been by to visit. She missed him.

Her father halted in the act of opening the door. "By the way, a joker calling himself Seth London dropped by a couple of times and left a sheaf of messages with the nurse. London. Paris. Huh," he sniffed. "Obviously a false name. Then he tried to tell me his name was Cooper and showed me some ID proving he was a pilot with Northern Lights Air. Isn't he the pilot that crashed the plane which landed you in hospital with CO poisoning? I told him to get lost. You don't want to get mixed up with the likes of him. I ordered the nursing staff to keep him away from you."

Petra groaned. Having a protective father in her life again might present some challenges. "I love you, Dad."

"I love you too, sweetie," he beamed, leaving her the privacy to use the facilities and nap.

* * * * *

Hours later an orderly with her evening meal on a tray pushed open her door. Seth slipped in behind him and waited until the other man arranged the tray on the sliding table, fluffed the pillows, and wheeled his food cart down the corridor to the next room.

Her pulse galloped at the sight of her handsome lover. A thick dark lock of hair drooped over tired eyes that brightened as he absorbed her grin. She held out a hand and he gripped the tips of her fingers, as eager as she was for the physical contact.

"The doctor refused to allow me in here until I informed him that I'm your fiancé." The anxious set of his shoulders, a hesitant tilt to his head, and expectant alertness on still features expressed more than his words.

She ruminated a moment. She wasn't a traditional girl, and didn't expect a traditional proposal. However, some traditions weren't optional. "Where's my ring?"

His shoulders relaxed. "You being a geologist and all, I expect you'd prefer to choose the rock."

She rearranged her legs when he moved to sit on the bed, to lay a hand along her cheek, to trace his thumb over her bottom lip. Her cheeks warmed at the memory of where that thumb had worked its magic in the shower.

"It's not as though there's a shortage of diamonds around here," he continued. "A cutting and polishing facility is located in an industrial park beside the Yellowknife airport. But you'd probably prefer another type of gem. A diamond will remind you of—" He cleared his throat, haunted by the memories of the previous week. "Of the incident." And left unsaid when you almost died.

Happiness left her speechless. He acknowledged her effort to bring her emotions under control, gave her a moment.

"The mine will need a replacement chief geologist," he mused aloud. "Carter has been charged as an accomplice."

Petra shook her head. "Poor Carter." She'd cared for the guy, but he'd never work in the industry again. Then the significance of Seth's observation clicked. With her Excelsior Board connections, the year-round job would be hers for the asking. She'd do it to be with Seth. "And a new chief of security," she lobbed back.

They stared at each other, intuiting the other's thoughts—two weeks on, two weeks off.

"Another charter outfit might take me on part time if I grovel—" Or not. He pushed out his bottom lip, fairly certain that once word of the Cessna's burnt-out shell spread to the far corners of the Arctic, odds were he'd never fly for a northern firm again.

"I could do some prospecting. I hear they discovered emeralds on the other side of the Mackenzie Mountains in the Yukon."

Seth half rose from the bed. "Over my dead body. The region is crawling with grizzly bears. They can tear a tent to shreds and eat you for a midnight snack," he growled.

Her brow knit and she gingerly crossed her arms. "What do you plan to do? Lock me up between two-week rotations? This is my career we're talking about."

He decided to change tactics. "What about kids?"

"Maybe in five years." The compressed line under her nose proclaimed that dynamite wouldn't budge her.

He eased back into his chair, satisfied. With a couple of spirited kids to handle, she'd eventually have to take a break from hunting gem deposits in the back of beyond and he could relax.

It dawned on him that to protect her in the meantime he'd have to stick to her like Velcro.

"All right, I cave, but on one condition."

Her eyes narrowed. "What's that?"

He stuck a thumb toward his chest. "We buy a plane and I fly you in and out of exploration camps myself."

A smile kindled amber sparks in her irises. She reached for him. "Deal," she said. "I trust you."

"With your life?" He gathered her close.

"No," she said gently. "My choices as to what to do with my life are my own responsibility." She snuggled against his broad chest. "But my heart is in your safekeeping," she whispered against his lips. "I trust you with my heart."

After a fervent kiss that shimmered with understanding and acceptance, Petra had one last question.

"Is your real name London?"

"Lunden," he agreed as he savored her earlobe, sending rippling shocks to her center. "With a 'u' and an 'e'. Cooper and undercover assignments are history. You are my priority from this moment forward."

She snuggled into the crook of his neck and blissfully inhaled his scent, knowing in her heart that she belonged with Seth. As a kid, when other girls her age dressed their dolls as bride and groom, hers acted out explorer and astronaut scenarios. An expensive engagement ring and fancy wedding had never figured in her fantasies of the future. But although a diamond ring was a universal symbol of commitment, in the past week diamonds had come to represent so much more.

"I do want a diamond," she said, meeting moist eyes glittering with emotion. "Rough diamonds brought us together. Diamonds are how you found me, not almost lost me. A diamond is the hardest mineral. It cuts through anything. Together you and I are that strong."

**The End**

# About the Author

Madelle Morgan began her engineering career in Yellowknife, Northwest Territories, Canada, known as the Diamond Capital of North America. For five adventure-filled years she took charter and scheduled flights to construction projects throughout the Arctic. Years later she "mined" her experiences to write *Diamond Hunter*. The extraordinary people and places of Canada's far north are like no others on earth.

Now retired, Madelle writes contemporary romance as well as mystery/suspense. Her new novella series is set in beautiful Muskoka, Ontario, Canada, Canada's premiere summer playground. The National Geographic Traveler magazine chose Muskoka as one of the Best of the World – Must-see Places for 2012. Canada's Arctic is wild and dangerous, but hearts aren't any safer in Muskoka!

Subscribe to blog posts, announcements of new releases and deals, and more at www.MadelleMorgan.com
Follow her on www.facebook.com/madellemorganauthor
See Pinterest images that inspired the writing of Diamond Hunter
Connect on Twitter @MadelleMorgan